31 — GALE 8·28·18

CRIME & PUNCTUATION

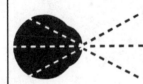

This Large Print Book carries the
Seal of Approval of N.A.V.H.

A DEADLY EDITS MYSTERY

CRIME & PUNCTUATION

KAITLYN DUNNETT

THORNDIKE PRESS
A part of Gale, a Cengage Company

Farmington Hills, Mich • San Francisco • New York • Waterville, Maine
Meriden, Conn • Mason, Ohio • Chicago

Copyright © 2018 by Kathy Lynn Emerson.
A Deadly Edits Mystery.
Thorndike Press, a part of Gale, a Cengage Company.

Thorndike Press® Large Print Mystery.
The text of this Large Print edition is unabridged.
Other aspects of the book may vary from the original edition.
Set in 16 pt. Plantin.

LIBRARY OF CONGRESS CIP DATA ON FILE.
CATALOGUING IN PUBLICATION FOR THIS BOOK
IS AVAILABLE FROM THE LIBRARY OF CONGRESS

ISBN-13: 978-1-4328-5177-4 (hardcover)

Published in 2018 by arrangement with Kensington Books, an imprint
of Kensington Publishing Corp.

Printed in the United States of America
1 2 3 4 5 6 7 22 21 20 19 18

To the LCHS class of 1965

CHAPTER 1

"I don't know, Cal. It doesn't look good."

Always the silent type, Cal stared back at me with big green eyes and an enigmatic expression.

"You *should* be concerned," I said. "If I can't pay the bills, both of us will be reduced to eating cut-rate cat food."

That earned me what we used to call "the hairy eyeball."

"What do *you* know?" I muttered. "You're a cat."

Cal is short for Calpurnia. She's a seven-year-old calico. I'm Mikki Lincoln, her sixty-eight-year-old source of food, affection, and a warm place to sleep. She stretched out next to me on the loveseat as I once again scanned the handwritten numbers on the notepad on my lap. The totals hadn't changed. I'd committed myself to spending more than the sum of my various retirement incomes. I'd also well and truly burned my bridges, leaving me with a cat and a hundred-and-ten-year-old, three-story house to support.

In difficult situations, indulging in fantasy is a perfectly acceptable coping mechanism. I considered that as good an excuse as any for pretending that Cal and I were carrying on a conversation. Yes, I knew full well that I was talking to myself. I just wasn't ready to admit it.

"Come on, Cal. Help me out. Surely I have *some* marketable skill."

Desperation is the mother of inspiration, or if it isn't, it should be. Calpurnia had no useful suggestions to contribute, but the minute those words left my mouth, the proverbial light bulb went on over my head.

"That's it!" I hauled ten solid pounds of calico cat into my arms and gave her a celebratory hug. "There *is* something I know how to do!"

Calpurnia kicked me in the stomach, forcing me to release her. She jumped from the loveseat to the floor and stalked to the far side of the room. There, ignoring me, oblivious to the fact that relief and anticipation had replaced my earlier dismay and despair, she sat, lifted her back leg, and began to wash her nether regions.

Two Months Later

I'd forgotten how harsh our doorbell sounded until it broke the peaceful stillness of mid-morning, after the children attending the parochial school across the street were all snug in their classrooms. I wasn't expecting anyone. The contractors had finished giving me their estimates. The men hired to do the next batch of renovations wouldn't start work for another ten days.

Although I am not by nature a timid person, I took the precaution of peeking out through the drapes covering the picture window in the living room. For the past few months, I'd had to keep reminding myself that I was a woman of a certain age living alone. It didn't make sense to take foolish chances.

The line of sight was poor, but it was sufficient to let me see that the person standing on my front porch looked harmless. A short, plump, pretty blonde in designer jeans and a bright orange turtleneck sweater and boots with three-inch heels took a step back, shifting her weight from foot to foot as she waited for me to answer the door. *Young* and *eager* were my secondary impressions, and I couldn't help but notice that she had a bulky mailer, almost certainly containing a manuscript, securely tucked under one arm. Odds were good that I wasn't about to admit an ax murderer into my home.

"Ms. Lincoln?" she asked when I opened the door. The hopeful note in her voice was a match for the cautiously optimistic expression on her face. "I'm Tiffany Scott. I understand you're a book doctor."

That description always sets my teeth on edge. I schooled my features not to betray my distaste for the term and said only, "I edit manuscripts for a living," as I waved her into the hallway. "Excuse the mess. I'm remodeling."

Glancing into the living room as we passed the archway that opened into it from the hall, I winced. In preparation for the work to be done upstairs, it currently contained twice as much furniture as it should have. Teetering stacks of cardboard boxes added to the obstacle course. I'd tripped twice on my way to peek out the front window.

"This is a great old place." Tiffany sounded sincere. "My husband insists that everything in the house he built for me be brand-new. Sometimes I visit my grandmother just to remind myself how lovely antiques can be."

Since I was old enough to be Tiffany's

grandmother myself, I chose to take this as a compliment. In my own mind, of course, I am *much* younger than my chronological age and definitely not an antique!

"I bought it while I was still living in Maine."

Her eyes widened. "Sight unseen?"

"Not in the usual sense. I lived in this house until I was seventeen."

Unfortunately, in the fifty-one year interim, a series of owners had neglected to upgrade the wiring or plumbing or make significant repairs to the roof or to interior walls and floors. The old wooden siding had been replaced with aluminum at some point, removing the need for periodic scraping and repainting, but otherwise little had been done to modernize the structure. I shuddered every time I thought about how much work needed to be done to make the place fully habitable.

I'd already had a new roof put on. There hadn't been much choice about that, not when there was so much evidence that the old one leaked every time it rained. Now my contractor had lined up an electrician and a plumber to bring the basics up to code before winter set in. After that, there would be a million and one small renovations to complete, but I was hoping I could do some of them myself.

When Tiffany rang my doorbell, I'd been enjoying a second cup of coffee in the alcove off the kitchen that my mother always called "the dinette." It was as good a place as any for us to talk.

"Something to drink?" I indicated the coffee maker I'd bought right after I moved in. Most of the K-Cups I had on hand were the blend I drank every day, but I still had a few of the samples that had come with the machine — tea, hot chocolate, a half-caff, and a super dark roast that was way too strong for my taste.

"No thank you. Ms. Lincoln, I —"

"Better make that Mikki." Tiffany might be at least forty years my junior, but the relationship between writer and editor is a partnership best approached on equal terms.

Once we were both settled at the small, square table that filled most of the alcove, a little silence fell. I'd barely established a presence online and hadn't done any advertising locally. I didn't plan to, either. Potential clients were supposed to contact me by email. Having one show up on my doorstep was a trifle disconcerting.

To gather my thoughts, I stared out at my backyard through two side-by-side windows.

Very little light made its way in. What I remembered as a lawn with one big spruce halfway to the back property line was now a small forest. The lot wasn't all that big, but someone had planted trees — lots of trees of many varieties — in every available spot. I like trees. I used to live in Maine. But this was a bit much even for me.

"Mikki?" Tiffany's tentative tone of voice brought me back to the table and the manuscript she still clutched.

"If you don't mind my asking, how did you hear about my editing service?"

She relaxed at once. "Oh, you were easy to find. I did an online search for freelance editors, and when I saw you were based right here in Lenape Hollow, I knew you were the perfect one to help me. It was *meant*."

Tiffany's tendency to gush made her seem alarmingly naïve. I suspected that, like many novice writers, she was unaware of how easy she would be to cheat. She needed to be wary of bogus publishing companies and agents who charged a "reading fee," and those dangers were just the tip of the iceberg.

"Are you certain you don't want to query other editors before settling on me? It makes sense to compare prices and evaluate the various services available before you —"

"I want you." As if to prove it, Tiffany released the death grip she'd had on her oversize mailer and slid it across the table toward me.

"Here's the thing, Tiffany. Even though you seem certain I'm the right editor for you, I can't agree to take on a project until I know more about it. There are some genres, science fiction for instance, that I would hesitate to tackle. I'd be a very bad choice if that's what you've written."

"It's not science fiction. I've written a mystery novel. Your web page said you work with crime novels and women's fiction."

Feeling a bit more comfortable, I eased the manuscript out of the mailer and set the latter aside. "Do you want me to do copyediting, line editing, developmental editing, or all three?"

"I'd like you to read my novel and tell me what to fix so it will sell." She leaned closer, her voice earnest and her insecurities about her writing on full display. She looked heart-wrenchingly vulnerable. If I'd known her better, I'd have given her a reassuring hug.

"If I do developmental editing, that means I'd make suggestions for changes. After you revise your manuscript, maybe more than once, I'd do line editing, which is just what

14

it sounds like, and then, finally, copy editing, which is checking for typos, grammar and punctuation errors, and the like." I waited until she met my eyes. "All that could get expensive."

"I've got money. And I want you."

"Well, then, let's see what we have here." I wasn't quite ready to commit myself, but I was encouraged by Tiffany's attitude.

I treated the thick stack of printed pages as gently as a mother with a newborn. Measuring by eye, I estimated that she'd used almost a full ream of paper for the printout — five hundred pages. At about two hundred fifty words a page, that came to around 125,000 words. Unless every word was golden, she would have some cutting to do.

"Most writing needs to be trimmed," I warned her, and lowered my gaze to the first page.

After the words "Chapter One," Tiffany had added a dateline — 1937. That her novel was historical would present additional editing challenges. I'd have to be alert for anachronisms as well as for grammar and punctuation problems.

"I'm not an expert in this time period," I warned her. "It's your responsibility to make sure the details are right."

"I've done tons of research," she assured me.

I began to read. My eyes widened as an exceedingly graphic description of a murder unfolded. The writing was . . . vivid.

I love words, and Tiffany had chosen hers well in these first passages. She'd also avoided making any grammar or usage errors, something that would have jerked me right out of the story.

When I looked up, I saw that Tiffany's hands were clasped together so tightly that the knuckles showed white. I know that's a cliché, but it was also the literal truth. My client was scared to death that I might hate what she'd written.

I have to admit that I'm not fond of reading about blood and gore, but I could stomach a good deal of violence if her prose was all this memorable. Besides, her business, and the advance I was going to ask for, would be very welcome.

"Your opening certainly grabs the reader's attention," I said.

A smile blossomed on Tiffany's face, turning her cheeks pink with pleasure. "Oh, I'm so glad you like it."

I wouldn't go that far, I thought, but I could see how this book might appeal to fans of the hard-boiled end of the crime novel spectrum.

"You have a strong voice, Tiffany, and appear to have a good command of the English language. You've obviously taken the time to learn the basics of formatting a manuscript. That said, until I've read the entire novel, I can't offer specific suggestions for improving it. Tell me, do you belong to a critique group?"

She shook her head and her smile vanished. "Hardly anyone knows I write in my spare time."

"Not even your husband?"

She shook her head and avoided meeting my eyes. "No one in my family has a clue."

It was rare, these days, for someone to complete a book-length manuscript in a vacuum, but Tiffany appeared to have managed it. On further questioning, she admitted to reading how-to books and *Writer's Digest,* but she had never shared anything she had written.

"You're the first person ever to read my work."

"Okay, then. Tell me — why did you choose to focus on 1930s gangland killings?"

She shrugged. "It's part of the history of this area. If you grew up here, you must know that."

"Before my time," I reminded her, "but, yes, I have heard of Murder Incorporated."

Back in the 1930s, New York City gangsters regularly used our part of Sullivan County as a dumping ground for their murder victims. The body in Tiffany's scene had been killed with an ice pick, bound with sash cord and ignition wire from an automobile, tied to a rock and to the frame of a slot machine, and thrown into a local lake.

"Did you use details from a real crime?" I asked.

"Oh, yes. It's important to be authentic."

"You might want to consider losing the slot machine. What's true isn't always believable in a novel."

Her face puckered up as if she might burst into tears. To my relief, it cleared again the next moment. "Is that like 'kill your darlings'?"

"Exactly." I sent an encouraging smile her way. "Can you deal with the possibility that some of your favorite passages may be the ones that need to be cut?"

I could see she was torn, but she put on a brave face and stuck out a hand. "If you take me on as a client, I promise to listen with an open mind to all your suggestions."

We shook on it.

Having sealed the deal, we got down to basics. Although she had already seen my rates listed at my website, I went over those details again as I entered them into the simple contract a lawyer friend had helped me devise. Tiffany didn't even blink when she wrote a check for half the estimated cost of her developmental edit.

After we'd agreed to meet again the following week, I escorted her to the door. Then I did a happy dance all the way back to the kitchen. I celebrated my acquisition of a new client by taking myself out to a nice restaurant for lunch and bringing the leftovers home for Calpurnia.

CHAPTER 2

Three days later, Tiffany's manuscript sat beside my laptop as I typed. I was on my front porch, comfortably settled in a well-padded wicker chair. I was supposed to be working. Instead, I was sending jpegs to my sister-in-law.

Fall colors had just started to appear on the trees. No one could deny the scenic beauty of pictures that showed mountains and lakes. I felt certain Allie would also be struck, as I had been, by the similarities in terrain between the foothills of New York State's Catskills and the western part of Maine where I had lived for most of the last fifty years. I hoped that realization would reassure her that I knew what I was doing.

The entire family thought I was nuts to uproot myself at my age and start over somewhere else. They didn't understand how difficult it would have been to stay put.

The final photograph I attached to my

email showed a particularly brilliant sunset over Chestnut Mountain, a good-sized hill in the western part of Lenape Hollow. If I hadn't known better, I'd have thought it was the view from the road approaching our weathered farmhouse in Maine. I'd always thought that panorama quite lovely, especially in autumn.

As I pressed SEND and exited the email program, I debated whether or not to snap a few pictures of the village to go with my next message. To my delight, I'd discovered that downtown Lenape Hollow was looking pretty dapper. Many of the buildings had been newly painted. Although a few of the storefronts stood empty, signs in their windows read OPENING SOON rather than BUSINESS PROPERTY FOR RENT.

The signs themselves were a good indicator of increasing prosperity. One of the new businesses in the village was a state-of-the-art sign company. Their prices were high, but the results were stunning, large and durable and featuring easy-to-read lettering and clever graphics.

Only last week, the local newspaper reported that the town had approved spending nearly fifty thousand dollars to hire a public relations firm to market it as an ideal location to establish a small business. The new casino might have been awarded to another municipality, but Lenape Hollow was centrally located in the county and therefore well placed for economic growth. All in all, the future looked promising. Next time I went downtown, I would definitely take pictures.

The only place I was not prepared to share in photos was my house. There was a good reason for that. I was on the front porch with my laptop, at least in part because the room I intended to use as an office was not yet fit for human occupation. Although I was able to do some home repairs myself, there was too much that needed to be fixed for me to tackle it all. I meant to limit my activities to the small upstairs room where I'd already ripped up moldy carpeting to reveal a scarred wooden floor.

There were days — too many of them lately — when I wished I hadn't impulsively bought the house. On others, though, when I awoke full of optimism about the foreseeable future, I knew I had made the right decision.

You've got everything under control, I told myself. *Now get to work!*

I opened the attachment my very first client, a woman in Virginia, had sent that morning. It was the newest version of a short story she'd been working on for several weeks. The last time around I'd made suggestions for punching up the ending. I was curious to see if she'd taken my advice, but I'd only read the first two pages before I was distracted by the sound of a car pulling into my driveway.

Lenape Hollow rises on both sides of the main street of the village. My property is on the uphill side of Wedemeyer Terrace, with the house on higher ground than the garage. Since the porch railings are high and solid, I could see only the roof of the vehicle from my present position.

I stayed where I was, curious but unalarmed. I'd had several visitors since I moved in, mostly old friends from high school.

A car door slammed. A moment later, I heard the clump of footsteps as someone climbed the three steps cut into the side of the terrace and started along the flagstone sidewalk that ran the entire width of the porch before it reached an entrance. I could see the top of a head — no hat and thick, rust-colored hair — but its owner didn't notice me. I saw him pause to check the house number before mounting the five wooden steps leading onto the porch.

When he hove into view, I was able to

measure him against the height of the door frame. He was slightly over six feet tall and in good physical condition. He wore dress slacks, a blazer, and a loosely knotted tie. As I watched, he approached the front door and peered through the screen into the hallway. Since no one was visible, he looked to his right, located the bell button, and was about to jab it when I spoke.

"May I help you?"

His head swiveled in my direction, showing me a craggy, suntanned face dominated by a beak of a nose and piercing dark brown eyes. At a guess he was in his mid-thirties.

"Michelle Lincoln?" he asked.

The deep voice went well with the rest of the package. If I'd been forty years younger and the heroine of a romance novel, I'd have been instantly smitten. The man even had a cleft in his chin!

"That's right." Did I sound a trifle breathless?

The table holding my laptop, Tiffany's manuscript, and an assortment of old-fashioned writing paraphernalia was lightweight. I moved it out of my way and started to stand.

"Don't get up." Four long strides brought him to my side before I subsided. He held out his identification. "I'm Detective Hazlett with the Lenape Hollow Police Department."

My heart stuttered as I stared at his credentials. More bad news? Hadn't I had enough of that lately to last a lifetime?

The feeling of panic lasted only a moment. This visit could have nothing to do with anyone near or dear to me. All of them — my sister-in-law, her husband, their two kids and their spouses, and Allie's three grandbabies — were safe in Maine. My cell phone, on the table next to my laptop, hadn't rung all morning. I had the laptop set to ping if an email came in. Anyone trying to reach me would have had no trouble getting through.

I tamped down my irrational fears and studied his badge and photo carefully before nodding to indicate that I'd seen enough. Another worry niggled at me during the few seconds it took him to put his ID away. What if he asked *me* for proof of identity? I hadn't yet traded in my Maine driver's license for one from the state of New York. All the information on the old one was out of date, even weight and hair color. What if there was a deadline to register my car in New York? Had I inadvertently broken the law?

Without waiting for an invitation, the

detective appropriated the mate to my chair. He reached into another pocket and this time came up with what looked like one of my brand new business cards. It was hard to be certain. It was inside a see-through evidence envelope, but it had the bedraggled appearance of something that had been forgotten in a pocket and gone through the wash.

"Oh, my," I whispered. "This can't be good."

"You recognize the card?" He held it closer, and I nodded.

"It's one of mine. I've just started a new business." I had to pause to clear a lump in my throat. "I've mailed a few of those to clients in other states, but here in Lenape Hollow I've only given out one, to a woman named Tiffany Scott. Is she . . . has something happened to her?"

His eyes narrowed. "It would be best if you let me ask the questions, Ms. Lincoln."

I couldn't blame him for being circumspect. In spite of the fact that I'd grown up in Lenape Hollow, I'd been gone a long time. He didn't know me, and — let's face it — outsiders are always the first to be suspected when something goes wrong in a small town.

"When did you give Ms. Scott your card?"

26

he asked.

"Monday. Three days ago."

"Can you elaborate on the circumstances?"

"She brought me this printout of her novel." I indicated the manuscript. "She hired me to help her get it ready for publication."

"That's what you do? Fix other people's writing?"

I nodded. "I'm a freelance editor."

He glanced at the bedraggled card. "Write Right Wright?"

If I'd been younger, I'd have blushed. Instead, I kept my voice level and unapologetic. "I needed a catchy name for my business, and the Grammar Guru was already taken."

"So, Ms. Scott wrote a novel?" Detective Hazlett's brow furrowed as he scribbled in the small, spiral-bound notebook he'd removed from yet another pocket.

"That's right. She wrote it, and then she hired me to edit it."

"You mean fix her grammar? Catch typos?"

"That's one of the services I offer. She wants developmental and line editing as well — in simplest terms, someone to check her story for consistency and to point out areas that might benefit from revision."

Along with my business cards, I'd had flyers printed to describe the three kinds of editing I was prepared to do. I'd included a list of fees and a disclaimer to make clear that I could not be hired to rewrite someone's book. There was also a mini-biography designed to impress potential clients with my expertise. I located one of the flyers in the pile of papers on the table and handed it over.

"How did she find you?"

"Online. I have a website. She saw I was local. The personal contact seemed important to her. As a rule, I wouldn't expect to deal with walk-in clients, but I have no objection to them. She came by. We talked about her book, signed a contract, and I took down her contact information. She left the manuscript with me. We arranged to meet again next week."

Detective Hazlett took a moment to skim my leaflet. "Much call for this?" he asked.

"Not here in Lenape Hollow, no." When he said nothing but still looked doubtful, I found myself compelled to fill the void. "I taught language arts to seventh- and eighth-graders until I was sixty-five. Unfortunately, my retirement income doesn't stretch far enough to cover the repairs I need to make on this house. To cover the difference, I set up shop as a freelance editor."

Detective Hazlett put away his notebook and eyed Tiffany's manuscript. "What's it about?"

I hesitated, unsure how to answer. Why had I put off reading the book? I knew little more now than I had on Monday. "It's a murder mystery set in the 1930s."

"Nothing . . . controversial?"

"I wouldn't say so, no. Historical mysteries are quite popular with readers, and I —"

"I'll be taking this with me, if you don't mind. I'll give you a receipt."

I *did* mind, but I was hardly in a position to argue. Strictly speaking, the manuscript didn't belong to me. I waited a beat.

"How, exactly, did you acquire the business card I gave to Ms. Scott?"

He sent me a long, level look before answering. "It was on her person when we found her. I'm sorry to have to tell you this, Ms. Lincoln, but your client is deceased."

I had been afraid he was going to say something like that. It hadn't seemed likely he'd have one of her possessions any other way.

"What happened?" I asked. "Was it a car accident?" The day I met her, she had driven away in a sporty red convertible.

"No," he said as he handed over the promised receipt and scooped up Tiffany's manuscript. "We are investigating the possibility that she was murdered."

CHAPTER 3

An hour after Detective Hazlett dropped his bombshell and left, I was still too agitated to settle. Unable to go back to work, I gathered up my laptop and papers and carried them into the house. Calpurnia opened one eye when I deposited everything on the dinette table. She was curled up on a cushion on the wooden bench seat my father built many years ago to go over the radiator beneath the double window. The bench looked shabby now, the paint faded and the grill that allowed heat to rise so rusty that I feared it was about to disintegrate.

"Don't get up," I said to the cat.

Taking me at my word, Calpurnia closed her eye.

This time, talking to a cat did nothing to ease my stress and confusion. Consulting my late husband, who had also been my best friend, was no longer an option. The

31

gloomy thoughts I normally kept at bay saw an opening and flooded into my mind — doubts, regrets, sorrow . . . anger. In my mind's eye, I saw the house we'd shared in Maine. Tears welled up as I remembered how unbearable it had been to live there alone.

My husband and I had been married for forty-five years when he up and died on me. For forty of those years, we'd lived on twenty-five acres of land on the outskirts of a small Maine village. We had no close neighbors, but that had never been a problem for us. We enjoyed our solitude and each other's company. He took care of the heavy-duty chores like plowing our long, steep driveway and fixing things when they broke. I put meals on the table, did the laundry, and, with varying degrees of thoroughness, took care of the rest of the housework. We'd been anticipating a long, relaxing retirement during which we would have time to pursue new hobbies and travel a bit.

So much for carefully laid plans!

I slammed my fist on the table, making the papers jump. The pain brought me out of my funk.

"Get a grip," I said aloud. "There were practical reasons to leave."

I'm relatively fit for my age, but I've never had much in the way of muscles. The idea of fending for myself, especially through a long, bitter winter, had been daunting. I suppose I could have learned how to drive the John Deere tractor with the snow blower attachment, but to be perfectly frank, I had no desire to be *that* self-sufficient.

I'd considered various options, everything from finding an apartment in one of the nearby towns — walking distance from post office, bank, and the local Food City — to buying a condo in Florida. Then an invitation to my fiftieth high school reunion arrived in the mail.

I hadn't given much thought to Lenape Hollow for decades. My parents moved to another town at the same time I left to start college, so I'd never gone back for holidays. Two weeks after I received my bachelor's degree, I was married in the college chapel. Since my husband was a native Mainer, that's where we settled. The only time the Empire State had been on my radar after that was when the Red Sox played the Yankees. Having been raised by a loyal fan of the Dodgers — *before* dem bums left Brooklyn — I had no difficulty picking which team to root for.

Once I decided to attend my reunion,

curiosity got the better of me. I looked up the local newspaper online. Almost the first thing I saw was a real estate ad for a very familiar house.

So, here I was, starting over. Today that depressed the heck out of me.

Rather than stay home and brood about death — Tiffany's or my husband's — I grabbed my keys and I headed for my friend Darlene's house.

When I pulled into her driveway, I saw that her van was in the garage, although her husband's car was missing. Frank Uberman had been in the class ahead of us in high school. Darlene had married him while they were still in college.

She had given me her house key when I first moved back to Lenape Hollow. I used it, but I stopped just inside the front door to call out a greeting.

"In the kitchen," came the answering shout.

I made my way from the entry hall through her spacious living room and equally large dining room, steering around a laundry basket full of clean, folded clothing that had been abandoned in the middle of the floor of the former and a mobility scooter tricked out with all the latest amenities that nearly blocked the door from the latter into a

34

cheerful, sunlit kitchen.

The battery was missing, and I didn't see the bag Darlene kept it in when she wasn't using the scooter, so I assumed it was being recharged. All in all, that was an excellent sign. So was finding Darlene standing in front of the stove, stirring something that smelled deliciously of tomatoes, garlic, and onions.

"You're having a good day."

She glanced over her shoulder, shrugging as she did so. "So-so. Don't fuss. It won't kill me to be on my feet for a while."

"I didn't say a word."

It had come as a shock to return to Lenape Hollow and discover that one of my closest friends from high school, Darlene Uberman, née Misner, suffered from arthritis so severe and in so many joints that she'd been forced to take early retirement from her job as head librarian at the Lenape Hollow Memorial Library. On her best days, she could walk without so much as a cane for balance. On her worst, she could barely get out of bed. How much she was hurting depended upon the weather and the effectiveness of the meds she took for pain.

Over the years, she'd accumulated the full assortment of mobility aids. When she had to "walk" a considerable distance or simply

35

wanted to save her strength, she used the scooter, what she liked to call "motorized transport." At other times she relied upon her cane, her walker, or a lightweight wheelchair. Fortunately, she could still drive a car, giving her an additional degree of independence, but she was obliged to rely on others for the heavy lifting.

Darlene's physical challenges had made her look older than she was. Chronic pain etched lines into her face, but they were right next to others that came from frequent smiles.

We'd started life very similar in appearance — brown hair, blue eyes, average height and build, although at five-foot-seven I'd ended up being two inches taller than she was. That had equalized with age. I'd shrunk a bit since senior year in high school, and Darlene now wore orthopedic shoes that gave her an additional inch.

As usual, she was perfectly turned out. She'd always been a Rembrandt when it came to applying makeup so that it looked as if she wasn't wearing any at all. She probably hadn't needed to. Boyfriends called her eyes "cornflower" blue while mine, partially hidden behind glasses, never made it past an ordinary and uninteresting adjective, usually "pale" or "light." Darlene had a cute, albeit snub, nose. Mine was just a little too long. Even now, I envied her stylishly coiffed, fluffy white hair and her ability to make anything she wore look good. Today she was clad in jeans and a sweatshirt. I can dress in my best, freshly pressed and pristine, and within five minutes, I look as if I've slept in my clothes. Don't even talk to me about scarves! No matter how I tie them, they just hang there, limp and unflattering, feedbag instead of fashionable.

At around age fifty, such things stopped bothering me, although I still noticed them. I gave up trying to impress other people with my appearance. I never wore much makeup to begin with, so it wasn't hard to give that up. I let my hair grow long as, gradually, it turned from brown to the sort of gray that, in some lighting, makes me look like a blonde. I wear it shoulder length, with bangs, in contrast to Darlene's short hairdo. The style would do a good job of hiding my hearing aids if I didn't habitually tuck it behind my ears.

These days Darlene and I do have one thing in common. We've both . . . filled out since high school. I refer to my build as "sturdy." She maintains she's twice the woman she used to be — literally. The weight doesn't help her arthritis, but I ask

37

you, how on earth is she supposed to lose pounds when she can't walk any great distance, let alone jog or work out at a gym? Still, from what I observed at our fiftieth high school reunion, we were both aging a lot more gracefully than at least half of our classmates.

"Where's Frank?" I asked as I settled in at Darlene's kitchen table.

"Playing golf. Where else?" She gave the contents of the pot a last stir with a wooden spoon, turned, and got her first good look at my face. Her smile faded. "What's wrong?"

So much for casually leading up to the subject!

The story spilled out none too coherently, but Darlene didn't have any trouble following it. By the time I was finished, she'd joined me at the kitchen table and supplied me with a steaming cup of coffee and a huge portion of homemade streusel.

"Tiffany Scott," Darlene repeated. "Huh!"

I nodded. "Did you know her?"

My friend shifted uncomfortably in her chair. "I know who she is. Was. Are you sure it was murder?"

I considered her question for a moment. "Detective Hazlett seemed to be hedging his bets. He said there was a *possibility* she'd been murdered. But, Darlene — why would he be asking me questions if it there wasn't something suspicious about her death?"

"Sad," Darlene said instead of answering. Looking thoughtful, she took a long swallow of her coffee.

"She was very young."

"She was an adult."

"Well, yes, but surely she wasn't any older than her mid-twenties. She had her whole life ahead of her, and she was so excited about her novel."

"Was it any good?"

I had to admit I'd only read the first few pages.

"So it might not have been publishable?"

I shrugged. "These days, I'm not sure there is any such thing. She could always have brought it out independently, as an e-book original. Anyway, that's not the point. It's a tragedy when anyone is cut off before their time."

"Why are you taking this so hard?" Darlene asked. "I don't mean to seem callous, but it isn't as if you were close friends with Tiffany Scott and are devastated by her death."

"I liked her, and I'm sorry she's dead." I narrowed my eyes as Darlene topped off her coffee from the French press she'd brought to the table and downed half the cup as soon as she'd added cream and sugar. "You don't usually drink more than one cup, especially in the afternoon. What is it you aren't telling me?"

"I suppose you'll find out anyway. Tiffany Scott was Ronnie's granddaughter."

"Ronnie? Veronica Rappaport?"

"Veronica North these days." A faint smile flickered and was gone. "She tried out two other husbands before she latched onto Cal North. She had a son by one of them. He's Tiffany's dad."

Following Darlene's example, I took a sip of coffee while I digested this new information. I'm not much of a drinker, but in that moment I found myself wishing for something much stronger.

Ronnie Rappaport had been the bane of my existence in high school. In a politically correct world, she'd be singled out as a bully and warned to mend her ways. Back in the day, attitudes were different. Kids were expected to suck it up and cope with taunts and put-downs on their own.

More than fifty years after the fact, telling myself I was being mature, I had chosen to ignore Ronnie at our reunion banquet. Even though only thirty members of our class showed up, and only half of them brought spouses, it hadn't been difficult to stay out of her way. Now that I thought about it, I wondered if Ronnie had been doing her best to avoid me, as well.

My husband and I had chosen not to have children. That pretty much took grandchildren out of the equation, but it didn't keep me from feeling empathy for Ronnie. "Were they close? Ronnie and Tiffany?"

"I have no idea." As if her coffee had suddenly lost its appeal, Darlene shoved her cup aside. "I don't move in the same social circles as the Norths or the Scotts, but I expect Tiffany's choice of a husband pleased her grandmother. Ronnie always set great store by success."

I remembered Tiffany mentioning a husband. He liked modern décor, and he hadn't read her novel, but that was all I knew about him. "Who did she marry?"

"Only the richest man in town. His name is Gregory Onslow. He owns Mongaup Valley Ventures."

Neither name meant anything to me, and I said so.

"I've got a brochure somewhere. He's been promoting a major construction project that's created quite a stir in town." She waved off my next question. "It would take too long to explain, and I doubt it would

41

cheer you up to hear about it. That's why you came here, isn't it? So I'd help you pull yourself out of the dumps?"

"You do tend to look on the bright side of life." I threw out the sarcastic reference to *Monty Python's Life of Brian* with a deadpan expression on my face.

She caught it, gave a snort of laughter, and dipped into Voltaire's *Candide* for a comeback: "After all, this is the best of all possible worlds."

I smiled in spite of myself. "I guess I should count my blessings and not dwell on someone else's misfortune."

"Works for me. Look at the plus side — if Tiffany found you on the Internet, others will, too. How many people have hired you since you went live?"

"Six. Tiffany's was the biggest project. I was looking forward to working with her."

"I thought you said you hadn't read much of her book."

"No, but the signs were promising. Good word choices. No glaring grammar errors. Plus, she knew how to format correctly. The manuscript was printed in twelve-point Times New Roman with one-inch margins and proper spacing after periods and between paragraphs. And she used the Oxford comma."

Darlene lifted an eyebrow. "Is that some word nerd thing?"

I chuckled. "You would not believe how much controversy there is over something as simple as whether or not to put a comma before the word 'and' at the end of a list."

"You should definitely blog about that, then."

"Darlene, I'm not starting a blog. If all goes well, I won't have the time."

"It will attract more business. So will having a presence on social media."

"Don't even start! I can't do everything, even if I wanted to. And I don't."

"Stick with just the blog, then. You can call it *The Write Right Wright Writes,* or maybe *Lincoln's Language Log.*"

A spirited discussion ensued and, true to form, the visit with Darlene lifted my spirits. By the time I drove home, I was in a much more cheerful frame of mind.

CHAPTER 4

Neither the local evening news on television nor the next day's local newspaper — the biweekly that comes out on Tuesdays and Fridays — carried any details about Tiffany Scott's murder, only reporting that she'd died unexpectedly and that the police were investigating because it was an unattended death. There was no mention of foul play or suspicious circumstances, but I couldn't get the image of my waterlogged business card out of my mind. The idea that Tiffany might have been drowned like an unwanted kitten made me shudder.

Although I took swimming lessons as a kid, I'm not fond of water. That may be *because* I took swimming lessons as a kid. I had to remove my glasses, which meant everything around me abruptly became a blur. Then, as soon as I dove into the water, it went straight up my nose. As a solution, my mother insisted that I wear a nose guard.

All that did was give everyone else at the swimming hole a good laugh.

I tried to tell myself that the cause of Tiffany's death was none of my business. I did not need to know the details. I vowed to forget all about her book and erase the memory of an aspiring young author full of enthusiasm.

It didn't work. When I sat down at my dinette table for breakfast the next morning, I remembered all over again the way she'd looked sitting opposite me. Her face had been aglow with hopes and dreams that would never be realized.

I was badly in need of a distraction, and the visit from Detective Hazlett had reminded me of a task I'd neglected. During that brief moment of panic when I'd thought I must have done something to warrant a visit from the police, I'd realized that I was, in fact, guilty of breaking the law. A few minutes online confirmed that I should have registered my car within thirty days of establishing residency in New York State.

Oops.

Just to make matters more complicated, I also discovered that I had to have a New York State Insurance Identification Card before I could register my vehicle. Fail to present this ID and you'd be required to surrender your plates. Not only that, if you had a lapse in insurance of more than three months, you risked having your driver's license suspended.

"Wonderful," I muttered. "I was right to panic when that cop showed up."

Always one to look for the positive in a situation, I decided to see this as a way to keep my mind off Tiffany's death. Making myself and my car legal would certainly occupy the entire day.

My first stop was at the insurance agency where I'd bought my homeowner's insurance. I traded in my old automobile policy for liability, no-fault, and uninsured motorist insurance from a company approved by the state of New York. Then, armed with two freshly issued insurance ID cards, the original and a copy, I got in the car and headed for the nearest Department of Motor Vehicles office.

That meant a trip to Monticello, the county seat. By the time I drove there, my insurance agent would have notified the DMV that I was covered. Apparently there is a lot of car insurance fraud in New York State. The DMV would not only take possession of one of my two ID cards before they let me register my vehicle, they'd also have to have electronic verification of insurance.

46

What is it about dealing with government agencies that makes honest people so nervous? I was a wreck by the time I parked at the Sullivan County Government Center and collected the paperwork I'd brought with me. I checked everything one last time. Vehicle Registration Application printed from the DMV site and filled in. Check. Proof of my identity. Check. Proof of car insurance and ownership. Check. Checkbook to pay title fee, license plate fee, and tax. Check.

I planned to get a new driver's license while I was there, too. According to the online instructions, that was a simple matter of trading my Maine license, not due to expire for another year, for one from New York. I wouldn't have to take a written test or prove I could parallel park. I shuddered at the thought of the latter. I couldn't remember the last time I'd attempted that particular maneuver.

My father taught me to drive. He'd had me steer his big old Buick in circles in an empty parking lot on a Sunday afternoon. He was a good teacher. I'd been pretty confident of success the day I went in to take my driver's test . . . and devastated when I didn't pass. I no longer remember the reason I failed on that first attempt, but I do recall that most of my high school friends were in the same boat. To make ourselves feel better, we decided that the DMV must have a policy to flunk everybody under eighteen at least once before letting them have a license.

Think positive, I ordered myself. I'd completed the application form. I had my passport with me for additional proof of identity. I'd even dug out my Social Security card, since the information online indicated that I might need to present that to the powers-that-be to prove I was who I said I was. Belatedly, I wondered if I should have brought a copy of my birth certificate, too. No, I decided. That wouldn't help. Then I'd have to have my marriage certificate to prove that Michelle Greenleigh and Michelle Lincoln were the same person. Clearly I was overthinking this.

Taking a deep breath, I tucked everything into my shoulder bag and got out of the car. The DMV office was easy to find, since it was on the first floor of the government center and clearly marked, but I had to repress a sigh when I saw how many others were already waiting, seated on several rows of long, blue, uncomfortable-looking benches. There were even two people ahead of me in the line to get a ticket. A moment after I joined the queue, a middle-aged woman with a sour expression on her face crowded in behind me. She was muttering under her breath.

After I'd taken a number and a seat, I studied my surroundings. The institutional décor was not designed to offer comfort. The only adornments on the bland walls of the waiting area were a few signs, mostly warnings. There was, however, a child-size desk with two wooden chairs in front of it, neither occupied at the moment. It was supplied with what looked like a coloring book and a box of crayons. I stifled a snort when I shifted my gaze upward and noticed the sign directly above the little desk.

LEARNERS PERMITS
9:00 A.M. TO 3:00 P.M. ONLY

The numbers of the lucky persons being served appeared beside the windows where they were to stand, barred from direct contact with a clerk by a counter topped with a wall of glass. After a glance at my ticket, I was glad I'd thought to tuck my iPad into my shoulder bag. It looked as if I was going to enjoy a nice chunk of reading time.

The next hour passed slowly. My e-book didn't hold my interest, and most of the people seated near me were careful to avoid eye contact, discouraging me from trying to start a conversation. The only exception was the woman who'd been in line behind me. She'd taken a seat on the same bench, leaving only about a foot of space between us. Every time I glanced her way, my gaze was met by a hard, unfriendly stare.

I've never been good at waiting, and the sensation of hostile eyes watching me made matters worse. By the time my number came up I had a bad case of the jitters. I hopped off the bench with more speed than grace and made tracks for window three.

"I'm number one-oh-seven," I told the bored-looking clerk on the other side of the glass partition. And then I blurted out what had apparently been niggling away at the back of my mind the entire time I'd been sitting there. "Did you know you're missing the apostrophe in your sign?"

She answered my question with a blank stare.

I should have dropped the subject, but on occasion my mouth operates without consulting my brain. "The sign that says LEARNERS PERMITS — it should have an apostrophe after the word *learners*. It's possessive, you see. The permits belong to —"

"Ma'am, do you have business with the

DMV?" The bored look had been replaced by one of mild irritation.

If I'd been twenty years younger, or even ten, my face would have turned crimson with embarrassment. No one likes to be lectured to, and annoying the person whose cooperation I needed was a very bad idea. "Sorry. I just moved here. I need to register my car and trade my Maine driver's license for one from New York." I fished the documents out of my shoulder bag and placed them in a neat pile on the counter.

Despite the shaky start, the registration went smoothly. Once I had my brand-new license plates in hand, the clerk moved on to Part B. First she had me read the eye chart on the wall behind her. Since my glasses were less than a year old, I passed that test with flying colors. Then she took my picture. I didn't expect much there. ID photos are rarely flattering, but I was unprepared for the process to come to a dead stop when she examined my Maine driver's license.

"This isn't valid."

"Excuse me?"

"This license. It's not a Real ID."

Belatedly, I realized that the clerk's objection had nothing to do with proof of my ability to drive a car. I sighed. I was going to have to deliver a little lecture after all.

"Maine is one of five states who initially refused to meet the requirements of the Real ID Act. It was only when residents could no longer get into a federal building without a passport that legislators enacted a compromise. The upshot is that this is still valid and your web page states that New York and Maine have reciprocity on drivers' licenses."

She squinted at the object in question, a doubtful look on her face, and didn't say a word.

Compelled to fill the silence, I kept talking. "It would have cost a bundle to comply with the federal law, and Maine's legislature is frugal as well as paranoid about sharing information. Even now drivers can opt out of a Real ID. I hadn't decided what I was going to do when this came up for renewal." I ground to a halt. "Perhaps you could check with your supervisor?"

She continued to fix me with a suspicious look, the kind that made me think she was about a nanosecond away from calling security. There was no guard in the DMV office, but there had been a uniformed sheriff's deputy in the lobby. Meanwhile, the sour-faced woman from the line to get a number had taken her place at the adjacent window. While she waited for the clerk to process her application, she eyed me up and down with a sneer on her face. She seemed to have taken a personal dislike to me. For some reason, that rattled me almost as much as the clerk's recalcitrance.

Almost. The low point of my day was when the clerk disappeared into another room, taking my Maine license with her. I was certain that when she returned she was going to deny me a new license *and* confiscate the old one. I wondered how I was supposed to drive home then.

It took another quarter of an hour for everything to be straightened out. My application was approved and in exchange for my Maine driver's license I was given a temporary one from the Empire State. The official one would be mailed to me. After all the hassle, I had to fight an urge to break into a run as I left the office. I was half convinced they could still change their minds. Instead, I proceeded at what I hoped was a decorous pace along a long corridor lined with blue doors and gave a sigh of relief when I finally exited the government center.

I really hate bureaucracy. It has a numbing effect on the brain. I stood there, mind blank, for a full minute before I could remember where I'd parked my car.

As I drove home, once more the good, law-abiding citizen, I mentally composed a letter I would never send. In it I made several suggestions about areas where the training of DMV employees could be improved. First on the list was a remedial lesson in basic grammar and punctuation with an emphasis on the use of apostrophes.

CHAPTER 5

I spent the weekend working on the small room that was my DIY project. Steaming wallpaper is a boring job. So is sanding a floor. I had plenty of time to think, and I was of two minds about attending Tiffany's funeral. It was to be held on Monday afternoon at the same church I'd attended as a child and at which Darlene was still an active member. She had called to ask if I wanted to go with her. I'd agreed, but as soon as I hung up memories had rushed in. The last funeral I'd attended had been my husband's. I'd reached for the telephone, intending to call Darlene back and cancel, but something had stopped me.

While I worked, I came to the conclusion that it hadn't been a need for closure. It hadn't eased my sense of loss one iota to "celebrate" James's life after his death. He'd always maintained that funerals were a waste of time and money. After the fact, I

55

had to agree with him.

No, the truth was simpler than that. I'd agreed to go to Tiffany's funeral out of crass curiosity. I was hoping to get a look at her entrepreneur husband, perhaps even have the opportunity to ask him if the police had told him about Tiffany's novel. Imagining the manuscript in some police evidence room, forgotten and gathering dust, bothered the heck out of me.

She had told me that her husband didn't know she was writing a book, but it seemed to me that he might want to have possession of it now — a legacy of sorts. If James had written a novel in secret, I'd certainly jump at the chance to read it! Besides, since I was no longer in a position to edit Tiffany's book, I felt obliged to refund the money she had paid me as an advance.

So it was that on Monday, at the First Presbyterian Church of Lenape Hollow, I trailed after Darlene as she steered her scooter expertly up the ramp and into the sanctuary. The side aisle was wide enough to allow her to pass without difficulty, but to avoid blocking anyone else's way, she headed straight for the pews closest to the altar. When I had settled into the third row with Darlene parked beside me, I had a clear view of the family of the deceased.

Gregory Onslow, Tiffany's husband, was a good ten years older than his late wife. Either that, or he had deliberately added white streaks to his hair in an attempt at gravitas. He wore a dark gray pinstriped suit that screamed "custom made" and kept his eyes straight ahead so I couldn't get a good look at his face.

In the same pew, but with a marked distance between them, sat Tiffany's grandmother, Veronica North. At our reunion banquet I'd only seen her from a distance and in dim illumination. Sunlight filtering in through the stained glass windows struck hair of an improbable matte black, a far cry from her natural color. This was so obviously a dye job that it was painful to look at, and when she turned slightly, to the accompaniment of a whisper of silk, she revealed tightly stretched skin that shouted, "Facelift!"

"Where are Tiffany's parents?" I whispered to Darlene, recalling that she'd told me Tiffany's father was Ronnie's son.

"They moved to New Zealand."

I started to ask why, but just then the minister appeared to launch into a surprisingly brief service. He did not ask anyone to share their memories of Tiffany, and he kept prayers to a minimum.

When it was over and I stood to look toward the exit, I was surprised to discover that the church was packed. I repressed a sigh. Between Darlene's need for maneuvering space and the fact that we were seated so far down front, it was going to take a while to escape. Everyone parted for the minister, the widower, and the grieving grandmother, but the ranks closed in again as soon as they passed.

A steady murmur of hushed voices hummed in the air, broken here and there by a stifled laugh or a cough. The pungent smell of the flowers — that odd mix that comes from too many fancy arrangements — had me longing for fresh air. I tried to distract myself by searching among the mourners for familiar faces.

There was no sign of Detective Hazlett. I wasn't sure what to make of that. Cop shows on television always give the impression that homicide detectives make a practice of attending the victim's funeral, hoping the killer will show up and somehow give himself away. Another myth shattered.

Or, just maybe, there was no homicide involved. From what little I could overhear of the quiet conversations around me, no one was speculating about murder.

"I hear she died at home," one woman

whispered to her companion.

"A fall?"

"Slipped in the shower or some such. Terrible way to go."

A shower, I thought, would only account for that soaked business card if Tiffany went into it fully clothed.

"Found in the woods behind her grandmother's house," someone on the other side of me said. "Slipped on a rock and cracked her fool head open."

I turned and tried to pick out the speaker, but there were too many people around.

In the crush, I did spot several classmates, together with one or two others who looked vaguely familiar, but I felt no particular urge to push my way through the crowd to talk to any of them. I jumped when someone tapped me on the shoulder.

"Michelle? Michelle Greenleigh?"

"Yes. Well, Michelle Lincoln now." I turned to find a tall, slender woman standing behind me. She appeared to be a few years my senior.

"You won't remember me," she said, "but I started teaching at the high school your junior year. I was Clarice Browne then. Now my last name is Cameron." She gestured toward the exit, where the minister was shaking hands with parishioners on their way out. "That's my husband. He's been the pastor here for the last four decades."

"That has to be some kind of record," I blurted. I could remember three different pastors during my first eighteen years.

"He is much revered." She sounded a trifle defensive.

"I'm sure he is." We'd moved out into the aisle, but there were still too many people ahead of us for Darlene's scooter to get through.

"I had heard you moved back to Lenape Hollow," Clarice said. "I'm surprised I haven't seen you in church on Sunday. I don't believe you ever gave up your membership in this congregation."

"In that case, I must owe a fortune in back offerings."

That quip went over, as we used to say, like a lead balloon.

"Your spiritual well-being is nothing to joke about." The evangelical gleam in her eyes had me backing up a step. "What church did you attend during your time away?"

I was tempted to tell her I'd become a Buddhist or a Scientologist just to discourage her recruitment effort, but the truth was that I'd simply stopped attending worship services of any sort a long time ago. Her aggressive attempt to lure me back into the fold only made me dig in my heels, more determined than ever to avoid organized religion. My faith was a private matter, one I had no intention of discussing.

"Fore!" Darlene called out as she spotted an opening and shot toward it on her scooter.

I jumped to one side, narrowly avoiding damage to my toes. Clarice backpedaled rapidly, going in the opposite direction. Before the minister's wife could buttonhole me a second time, I hurried after my friend.

In Darlene's van, we followed the hearse to the cemetery for a brief graveside prayer. Afterward, I felt obliged to join the queue offering condolences to Ronnie North.

"I'm so sorry for your loss," I told her when my turn came. "I only met your granddaughter once, but she seemed like a lovely person."

Ronnie looked down her nose at me. She has a fine patrician proboscis and does this well. In high school, that look and the superior smirk that went with it always made me feel like a bug about to be squashed.

"How kind of you to say so," she murmured in a pleasant contralto that was huskier than I remembered but sounded just as insincere. When she turned her attention to

61

the next person waiting to offer condolences, I got a whiff of her signature perfume. I've never cared for Emeraude. I suspect Ronnie is the reason.

Dismissed, I looked around for Gregory Onslow. My gaze fell on a sandy-haired fellow in a gray suit that looked expensive but *not* custom made. In his late twenties, he stood a little apart from the rest of the mourners. A cell phone was pressed to his ear. I shook my head over his rudeness. He clearly had no clue how to behave at at funeral.

Onslow, like Ronnie, was surrounded by people offering sympathy. I'd have to wait before I could speak with him.

It didn't bother me to linger in a cemetery, especially this one. When I was a little girl, my grandfather used to bring me here and tell me stories about our ancestors. Greenleighs and twigs from several other branches of the family tree had been buried in Lenape Hollow Cemetery for generations. The first was John Greenleigh, one of the duly elected fence viewers for the village.

As a youngster, I thought a fence viewer must be a surveyor. It turned out I was almost right. The job involved making sure people's fences were in compliance with the local laws and also dealing with complaints about livestock that crossed a fence or stone wall onto the neighbor's property. This was a big deal in colonial New England and New York; I don't know about the rest of the country. Anyway, John Greenleigh went to his reward back in 1810 and I wandered over to his weather-worn headstone to pay my respects.

The graves were well cared for, thanks to an endowment to the cemetery association that paid for mowing the grass and making minor repairs. If there had been a problem with vandalism, as there was in some cemeteries, it was not evident here.

I'm not certain how long I spent ruminating on family history, but when I glanced toward Darlene's van I saw that she'd already stowed her scooter in the back and was in the driver's seat. Even from a distance, I could tell she was fidgeting. I signaled that I'd only be another minute or two and looked around for Tiffany's husband.

Only a few mourners remained. Ronnie had left. Onslow, however, was still present, talking to a man I didn't recognize. With a determined stride, I headed their way, only to be brought up short when I heard the venom in Onslow's raised voice.

"Don't you know who I am?" he demanded, looming over the smaller man in a threatening manner.

"I am well aware of your reputation, and I am not impressed. Just because you have money — a good deal more of it now than you did before your wife's death — doesn't mean you can have everything your own way."

As I watched, a dull red wave crept up the back of Onslow's neck. His hands clenched into tight fists at his sides. "Try to stop me, and you'll regret it."

I turned tail and fled. Obviously, this was not an opportune moment to talk to the widower about his late wife's hopes and dreams. I wondered if there ever would be a good time to do so. Who knew how he'd react? Having witnessed the intensity of his anger, I couldn't help but speculate that Onslow's short fuse might have been the reason Tiffany had never told him about her writing.

CHAPTER 6

Although I had not been invited to Ronnie's house after the funeral, Darlene had. She insisted that I accompany her. I thought about making my excuses and walking home. It wasn't far. Lenape Hollow isn't all that big. Instead, I climbed into the passenger seat of the van and kept my mouth shut.

Only after we were under way did it occur to me that I had no idea where Ronnie lived. In high school, her family had owned a one-story, cookie-cutter house in the village's sole housing development. Since Tiffany had said something about her grandmother's place being full of antiques, I could only suppose quite a few things about Ronnie's life had changed in the course of half a century.

A few minutes later, Darlene left a quiet street on the west side of the village and pulled through open wrought-iron gates to climb a long, winding driveway toward a

Victorian mansion. I remembered the property as belonging to a miserly old woman named Laverne Levine. On Halloween, kids used to dare each other to climb over the wall — the gates were always closed and locked — and knock on her door. The bravest of the boys tossed firecrackers onto her porch before they took off running.

I was still smiling at that memory when we entered what was now Veronica North's house, and I caught sight of Mike Doran. Speak of the devil. I sidled up to him. "Any firecrackers in your pockets, Mike?"

His blue eyes twinkled, but he managed to keep a straight face. "Why, Mikki Greenleigh, as I live and breathe. I don't know *what* you could possibly mean."

"You being a respectable senior citizen and all?"

"Exactly."

We hadn't talked much at our reunion banquet, but I knew my old classmate had gone to law school and set up his practice in Lenape Hollow. "How are you keeping busy, now that you're retired?" I asked.

He shrugged. "By not entirely retiring. I keep my hand in with the occasional interesting case."

"Michael!" Ronnie's imperious tone put an abrupt end to our conversation. She beckoned, and he trotted over like a good dog, abandoning me without a backward glance.

It had been that way in high school, too. He'd asked me out a couple of times and then dumped me to date her. I'd been philosophical about the breakup even then, joking that we wouldn't have lasted as a couple anyway. Simply being known as "Mikey and Mikki" would have killed the romance.

I helped myself to a cup of oversweetened punch and a cookie and looked around. I recognized quite a few faces from the church and the cemetery, including the sandy-haired man with the phone glued to his ear. He was still yakking on it.

"Who is that guy?" I asked Darlene.

In deference to the crowded conditions in Ronnie's house, Darlene had left her scooter in the van and was making do with her walker. "Dip me up a cup of that punch and I'll tell you."

After I obliged her, she took a sip, made a face, then downed a longer swallow before she answered my question. "That's Alan Van Heusen. He's Greg Onslow's flunky. Onslow sends Van Heusen in when he doesn't want to get his hands dirty."

"Sends him to do what? Break kneecaps?"

"What a lively imagination you have!"

Van Heusen was tall and muscular. When he turned slightly, I saw that he had big brown eyes and a face that was quite pleasant looking. No scars. No sign that his nose had ever been broken. Nothing, in fact, to mark him as anything but a legitimate businessman.

That didn't change my opinion of his manners. His boss's wife had just died, and he was in the home of her bereaved grandmother. Out of respect he should, at the least, go outside to conduct business. Better still, that phone call could have waited until he was back at his office.

"I suppose, now that I think about it," Darlene mused, her voice wry, "that Onslow *did* make a few offers folks couldn't refuse."

My eyebrows shot up.

"More than a year ago, Mongaup Valley Ventures bought up several buildings on Main Street, all the ones currently sporting signs that say they'll be opening soon. New ownership seemed like a good idea for most of them, the ones that went out of business ages ago, but a couple were doing okay as they were. Now those shops are boarded up, too, and if anyone knows what's scheduled to replace them, they're not saying."

"Are you telling me that Onslow forced the owners to sell?"

Darlene frowned into her cup. "I don't like to spread unfounded rumors, but I know for a fact that in one case there was another prospective buyer in the picture, someone who had definite plans to move right in. Onslow stepped up at the last minute with a preemptive bid."

As we talked, I continued to watch the people around us. It didn't take me long to realize there was something peculiar about their behavior. There was no casual flow of movement. Conversation, too, seemed oddly static. True, it was an occasion for hushed voices, but I sensed an undercurrent I was at a loss to understand. It didn't feel like sadness or grief. It felt like anger. The tension in the air was thick enough to choke a horse.

"Darlene, what's going on here?"

She followed my gaze to the group gathered around Ronnie. A glance in Onslow's direction revealed another cluster of people congregating near him. Judging by the glares and the ominous muttering coming from both sides, these folks were ready to rumble. The man I'd seen Onslow try to browbeat at the cemetery was whispering in Ronnie's ear. She looked as if she'd just bitten into a particularly bitter piece of fruit.

"Do you remember me mentioning that Onslow's company has a construction project planned, one that has a lot of people riled up?"

"So what?" As guests in Ronnie's house, these folks ought to be able to keep a lid on their feelings. Did no one feel any respect for the dead?

"Tiffany's grandmother is the leader of the opposition." Darlene nibbled a cookie.

"I thought you told me Ronnie approved of her granddaughter's choice of a husband."

"She probably did, at first. Financially and socially, Onslow is a good catch. But then he came up with a scheme to build a theme park in Lenape Hollow. With the legal gambling issue finally settled, he thinks he can bring prosperity back to this part of Sullivan County, too — restore the town to the tourist mecca it was when we were teenagers."

"With a *theme* park?" Visions of the Wizarding World of Harry Potter and Santa's Village danced in my head, and neither fit well into Lenape Hollow. To say the concept boggled my mind was an understatement.

Darlene's lips twisted into a wry smile.

"Ever since our little town was passed over as the site for Sullivan County's new casino, local people have come up with all kinds of crackpot suggestions to improve our economic situation. The difference in Onslow's case is that he has the money to back up what he wants to do. Mongaup Valley Ventures bought up two hundred and sixty-five acres on Chestnut Mountain, including the old hotel grounds."

I had only the vaguest memories of a Victorian-era hotel on the highest point of land in the area. It had burned down when we were kids and had been closed for decades before that.

"This is on top of the businesses on Main Street?" I asked.

"All of Onslow's plans veer toward the grandiose. Remind me to give you that brochure I mentioned the other day. You can read his prospectus for yourself."

"Why don't we head for your place now," I suggested, "before someone tries to sucker me into taking sides."

Darlene said nothing more as she drove from Ronnie's dooryard to the end of the driveway. When we reached the street beyond, I expected her to turn left. Both her house and mine were in that direction. Instead, she hung a right, went about a hundred yards uphill, and turned right again, stopping in front of a heavy wooden gate not much smaller than the one in *Jurassic Park.*

"*Someone* likes their privacy." I tried to make a joke of it, but the size and solidity of that barrier made me uneasy. "Who built here? When old lady Levine lived in Ronnie's house, she didn't have any near neighbors."

"This," Darlene announced, "is the reason Ronnie is so up in arms. It's the entrance to Greg Onslow's proposed theme park, the one he claims will make Lenape Hollow 'the Orlando of the Northeast' and bring fame and fortune to us all."

CHAPTER 7

The next day, having wasted the previous evening reading the flyer Darlene gave me and speculating about Tiffany Scott's relationship with her husband, I was determined to focus on work. There was nothing I could do for Tiffany, and the last thing I needed was to involve myself in a fight between a local developer and my old nemesis. More to the point, this was one of the last peaceful mornings before a horde of workmen descended on the house.

My business had been showing modest signs of growth. I had eight aspiring writers as clients, each of whom had sent me an electronic file of a manuscript in need of editing. For three hours, I worked with due diligence, but when the carillon in the Episcopal church tower began its regular noontime concert, I stood up and stretched. A glance out the window showed me another fabulous fall day.

One of the resolutions I'd made after my husband's death was to take better care of myself — healthier eating habits, more regular exercise, less stress. Lately I hadn't done too well in any of those areas. Determined to make a new start, I left my temporary desk — the dining room table — snagged the sweater I'd tossed over the back of a chair, tucked my keys, a couple of tissues, and a ten-dollar bill into the pocket of my jeans, and headed for the door. At the last minute, I went back for my smartphone, not because I planned to call anyone but because of its handy camera feature. Since I was going for a walk, I could also take more pictures to send to my sister-in-law.

Earlier forays around Lenape Hollow had taken me downtown on several occasions. *Down* is the operative word. To reach Main Street requires descending a steep hill. At the top of my porch steps, I hesitated. Across the street, the slope starts gently enough, but toward the bottom the angle of descent abruptly increases. That's great, if dangerous, when you're ten years old, the road has not yet been plowed, and you're trying out that new sled you found under the Christmas tree. Otherwise? Not so much.

Once I reached Main Street, the going

would be easier. It's relatively straight and flat. Returning home, however, would be an uphill slog. I do not exaggerate when I make reference to mountain goats. There are several streets that run between Main Street and Wedemeyer Terrace. One of them ascends at such a sharp angle that the town fathers installed a railing for pedestrians to grab on to. Walkers in far better shape than I am regularly pull themselves along hand over hand as they make the climb.

In my girlhood, my friends and I used to go everywhere on foot. When we weren't walking, we rode our bikes. I can't imagine where we found the energy. Just contemplating the return journey sent my enthusiasm into a tailspin. I'd walk later, I decided. Today was a good day for a drive.

Once in the car, I changed my mind yet again. Instead of going downtown, I drove back to the spot Darlene had shown me to the previous day. I don't know why I went there. Idle curiosity, I suppose. Those big wooden gates were as daunting as they had been at first sight, but this time I got out of the car to take a closer look.

Darlene had been right when she'd called Greg Onslow's scheme grandiose. *Deranged* might have been a better word choice. According to the brochure from Mongaup Valley Ventures, Wonderful World, "the Orlando of the Northeast," would have five separate venues. First up would be Frontier America, featuring a train ride to a lost Indian lead mine. Then there would be a year-round county fair with rides, restaurants, and carnival booths. The Land of Make Believe, an Animal Kingdom — wild animals in their natural environments — and the Kingdom of the Future would round out the list of attractions.

Each proposal struck me as more outdated than the last, like leftovers from the era of the original Disneyland. If Onslow was trying to bring back our heyday, this wasn't the way to do it. Even back then, the project would not have had much hope of success.

From the 1930s until around 1970, tourists had flocked to the foothills of the Catskill Mountains. They came to escape the heat of New York City in the summer, and because what became known as the "Borscht Belt" offered them everything they could possibly want: luxury accommodations, good fellowship, and free entertainment. I refuse to cite *Dirty Dancing* as an accurate representation of that time. The movie did get some things right, but I had a different perspective on things. I was one of those locals who didn't have anything to do with the big hotels or the bungalow colonies or the summer camps. When I was old enough to work, the job I took was with the local telephone company as a long-distance operator. My closest friend was a sales clerk at Woolworth's, and another pal waitressed in a downtown restaurant.

A soft breeze ruffled my hair as I stood staring up at the enormous wooden barrier. Colorful leaves rustled over my head, and a few drifted down to join those already on the ground. The only other sound was the faint murmur of the brook that ran along the edge of Ronnie's property.

When I looked toward that side of the gate, I spotted what appeared to be a narrow path. Curious, I moved closer and pushed aside a low-hanging branch. The track was wider than I'd expected and ran parallel to a high wooden fence. Since I hadn't seen any NO TRESPASSING signs, I promptly gave in to temptation.

The going was uneven but not treacherous. Other feet had already packed down the earth beneath my walking shoes. At first, the height of the fence prevented me from glimpsing anything on the other side, but after a little while that solid barrier gave way to old-fashioned posts and barbed wire.

I kept going. *Good exercise,* I told myself.

Eventually, I came to a spot where the barbed wire had been cut. That didn't surprise me. Local teenagers had probably been responsible. What youngster would be able to resist the urge to sneak inside and explore? I might have done the same thing when I was younger.

Who was I kidding? I had no hesitation about snooping at *my* age. Feeling quite pleased with myself when I managed to make it through the opening without snagging my sweater, I set off to reconnoiter, snapping pictures as I went.

It didn't dawn on me where I was until I came out on a ridge that looked down on a small lake. With a sense of shock, I recognized it as the one where I'd taken swimming lessons as a child.

It was easy enough to understand why I hadn't caught on to my location sooner. The *Jurassic Park* gate was new. The old entrance to what had then been called Chestnut Park was on the far side of the property. Back then, this parcel of land had belonged to the village. It had provided local residents with a swimming hole and picnic area — a place of their own for summer activities. Tourists were not allowed in.

I wondered if Mongaup Valley Ventures

had made the mayor an offer he couldn't refuse.

Looking down on it in the present, I thought Chestnut Lake seemed smaller than it was in my memories. There was no trace left of the dock or the rough log building that had housed the changing rooms. Still, it wasn't difficult for me to pick out the area of higher ground on the opposite side of the water where the picnic tables had been set up to take advantage of the shade of oak, ash, and maple trees. Beyond that, out of sight from where I stood, there used to be a paved parking lot.

I descended to what passed for a beach, arriving slightly out of breath. One landmark remained unchanged, a large boulder supposedly deposited eons ago by a glacier. It rose up out of a tangle of weeds, exactly the right size and shape to use as a bench.

With a nostalgic sigh, and no doubt a sappy grin on my face, I plunked myself down on this convenient seat and took a few more photos before tucking the phone into the pocket of my sweater. Bracing my hands behind me, I leaned back, content to enjoy the colorful, rustic view. Memory provided the sound of children's laughter and the sight of swimmers racing from one side of the lake to the other. Sometimes we'd played volleyball on the not exactly sandy shore.

My peaceful contemplation of the scene was cut short by an angry shout.

"Hey, you! This is private property!"

I stumbled to my feet, off balance and ungainly, to find a behemoth in a private security uniform trundling down the hill toward me. He had a nightstick in one hand and a portable radio in the other. I put both hands out in front of me with the palms toward him. It didn't surprise me to see that they were shaking or to discover that my heart was racing and my throat had gone dry. I considered myself lucky that my trembling knees kept me upright long enough for the guard to reach me.

I had to take a couple of deep breaths before I was able to speak. "I didn't see any signs," I gasped. "I was just paying a visit to the old swimming hole."

Slowly, he lowered the truncheon. Although he wore no name tag, his shoulder patch identified him as an employee of Mongaup Valley Security. It wasn't much of a leap to guess that this was a subsidiary of Mongaup Valley Ventures. After a moment's hesitation, he stuck both the nightstick and the radio back into their slots on his utility belt. I felt my eyes widen when I saw that it also held a canister of pepper spray and a gun.

"You got to leave now, lady. Mr. Onslow don't like people wandering around his property."

This time I had to swallow convulsively before I could manage to utter a single word. "Yes." I swallowed again. "Of course. I'm going."

I shifted my gaze from the gun to the guard's face. His hard-eyed, unyielding expression, lips tightly compressed and nostrils flaring like a bull about to attack, encouraged me to cooperate when he herded me toward a newly built road I hadn't even realized was there. It took us straight to the massive gates Onslow had installed.

For some reason, I'd imagined a heavy bar holding this wooden barrier closed, but the smooth surface was unbroken. It seemed downright anticlimactic when the guard pulled what looked like a garage-door opener out of his pocket and depressed a button.

Eerily soundless, the gates swung open, revealing my parked car and a glimpse of the street beyond. In the distance, I could hear the hum of an engine as another vehicle inched its way up the steep hill.

"Get going." The guard gestured, and I

obediently trudged toward my car.

The sun had been beating down on the windshield while I was exploring the remains of Chestnut Park. As soon as I opened the unlocked driver's side door, a wave of heat eddied out. I shrugged out of my sweater, knowing I'd be too warm if I left it on, and was about to toss it into the backseat when I remembered my phone. Arresting the movement, I fished it out of the sweater pocket . . . and jumped a foot when the guard shouted at me again.

"Hey! You been taking pictures?"

I spun around to find him bearing down on me once again. My immediate reaction was to thrust the phone behind me. The car door was between us, but even as solid as it was, it didn't offer much protection against a guy that big.

"Give it here."

He reached for me with his enormous hands, eliciting a squeak of alarm on my part, but before he could grab hold of anything, the car that had been passing by screeched to a halt a few feet beyond the future entrance to Wonderful World. The guard and I turned to watch as the vehicle backed up at reckless speed, stopped again, and roared in our direction, coming to a second abrupt stop just inches from my rear bumper.

It took me a moment to identify the driver. Mike Doran was so furious that his face was contorted out of all recognition. He flung himself out of the car and charged toward the security guard. "What the hell do you think you're doing? Leave her alone!"

An overwhelming wave of relief swept the last of the starch out of my limbs. I collapsed onto the car seat. A moment later, taking advantage of the guard's distraction, I swung my legs inside, jerked the door closed, and hit the lock button.

Through the window, I could hear sputtered excuses. Clearly, my tormentor knew who Mike was, and that he was a lawyer. It's amazing what the fear of being sued will do to change someone's attitude.

"I don't care if she *was* taking pictures," Mike bellowed. "You don't go around threatening defenseless women."

The guard apologized again before he retreated to the far side of the gigantic gates. In slow motion they swung closed, hiding him from view.

Mike gestured for me to roll down my window. "You okay?"

"I'm fine. And I'm *not* defenseless."

Now that the danger had passed, I was a

trifle miffed that he'd thought he had to rescue me. If he hadn't come along, I was sure I'd have found a way to deal with that bully on my own. At worst, I'd have had to relinquish my cell phone and watch him delete my pictures.

Mike chuckled at my chagrin. "C'mon, Mikki. Let me have my knight-in-shining-armor moment. They don't come along all that often."

"I do appreciate the help." If I sounded grudging, he chose to ignore it.

"Good. How about you reward me by meeting me for coffee tomorrow?"

He looked so eager, so much like the Mikey I remembered from high school, that I had to smile. "I'd love to," I said, and I meant it.

We agreed on a time and place. He started to leave, then turned back again. "Why was he so intent on getting hold of your camera?"

"Beats me. I only took a few nature shots to send to my sister-in-law. Scenic views. Autumn colors and all that. I *was* trespassing, though."

"You and half the kids in town. I guess it's only natural you'd be curious."

"Lots of memories," I agreed, "especially down by the lake."

A peculiar expression came over his face. "What?"

"You mean you don't know?"

I hesitated, suddenly uncertain whether or not I wanted to hear his answer. After a moment, curiosity won out. "Know what?"

"That's where they found Tiffany Scott's body. She drowned in Chestnut Lake."

CHAPTER 8

I didn't sleep particularly well that night. I dreamed about bodies floating in water. One was Tiffany's. The other was the victim she described in the first scene of her novel.

There was a nip in the air the next morning, and I set off at a brisk pace down the Alley. This isn't a street, but rather a wide driveway that runs from Wedemeyer Terrace, at a point almost directly across from my house, down to Main Street. The Catholic school uses it as a playground at recess, and near the bottom of the hill it flanks the rectory. The church is a bit farther away, off to my right as I descended the last, steepest bit.

Mike had suggested we meet at a place called Harriet's. It hadn't been in business when I last lived in Lenape Hollow, but he'd assured me I couldn't miss it. It was located just a few doors past the gas station that was across the street from our old redbrick elementary school.

What Mike had neglected to mention was that the coffee shop was situated *directly* opposite the new-to-me police station. From the table he'd chosen by the window, I had a clear view of the entrance and the sign that read LENAPE HOLLOW POLICE DEPARTMENT. I hadn't been seated for more than ten minutes when Detective Hazlett parked his unmarked car on the street in front of the building and went inside.

Mike saw me wince and frowned. "What?"

"Nothing."

"It's not nothing. Tell me."

I gave him a brief recap of my business dealings with Tiffany before telling him about my encounter with Detective Hazlett. "He showed up on my doorstep to ask questions after they found her body. He said he was investigating her death as a possible murder, but then, only a few days later, everyone was saying it was just a tragic accident."

"Or suicide. I've heard people bandy about that theory, too."

"Not likely. She wasn't the type."

His eyebrows shot up. "And you know this because you spent, what, twenty minutes with her?"

"I trust my instincts, and they're telling

me that there is something odd about Tiffany's death. Why else would there have been so much speculation, even at the funeral? You tell me she drowned in the lake. Other people think she fell inside her house or while walking in the woods near Ronnie's place."

On Ronnie's property, I wondered, or on Wonderful World land?

"The family wants to keep the details out of the media." He shrugged. "There's nothing wrong with asking for a little privacy in which to mourn her death."

He had a point, but I didn't believe I was imagining things.

"Tiffany's novel starts with a drowning," I said slowly. "That . . . bothers me."

"You're a good person, Mikki." He contemplated his Danish as he added, mumbling the words, "Biggest mistake of my life was when I broke up with you."

A short bark of laughter escaped before I could stop it. "The Mikey and Mikki thing would have split us up eventually. As a couple, we'd have been just too precious for words. Besides, Ronnie was waiting in the wings, determined to get her claws into anything I had. You didn't stand a chance against the dragon lady."

He pretended to shudder at the memory

and then took a big bite out of his pastry. After he'd chewed and swallowed, he changed the subject. I had no objection. In fact, I encouraged him to talk about himself, curious to know how the boy I remembered — skinny and kind of dopey-looking and voted class clown — had morphed into a heavyset, self-confident, clearly prosperous professional man. It turned out that Mike's law practice had specialized in divorces, including two of his own.

"I should never have let you go," he said again after he'd hit the highlights of his life since high school.

"Nonsense! I'd have made you miserable, and you'd now have three divorces behind you instead of only two. Is there a current Mrs. Doran?"

He admitted that there was and added that he, like me, was childless.

"Your turn," he said. "Tell me more about this new business venture of yours."

"The short version is that I needed extra income to pay for repairs on the house, and editing manuscripts seemed like a logical choice. I have a good friend back in Maine who writes romance novels. I've read drafts of her work for years to give her feedback. That's not quite the same as editing, but it was good practice, and my background as a language arts teacher — what we used to just call English — has conditioned me to spot errors. You wouldn't believe how careless people have become about word choices and good grammar. It drives me crazy when I find obvious mistakes in published books, and I don't even want to think about the howlers that creep into news stories."

"Let me guess — you proofread your emails."

Mike's quip interrupted what might well have turned into a rant. I sent him a stern look but then made him laugh by mimicking the high-pitched, nasal voice of one of our old high school teachers, Miss Blumberg: "There would be far fewer misunderstandings if everyone did. Neither emoticons nor emoji are sufficient to clearly convey what the writer means." I wagged my index finger at him, just as she used to.

Still smiling, he said, "So now you help aspiring writers avoid mistakes."

"Exactly."

He asked more questions, and I answered. I was flattered by his interest . . . until I realized that he had gradually shifted the conversation away from my editing business and back to Tiffany's book. He seemed very curious about her novel.

"I'm surprised to hear that her story takes

place in the nineteen-thirties," he said. "I'd expect her to be more interested in writing about what's going on in the present."

"I only had time to read a short section before Detective Hazlett took possession of the manuscript, but that was definitely historical." I paused. "Did you know Ronnie's granddaughter well?"

He stared out the window for a long moment before he answered. "It's a small town. I know most of the people who live here." He glanced at the clock on the wall of the coffee shop. "I need to get going, and I'm sure you do, too."

"You're right," I agreed. "Working for myself doesn't mean I can spend the whole day goofing off."

He offered to drive me home and looked disappointed when I said I'd prefer to walk.

"I need the exercise," I joked, nodding at my empty plate. I'd scarfed down two glazed doughnuts while we were talking.

I *did* intend to go home and buckle down to more editing, but when I stepped outside, there was the police station, right in front of me. I waved to Mike as he pulled away from the curb, watched the car until it was out of sight, and then crossed the street.

"I'd like to speak with Detective Hazlett," I told the young man on the other side of a glass partition. *Bullet resistant?* I almost asked before I decided that question might be taken the wrong way.

A few minutes later, I was shown into a cramped little office that smelled of coffee and cinnamon but was almost painfully neat. Even the takeout bag in the wastepaper basket had been neatly folded. The logo identified it as coming from Harriet's, making me wonder if they delivered. I was certain Hazlett had not come in for food and drink while Mike and I were there.

In contrast to his surroundings, the detective was in shirtsleeves, his tie dangling. He reached for his jacket but abandoned the effort to shrug into it when I told him not to bother.

"I only need a moment of your time."

He waved me into a visitor's chair that was every bit as uncomfortable as it looked. "What can I do for you, Ms. Lincoln?"

"It's about Tiffany Scott's manuscript."

"You want it back?" His brow creased into a frown.

"No. That is, I think it should go to her family. But what I really wanted to ask is if you read it. It starts with the discovery of a body in a lake and I wondered . . ."

My voice trailed off at the look on his face. It revealed his opinion of me as plainly as if he'd spoken aloud. He thought I was a crackpot, or a conspiracy theorist, or perhaps just a woman of a certain age who was cursed with an overactive imagination.

He cleared his throat. "Ms. Scott *was* found in a lake," he admitted. "She drowned while swimming. It was apparently her habit to swim at that spot in good weather. She was not stabbed with an ice pick, nor was her body weighted down with a rock or a — what was it?"

"Slot machine." I sent him a wry smile to assure him that I got his point.

"If that's all . . . ?"

I stood, but I still had one more question. "How did my business card get wet? Surely she didn't go swimming fully clothed?"

Detective Hazlett stared at me in stone-faced silence.

"Unless it *was* suicide."

"It was not, and I can assure you that Tiffany Scott was not a latter-day victim of Murder Incorporated."

"Case closed?"

"Is there anything else I can do for you today?" He rose from his chair, his face grim, clearly prepared to boot me out of his office — literally, if that became necessary.

I stood my ground. "What about Tiffany's novel?"

"I'll see to it that the manuscript is given to her husband."

Too late, I wished I'd asked to have it back. Then I could have turned it over to Greg Onslow *after* I read it. Since that ship had sailed, I thanked the detective for his time, wished him a good day, and went home.

Five minutes after I walked through the front door, my phone rang.

"You have some nerve," said an accusing voice.

"Ronnie?"

"Why did my granddaughter go to *you* for help?"

"Because I'm a book editor and she had written a book."

"Did she give you anything besides her manuscript?"

Ronnie sounded so pissed off that I wasn't sure whether to be amused or annoyed. Surely she couldn't be jealous of the short time I'd spent with Tiffany.

"No," I told her. "Why would she?"

"Are you certain? Nothing to do with Wonderful World?"

"The theme park? No. Tiffany's novel was historical fiction, and that's *all* we discussed."

I don't know if Ronnie believed me or not,

but she slammed the receiver down on her old-fashioned landline with enough force to make me wince.

CHAPTER 9

The next day my house was overrun with carpenters, electricians, and plumbers. In an effort to complete the most essential renovations before the snow flew, the contractor I'd hired had marshalled his troops and launched all three types of work simultaneously. I hid out in the dining room with my laptop and cell phone, closing both the pocket doors to the wide-open living room and the ordinary door that led to the kitchen. Even so, workmen kept popping in, usually with questions I couldn't answer.

When the pocket doors slid open for what felt like the hundredth time, I ignored the faint sound and kept my focus on the screen in front of me. I was using track changes to comment on the first chapter of what might yet become a taut, fast-paced thriller . . . *if* my client could untangle the peculiarly twisted sentence structure he insisted upon using. I suspected he was trying to sound literary, an attempt that had backfired rather spectacularly. Any editor reading what he'd written so far would toss the manuscript aside, convinced the author needed a refresher course in basic grammar. Sadly, that wouldn't help — not until schools once again made diagramming sentences part of the curriculum.

After I finished typing my latest suggestion, I looked up. I expected to see any of a half dozen anonymous men in work clothes. I'd been introduced to them all that morning, but as soon as I sat down to work, most of their names had flown right out of my head.

Instead of an electrician or a plumber, Gregory Onslow's right-hand man stood just inside the pocket doors. I couldn't remember his name, either, but my throat closed up when I saw that he'd shut those doors behind himself. I knew he worked for Mongaup Valley Ventures, but he was still a stranger and we were isolated here, out of sight of everyone else in the house. Above all the noise of hammering and clanging pipes, even a full-voiced scream might not be heard.

He's harmless, I told myself. *You have no reason to panic.*

But he stood alarmingly close to me. My

dining room is not large, and the table took up most of the available space. I was seated with my back to the door to the kitchen. My unwanted visitor, even though he was barely inside the room, was less than two feet away from me. Only one corner of the table separated us.

I spoke in a reproving tone of voice. "I didn't hear you knock."

"Your front door was open."

I gestured toward the pocket doors. "Those weren't, although I'd just as soon they were now."

Without turning, he reached behind himself and slid them apart, revealing my living room and the picture window that looked out over the front porch to the street beyond. "Happy now?"

"Delirious. Is there something I can do for you?" I started to shove my chair away from the dining room table so that I could stand.

He was too quick for me. It took him only a couple of steps to reach my side. Then his hand settled on the chair back, preventing me from rising.

"No need to get up."

The words sounded friendly, but I didn't care for the way he was invading my personal space. I shoved harder, dislodging his grip and giving myself room to scramble to my feet.

He lifted both hands in a gesture of surrender. "Truce, okay? I just —"

A yowl and a hiss interrupted him. Calpurnia had been asleep on the floor near my feet. When he'd backed up a step, he'd managed to step on her tail. All affronted dignity, she levitated to the top of the table, back arched and fur fully fluffed.

He grinned. "Your ferocious guard cat, I presume."

"Sic 'em," I said under my breath. When I reached out a hand to soothe my brave protector, I got a scratch across the knuckles for my trouble.

The intruder chuckled.

I glared at him. The man had walked into my home, bold as brass, and now he was laughing at me? When he reopened the pocket doors, my anxiety level had dropped from red alert to merely wary, but that smirk on his face triggered another abrupt shift in mood. I was irritated. Make that *extremely* irritated.

"Do I know you?" I demanded.

He reached into the breast pocket of his suit coat for a business card and handed it over. "Alan Van Heusen at your service, Ms. Lincoln. I work for Mongaup Valley Ventures. I'm Mr. Onslow's chief assistant and general factotum."

Flunky was the term Darlene had used. Van Heusen was the one who did Onslow's dirty work for him. His card identified him as Director of Public Relations.

"And you're here because . . . ?"

"It has come to Mr. Onslow's attention that his wife consulted you about a novel she had written." He sent a smarmy smile in my direction. "I'm here to retrieve anything she left with you."

Calpurnia, ignored, stalked to the far end of the table. She made her displeasure known by upsetting a small plastic container full of paper clips, after which she jumped down to stand in front of the closed kitchen door until I reached over to open it and let her through. Only after I'd closed it again did I turn back to my uninvited visitor.

"You've wasted a trip, Mr. Van Heusen. Detective Hazlett took everything Tiffany left with me."

Thunderclouds scudded into Van Heusen's face so fast that I expected it to start raining at any moment. My uneasiness about being alone with him returned just as quickly.

"I'll be happy to show you the receipt." After I blurted out that offer, I moved a few steps closer to the kitchen door, wishing I'd left it open in Calpurnia's wake. Van Heusen still blocked my escape route to the living room.

"That won't be necessary. The police have already returned the manuscript to Mr. Onslow." His thin-lipped smile was patently false. "I'm here to make certain his wife didn't give you any other papers."

"If she had, I'd certainly return them. As a matter of fact, I've been meaning to refund the deposit she paid me, since I didn't have time to do anything to earn it."

"You're *sure* you haven't forgotten anything else?"

I permitted myself an eye roll. "There would be no reason for her to give me anything *except* her manuscript."

He hesitated, then asked, "Did you read it?"

"I had not yet started work on Tiffany's book when Detective Hazlett told me of her death. He found one of my business cards on her person," I added before he could ask.

Finally satisfied, Van Heusen was once again all charm. "We appreciate your cooperation, Ms. Lincoln. Please don't worry about refunding the money. Keep it for your trouble."

I stared after him as he walked away, taken

aback by his sudden generosity. I was equally surprised by the fact that I had lied to him about reading Tiffany's novel. True, I'd only looked at the first few pages, but in the usual way of things, I prided myself upon being scrupulously honest.

I couldn't imagine why he cared whether or not I'd read it. Did he think the book was a tell-all biography, or maybe a roman à clef that could somehow threaten his boss's reputation? This struck me as such a preposterous idea that I caught myself smiling.

What did it matter what Van Heusen thought or why he'd been so generous with Onslow's money? The sounds echoing through the rest of the house were a constant reminder that Tiffany's deposit would go a long way toward paying my bills. I wasn't going to quibble about keeping it.

Determined to forget the interruption and get back to work, I tried to focus. I even removed my hearing aids to cut down on distracting noises. Fifteen minutes later, frustrated and out of sorts, I exited the file I'd been editing, shut down my laptop, and popped the hearing aids back in. My concentration had been well and truly broken by Van Heusen's visit. I found it impossible to continue correcting grammar and sentence structure as if nothing had happened.

I *had* been honest with Onslow's flunky when I'd assured him that Tiffany had not given me anything besides her manuscript, but he was the third person in two days to ask if she'd left something else in my keeping. Mike had been the first. Then there had been Ronnie's phone call. Now Onslow, by way of Van Heusen, was checking to make sure I wasn't holding out on him. Why? What did they all think I might have in my possession?

I got up, stretched, and started to tidy up out of habit. The tabletop was littered with reference books, printouts of emails, and the mail I'd collected shortly before Van Heusen's arrival. I hadn't gotten around to opening any of it. I ignored the junk mail and the bills but reached for the padded mailer that bore my sister-in-law's return address.

The penny dropped the moment I pulled the tab to open it. Without looking at the contents, I tossed the thick envelope back onto the table.

If they arrive in good condition, I keep padded mailers, reusing them when I need to send something out by snail mail. The mailer that had held Tiffany Scott's manuscript had never been subject to the tender mercies of the U.S. Postal Service, making it an ideal candidate for recycling. I found it easily, since it was the only one in the bin that did not have labels or postage affixed.

I did not expect to find anything inside, but I felt a little thrill of anticipation as I turned the mailer upside down and gave it a shake.

Nothing fell out.

Just to make certain it was empty, I slid my hand inside. Way down at the bottom, my fingertips touched something hard. Scarcely daring to breathe, I grabbed hold and pulled it out. Even before I looked at it, I knew what it was that Tiffany had left behind.

The thumb drive was one of the smallest I'd ever seen, but it was big enough to hold an electronic copy of her novel . . . and much, much more.

CHAPTER 10

I stared at the thumb drive for a long time, wondering if this was what Alan Van Heusen had been after. It probably was, and it most likely accounted for those pointed questions from Mike and the phone call from Ronnie, too. Why any of them should think that Tiffany would give me something other than her manuscript remained a mystery, but I appeared to be holding the proof that she had done just that in the palm of my hand.

Calpurnia bumped her head against my leg, making me jump and almost drop the thumb drive. She'd circled around through the kitchen and hall into the living room and entered through the pocket doors Van Heusen had left open. She stared at me with an inquisitive look on her face.

"You'd like to know what's on this, too, wouldn't you?"

As if she understood, she made a beeline

for my laptop. I followed more slowly, still hesitating to take the plunge. I had no way to tell what information Tiffany had stored on her thumb drive without looking at the menu. Surely I had reason to do that much. I'd be wasting everyone's time if it contained nothing more than, say, her grocery lists.

On the other hand, what right did I have to invade a dead woman's privacy?

Let me be honest. I was dying to take a peek.

What difference will it make if I do? I asked myself. It wasn't as if Tiffany's death had turned out to be a homicide. Detective Hazlett hadn't contradicted me when I'd said the case was closed. If I'd thought for a moment that he might be interested in these computer files, I'd have taken the thumb drive straight to the police station. As things stood, however, I could see no reason to curb my curiosity.

Looking back on the previous day's visit to the good detective, I was embarrassed to have disturbed him. Don't get me wrong. I didn't regret pointing out the similarities between Tiffany's death and the murder in her novel, but in retrospect I had to admit that he was right to dismiss my half-baked theory that the two were somehow connected.

Hazlett had given Tiffany's manuscript to her husband, and it made sense that he was her heir. A small sigh escaped me as I sat down in front of my laptop. Alan Van Heusen's business card was on the table next to it. I ought to call the number printed on it and make arrangements to surrender the thumb drive. There was no need to examine it further.

"This is just an electronic backup of Tiffany's novel," I said to the cat. "Onslow probably has the original on her computer, and I know Detective Hazlett gave him the printout."

Busy grooming herself, Calpurnia did not reply.

I stopped dithering and inserted the thumb drive into the appropriate slot on my laptop. The menu came up without password protection — careless of Tiffany, but good for me. A quick glance showed me that, yes, her novel was there. So were numerous files that appeared to contain her research. I opened one at random and found the text of an article by a local historian, John Conway, titled "The Corpse in the Grey Suit." It was immediately clear that this incident from 1937 was the inspiration for the first scene in Tiffany's novel, right down to the body tied to the metal frame of a slot machine.

Tiffany had changed the name of the victim, and I assumed she'd done the same for the gangsters who'd killed him. I promised myself I'd read more of her novel and find out. For the moment, though, I contented myself with skimming this account of the real crime.

I was torn between revulsion and amusement as I read that the victim, Walter Sage, had worked as an enforcer for the Brownsville gang run by Abe "Kid Twist" Reles. Sage was killed because he'd been taking an unauthorized cut of the profits from running slot machines in various Sullivan County hotels. Reles sent Irving "Big Gangi" Cohen, Abraham "Pretty" Levine, and Harry Strauss ("Pittsburg Phil") to deal with the problem, although it was actually a man from nearby Hurleyville, Jack Drucker, who didn't appear to have a catchy nickname, who stabbed Sage to death with an ice pick.

Shaking my head, I closed that file and opened the next. It was yet another account of a Murder Incorporated homicide, this one from 1939. This victim had also been found dumped in a lake. A third file detailed a case from 1936. The fourth file I looked at differed only in that it appeared to be notes from interviews Tiffany had conducted with an unidentified source rather than an online or newspaper article. One glance was enough to tell me that the story was similar to those I'd already skimmed. I closed the file without reading any more. I have a low tolerance for gratuitous violence.

The remaining titles in the menu indicated that many of the files contained similar material, but one file name caught my eye. When I clicked on "blackmail.doc" the screen filled with a list of numbers and dates — the days and months, but not the years. For the fruits of an extortion racket, the sums listed seemed low, leading me to conclude they came from the 1930s. If one of the characters in Tiffany's novel was a blackmailer, it only made sense that she'd draw up a fictional list of payments. Such details add verisimilitude to a story.

After I exited that file, I took another look at chapter one. The first scene was as I'd remembered it — well-written but packed with gory details based on a true crime. I only glanced at that part of the text. I'd have skipped it entirely if I hadn't wanted to refresh my memory about the names Tiffany had assigned to her characters. That established, I kept reading. Nearly an hour passed before I took a break.

By that time I was badly in need of one. Sad to say, Tiffany Scott made a mistake all too common with first-time novelists. Writers attempting to sell a work of fiction are typically asked to submit a synopsis and the first three chapters of their books and hold back the rest of the manuscript until an editor or an agent requests the entire thing. With that in mind, Tiffany had rewritten, revised, and polished chapters one, two, and three until they were alarmingly close to being overwritten. In the fourth chapter and beyond, she was as meticulous as ever when it came to grammar, spelling, and formatting, but her prose abruptly lost its luster. The story, too, went flat. She seemed to have mislaid the thread of her plot. Characters who had shown promise became wooden. The dialogue was stiff as well. Worst of all were the information dumps. Every scene was littered with them, ruining the pacing and repeatedly jerking me out of the story.

If I had been reading this manuscript while wearing my developmental editor hat, I'd have forced myself to continue and would have done my best to suggest ways to save the project. As things stood, I had no need to torture myself.

"Well, Cal," I said to Calpurnia, who had made herself comfortable atop the mail I'd left scattered across the tabletop, "the good news is that I don't have to worry about letting her down gently."

I winced when I realized how callous that sounded. Cal didn't care. She nuzzled my hand.

Idly, I scratched her behind the ears, but my thoughts were still on the contents of Tiffany's thumb drive. The real reason I'd given in to curiosity and taken a look at her files had as much to do with Van Heusen, Mike, and Ronnie as it did with Tiffany. They all seemed to think she'd left something with me, although none of them had been willing to specify just what that something was. Left to make my own assumptions, I'd come to the reasonable conclusion that one of Tiffany's files must contain information relevant to the present-day controversy over Wonderful World. When I'd recalled the hostile factions gathered at Ronnie's house after the funeral, it had seemed logical that the amusement park was at the heart of the matter.

So what? I asked myself. The conflict between Tiffany's grandmother and her husband was none of my business . . . unless it had led to her murder.

I suppressed a groan when I realized *that* was what had truly been bothering me all along. Despite the assurances of the police, I continued to believe that there was something odd about Tiffany's drowning. It didn't matter to me that Detective Hazlett was satisfied that her death was an accident. I couldn't forget that my business card appeared to have gone into the water with her. Did that mean she'd been murdered? Maybe not, but it certainly suggested that the case wasn't as simple as Hazlett thought. It would be a slog to read the entire novel and the contents of each of the research files, but until I had gone over every single word, I would not be able to let go of my suspicion that the police had been too hasty to dismiss the possibility of foul play.

As gingerly as if it were a poisonous spider, I removed the thumb drive from my laptop and stared at it. *Had* someone had a reason to silence Tiffany Scott? Was I holding proof of it in the palm of my hand?

Get a grip, I ordered myself. *You could be wrong. What do you know about solving crimes?*

Given how much material the thumb drive contained and how long Tiffany's novel was, it would take me a good many hours to read everything. Even after taking all that trouble, the odds were against my finding anything useful. And yet, if there was even the slightest chance that her death had been a homicide, my conscience would not let me ignore this opportunity to discover the truth.

The sound of heavy footsteps clumping down the stairs signaled that the workmen were finished for the day. It also reminded me that I was twenty-four hours closer to having to make a whopper of a final payment to the contractor in charge of the renovations. Going through the files on Tiffany's thumb drive would have to wait. My first responsibility was to the clients who were still among the living — the ones who could continue to provide me with a steady income.

"Back to work," I said aloud.

Any investigation into the death of Tiffany Scott would have to be conducted in my spare time.

CHAPTER 11

Once Tiffany's thumb drive was out of sight and out of mind, I managed to edit two short stories and an article about the best way to encourage houseplants to grow. By the time I was finished and had fixed myself supper, I was too tired to do anything but go to bed. I slept soundly, and I felt well rested when the alarm went off the next morning, in spite of the fact that I'd set it for an hour earlier than I did when I was expecting workmen to arrive.

Darlene had an eight o'clock appointment with her eye doctor. Since she had to have her eyes dilated and Frank, who would ordinarily have played chauffeur, was committed to a golf tournament at the local links, she'd asked me if I'd do the honors. I was happy to oblige. Darlene had done plenty of favors for me since I'd moved back to Lenape Hollow.

She greeted me with a cheerful, "You'll

never guess what I heard last night!"

"You're right," I said, stepping into her living room. "Why don't you just tell me." Despite her tone of voice, I could tell she wasn't feeling her best. She was seated in her wheelchair.

"Tiffany Scott made a will."

"I suppose that's a little unusual for someone her age, but —"

"She made it a week before she died, but that's not the kicker. Wait for it — she left all her shares in Mongaup Valley Ventures to her grandmother!"

I took a seat on the sofa. "Huh! Bad for Mongaup Valley Ventures. Good for the folks opposed to Wonderful World."

"Got it in one. Greg Onslow must be fit to be tied. I'm sure he expected to inherit everything."

Remembering the heated exchange I'd overheard at the cemetery, I had to agree. "I gather Tiffany was an heiress."

"She brought money to the marriage, that's for sure." Darlene shrugged. "We're not talking billions, or even millions, but for this neck of the woods, she was rolling in it."

"Did Ronnie get everything," I asked, "or just the shares?"

"Just the shares. I think." For some reason

115

that brought a frown to Darlene's face.

"How do you know all this? I didn't think you and Ronnie were that close."

"We're not, but Frank played a round of golf with Mike yesterday afternoon, and Mike is the one who had charge of the will."

"I thought he was a divorce lawyer. And retired," I added as an afterthought.

"Yes, and yes, but he's also an old family friend through Ronnie. He was close to her son and his wife and knew Tiffany from the time she was born. It's not all that surprising that she'd have gone to him on a legal matter, especially if it was something she didn't want one of her husband's lawyers to get wind of."

The more I heard about Tiffany and Greg's marriage, the more unstable it sounded. It occurred to me that if she hadn't made that will, the grieving widower might have found his wife's death very convenient, especially if she knew about illegal activities on his part. *Was* there something incendiary hidden on that thumb drive? Was that why everyone was so anxious to get their hands on it? I really needed to buckle down and read those files . . . but not this morning.

"We'd better get a move on or you'll be late for your appointment," I told Darlene.

"Will your scooter fit into the trunk of my car?"

"It would, if I were planning to take it. Breakdown takes less than a minute. The seat comes off, the battery comes out, and the rest folds up for storage. It's also surprisingly lightweight, but there isn't much room to maneuver at Dr. Shapiro's office, so I'm stuck using the wheelchair."

I got her settled in the passenger seat, collapsed the wheelchair, and stowed it in the backseat. As I made the turn from Darlene's street and headed down a steep hill toward Main Street and the eye doctor's office, I couldn't help but notice that the trees, so colorful only a few days earlier, were rapidly shedding their leaves. We were coming up on one of the most dismal times of the year.

It was when we were approaching the next intersection that Darlene picked up where she'd left off criticizing Greg Onslow. "The more I hear about that man's business practices, the more it ticks me off."

I came to a complete stop even though there was no traffic and turned to look at my friend. She held herself rigid, more stressed than I'd ever seen her. I couldn't tell if the root cause of her tension was something Onslow had done or if griping about him was just a handy valve to let off steam. Either way, her mood was infectious. I had to force myself to relax my death grip on the steering wheel.

"I'll bet he insisted everything Tiffany inherited be tied up in joint accounts. Or maybe he just conned her into investing it all in his company."

"That would explain why she owned shares."

Darlene made a strangled sound. "I wonder how much they're really worth? I wouldn't put it past that man to declare bankruptcy and hightail it out of here with his ill-gotten gains."

She continued grumbling in that vein until I pulled into the small parking lot in front of Dr. Shapiro's practice. It was housed in a plain clapboard building, painted white. When we were kids it had been a furniture store. Big plateglass windows gave me a clear view of the reception desk and waiting room.

I glanced at Darlene as I turned off the engine and removed the key from the ignition. "You don't like Greg Onslow much, do you?"

She shrugged. "Nobody does. If he's about to do a bunk, it won't be the first time people who invested in his schemes have lost their shirts."

The slight tremor in Darlene's voice tipped me off. "You and Frank?"

"It was a couple of years ago. And it wasn't all that much money, but it ticks me off that he took advantage of us."

"If he's a cheat, how is he still in business?"

"No proof. He claimed he took a loss, too." She gave a dismissive little laugh. "You know the old saying — if it sounds too good to be true, it probably is."

"I don't get it. If previous ventures were failures, why would anyone invest in a new one? How on earth did the Wonderful World project gain so much traction?"

"You haven't seen him in action. He's a smooth talker." Darlene reached for the door handle. From the look on her face, you'd have thought she was going to face a firing squad.

I got out and retrieved the wheelchair. By the time Darlene was settled in it, she appeared to have beaten back her black mood. A wide smile brightened her face. To someone who didn't know her as well as I do, it might even have passed for genuine.

CHAPTER 12

Darlene's rapidly shifting moods left me feeling uncomfortable. I had the strongest sense that something other than Greg Onslow had upset her, but it wasn't like her to hold back. If anything she had a tendency to over-share, which meant whatever was troubling her must be very serious indeed.

Preoccupied with that disturbing thought, it took me longer than it should have to realize that I knew the optometrist's receptionist. She'd changed more than a little since the days when we sat next to each other in homeroom.

Throughout junior high and high school, the row of Gs had begun with Gertzman, Gildersleeve, and Gips, and ended with Sarah Goldman and me, Mikki Greenleigh. These days Sarah Goldman was Sarah Shapiro. Belatedly, I put two and two together.

"You're married to the eye doctor?"

Unlike most of our classmates, Sarah had

not put on weight as she aged, unless you count the heavy makeup designed to make her look ten years younger. Scrawny and silver-haired, she wore trim black pants and a high-necked tunic. Eyeglasses I felt sure were in the latest style and expensive as all get-out dangled from a gold chain around her neck. She didn't appear to need them to see.

In response to my surprised question, she gave the same throaty chuckle I'd heard so many times when we were young. "Better. I'm his mother. Park yourself over there," she said to Darlene. "Benjamin will be with you in a minute."

As soon as Darlene and I were settled, I leaned close to whisper in her ear. "What's the story with Sarah? She's our age. Why is she still working?"

"Why are you?" Darlene shot back. "She divorced her husband when she was in her thirties and came back to Lenape Hollow with her son. She raised him on her own, put him through school, and she's never gotten out of the habit of looking after him. He's good at what he does, but he doesn't have the gumption to stand up to her."

I'd have liked to know more, but the office Sarah ran was extremely efficient. Dr. Shapiro's assistant rolled Darlene away to have her eyes dilated, leaving me on my own with a limited selection of slightly dog-eared magazines. Back home in Maine, I'd have been able to find a recent copy of *Down East* to read, but here it was *People, Readers' Digest,* or that day's edition of the Middletown *Times Herald Record,* what passed for a local daily newspaper despite the fact that it was published in the next county. Aside from a piece on activities at the high school — a football game the next afternoon and a dance that night — Lenape Hollow didn't rate a mention, nor did Tiffany, her husband, her grandmother, or Mongaup Valley Ventures.

Darlene returned a few minutes later to wait with me while the eye drops took effect. "I hate this part," she confided, "and sitting in a dimly lit examining room all by myself just makes it worse."

"You never did like sitting around with nothing to do."

I gave her a hard look, certain I'd been right to think that something was preying on her mind. I hoped it was as simple as having to leave her scooter behind. In comparison, the wheelchair was slow and clumsy to operate, and it had to be lowering to have to be pushed.

"Cheer up," I said. "You'll be back home

before you know it."

"This whole day is going to be a waste. I won't even be able to read until my eyes are back to normal. And you know the worst part? I can't stand to look at myself in a mirror once my pupils get big. That really freaks me out."

I could sympathize with her reaction, and with the whole not-good-at-doing-nothing situation, too. Furthermore, the more I thought about it, the more I could see how frustrating it must be to be dependent on other people so much of the time. Despite the fact that Darlene and I were friends, it must have galled her to have to recruit me as a driver. I was just glad she had. If she couldn't focus well enough to read, it would be a very bad idea for her to get behind the wheel of a car.

I was reading an article in a four-month-old *People,* and Darlene had fallen into a state of silent brooding when the outside door opened to admit a gust of autumn air and another patient. I looked up, glad of the distraction.

The newcomer was no one I knew, but the fact that she, like Darlene, was in a wheelchair, had me staring at her as she maneuvered it skillfully through the entrance. No one came in with her. She rolled herself over to Sarah's command center.

"It must be treat the halt and lame day," Darlene whispered. The snarkiness in her voice was impossible to miss.

"Darlene!"

"What? Don't look so appalled. It's only politically incorrect if *you* make fun of cripples. We're allowed to diss each other."

Since I didn't have a good comeback, I settled for shaking my head from side to side.

Ignoring my reaction, Darlene rolled herself over to the reception desk and pulled up beside the other wheelchair. "Hey, Linda, what kind of mileage do you get on that thing?"

Linda, a heavyset woman somewhere in her forties, directed a contemptuous look at Darlene's wheels. It was justified. Linda was operating a state-of-the-art deluxe model with all the bells and whistles. It was sleek, streamlined, sturdy, compact, and motorized, making it all the more obvious that Darlene's ride was more closely akin to what hospitals use to transport discharged patients from a room to a waiting car.

Darlene's eyebrows shot up. "What?"

"Oh, nothing."

"This is temporary. You think your chair is so great? I'll match my scooter against it anytime. I've had her up to ramming speed."

I listened to this boast in amazement. According to what Darlene had told me the first time she showed me her scooter, it couldn't go any faster than three-point-seven miles per hour. At that rate, I doubted she could do much damage to anyone but herself.

Linda looked as skeptical as I felt. "Speed isn't everything."

"Said the tortoise to the hare. Want to race? Even in this clunker, I bet I could beat you." She gestured toward the area where those needing new glasses selected their frames and had their faces scanned to be sure their new spectacles would fit correctly. "First one to circle those displays three times wins."

"Tempting," Linda said, eyeing the obstacle course with the beginning of a smile on her face.

"Honestly, Darlene," Sarah interrupted from her perch behind the counter. "Act your age."

"I will if you will," Darlene quipped without looking at her.

Sarah drew back as if she'd been slapped. She glared at the two women on the other side of the reception desk before glancing over her shoulder toward the examining rooms. No one else was in sight. I couldn't see what she was reaching for behind the counter, but my money was on an intercom button or a phone.

I had the sinking feeling that I was about to have to play traffic cop. Even though I hadn't been back in Lenape Hollow long, my friendship with Darlene had resumed so easily that it had seemed as if we'd never been apart. I'd thought I knew her, but this was a side I hadn't seen before. I couldn't tell if she was serious about her challenge to Linda or not. If she was, the sheer recklessness of her suggestion set off alarm bells. The space between the displays was barely wide enough for two people to walk side by side. The mental image of two wheelchairs careening wildly around the impromptu speedway was enough to have me tossing aside my magazine and heading toward the two would-be Indy drivers.

"Take a chill pill, Sarah," Darlene said as I came up beside her. "Now that I think about it, this baby is better suited to a monster truck rally than a drag race."

By this point, Linda had thoroughly mellowed. "Bring your scooter over to my place anytime," she invited, "and we'll see just who can go faster."

"You're on." Darlene grinned at her.

Before they could set a date, the eye doctor's assistant reappeared to call Darlene's name. My friend's good humor abruptly vanished. Shoulders hunched, she submitted to being wheeled away while I returned to my seat in the waiting room.

The faint hum of Linda's wheelchair followed me across the tiled floor, but since she promptly took out a book and ignored me in favor of reading, I made no attempt to engage her in conversation. Instead, I brooded.

I was more certain than ever that something was bugging Darlene. The look on her face just now made me think I could pin down the cause. It seemed reasonable to assume that she wasn't her usual calm, cheerful self because she was stressed about this appointment with the eye doctor. I concluded that she anticipated a bad report on her eyesight.

At our age, that wasn't unlikely. I have a friend who is slowly going blind from macular degeneration, a truly scary diagnosis. Another acquaintance has a macular pucker, what her eye doctor describes as "a wrinkle on the retina." I haven't escaped unscathed, either. To ward off glaucoma, I put drops in my eyes once a day to keep the pressure where it should be, and I have the beginnings of cataracts. My eye doctor back in Maine has been trying to convince me to have minor surgery that will leave me seeing well enough to discard my glasses. I keep putting it off. Okay, I admit it — I'm a coward. I'd just as soon avoid any kind of surgery. Besides, I'm used to wearing glasses. I got my first pair when I was ten.

As the wait stretched past the half-hour mark, I stood up to stare out the window at the parking lot. Across the street was one of those buildings with the OPENING SOON sign in the window. I frowned. There was a second possibility to explain Darlene's state of mind. I'd just as soon be wrong about her health, but it was equally disturbing to think that Darlene and Frank might be in serious financial difficulties because of the money they'd lost on one of Greg Onslow's schemes.

That train of thought brought me back to Tiffany's death. Passions had been high even before she died, and the provisions in her will were sure to set off fireworks. Greg Onslow hadn't struck me as the type to go down without a fight.

I wondered who would inherit the shares if *Ronnie* died.

Abruptly, I resumed my seat in the comfortably padded waiting room chair. *Rein in your imagination,* I ordered myself. *This isn't the nineteen-thirties. No one is going around bumping off people who are opposed to the theme park.*

Darlene reappeared a short time later. Now her mood was pensive, and she scarcely said two words to me all the way back to her house.

"You okay?" I asked after I'd pulled into her driveway and turned off the engine.

"Just tired. I'd ask you in, but all I really want to do right now is take a nap."

Unable to argue with that, I unloaded the wheelchair, saw her safely inside, and left.

CHAPTER 13

Darlene's black mood was infectious.

What I should have done was go straight home. It wasn't as if I didn't have plenty of editing waiting for me, and there were workmen in the house who might have questions for me. And of course, Tiffany's thumb drive still contained dozens of files that I had yet to open.

Instead, I headed out into the countryside and drove aimlessly, surprising myself by ending up at Bethel Woods, the center for the arts built on the site of the Woodstock Festival. I'd already been living in Maine that August weekend in 1969, blissfully unaware that history was being made within fifteen miles of my old stomping grounds.

Whatever Max Yasgur's dairy farm had been like during that long-ago happening, on this particular morning the site was a quiet rural haven. I promised myself I'd come back one day soon to explore the grounds, the museum, and the performance center, but for the moment I settled for taking a few pictures of what was left of the fall foliage. I tried my best not to think about anything other than the beauty of a pleasantly mild autumn day.

When my stomach growled, reminding me that it was lunchtime, I headed back to Lenape Hollow, but instead of going home, I detoured to Harriet's. In addition to coffee and pastries, the restaurant served a selection of soups and sandwiches from noon until two in the afternoon, at which time it closed for the day.

On this, my second visit to the place, I got my first look at the proprietor, a small woman wrapped in an overlarge apron. Since her sole waitress was on a break — not too surprising, since I was the only customer in sight — she came out in person to take my order.

"So you're Harriet?" I asked.

Her dark eyes twinkled. "There is no Harriet. Never has been. Only me. Ada Patel, at your service." Her accent placed her origins as somewhat south of Lenape Hollow — probably in the vicinity of Passaic, New Jersey.

A few minutes later, Ada slid a plate containing my turkey sandwich and fries onto the table in front of me.

"Anything else I can get ya?"

"I'm all set, but I'm also curious. Has this restaurant been here long?"

"About a year. For this burg, that's good going. You wouldn't believe how many eateries go in and out of business in a twelve-month stretch."

"I did notice a Thai place that was boarded up."

"They were nice folks. Too bad they knuckled under and sold out."

I quirked a brow at her, but she didn't explain.

The arrival of a new customer put an end to our conversation. Fishing an order pad out of her apron pocket, Ada went to greet the newcomer. I recognized him from somewhere. He was distinctive-looking with gorgeous olive skin and dark hair that fell in loose curls to his collar, but it took me a moment to place him as the man I'd seen quarreling with Greg Onslow in the cemetery and again later at Ronnie's house. Then he'd been wearing a suit. Now he was dressed in jeans and a sweatshirt. Catching his eye, I waved him over.

"If you'd like company while you eat, I'd be delighted to have you join me."

He stood beside my table with a look of

mild confusion on his face. "Do I know you?"

I introduced myself and explained where I'd seen him before. "I admit to issuing my invitation out of sheer nosiness. I'm curious to learn more about your opposition to the theme park."

"You sure know how to ruin a guy's appetite, don't you?"

"If you'd rather not —"

He sat down. "The more people we can persuade to support us, the better. I'm Joe Ramirez. I own a gas station here in the village, and I'm a member of the board of the local Chamber of Commerce."

"Mikki Lincoln. I just moved back to Lenape Hollow."

"Oh, yeah," he said. "I heard about you. You bought the old Kirkland place on Wedemeyer Terrace."

"I beg your pardon. I bought the old Greenleigh place. It was my home fifty years ago, and now it is again."

"So that's how you know Mrs. North."

"She was a classmate of mine."

I filed away the fact that she was "Mrs. North" and not "Ronnie." True, Ramirez was much our junior, but even five decades ago a lot of us called some adults — our parents' friends and even a few of our teachers — by their first names. Folks I'd met who'd been brought up in the South had been appalled by this practice.

"Terrific woman," Ramirez said of Ronnie after Ada brought him his lunch. "She does a lot for the community. Not just financially, either. She helped organize the village thrift shop and she volunteers at the food bank."

Philanthropy was not something I'd ever have associated with my nemesis, but people did change as they got older. I listened to him sing her praises for a few more minutes before I interrupted to ask what he had against Wonderful World. While we ate, he outlined the drawbacks to Onslow's plans, most of which had to do with the proposed location of the theme park and the disruption it would cause for its neighbors.

"Add to that, Onslow is dishonest," Ramirez said.

"Dishonest in what way?" I polished off the final bite of my sandwich and reached for the last of the fries.

"He's a con man. Everyone knows it, too. Unfortunately, we haven't had any luck proving it." He'd made short work of a cheeseburger but lingered over his coffee.

"If you have no proof, how can you be so certain it's true?" I thought this was a reasonable question.

He leaned across the table, lowering his voice even though there were no other customers to overhear what he said. "Tiffany Scott had proof. Now she's dead. What does that tell you?"

His insinuation had my eyebrows shooting up. "Are you telling me you think her husband drowned her?"

A look of disappointment on his face, Ramirez abruptly stood. "And that's what we're up against. No one wants to believe anything bad about the town's golden boy."

"Oh, I'm willing to accept that he's a shady character, even a crook, but a murderer?" Even though that possibility had already crossed my mind, it sounded preposterous when Ramirez said it aloud.

"I wouldn't put anything past him, but you're right. I've got no evidence, just suspicions." His face relaxed into a rueful half smile. "I guess there ought to be smoke before I yell fire, especially since it turned out I was wrong about him benefitting financially from his wife's death. He already had control of her money."

"Onslow threatened you," I said, remembering the quarrel I'd overheard.

Ramirez grinned. "Yeah. What was it? 'Try and stop me, and you'll regret it'?"

"You don't seem worried."

Ramirez just shrugged.

"Do you really think you can stop him building the theme park?"

"That's the plan." He mimed tipping a nonexistent hat as he backed away from me. "It's been nice meeting you, Mrs. Lincoln. Best of luck fixing up the old Greenleigh place."

I left Harriet's soon after Joe Ramirez did, driving home in a thoughtful frame of mind. I knew for a fact that there was no file named "TheGoodsOnMyHusband.doc" on Tiffany's thumb drive, but the possibility that she'd left behind proof of his corruption was an appealing one.

Back at my computer, I took a second look at "blackmail.doc." Could it possibly be something Tiffany had copied from Greg Onslow's files? The numbers and dates meant nothing to me, and once again I was struck by how relatively small the amounts were. I concluded that my earlier guess was probably correct — this had to do with fictional crooks rather than real ones.

For the next fifteen minutes I randomly opened other files. The fifth try brought up a spreadsheet that was even more incomprehensible than the contents of the blackmail file. Have I mentioned that I hate spreadsheets? I have trouble making sense of them even when I'm the one creating them. This one appeared to be a record of expenses. I squinted at the screen, hoping for a breakthrough. That's when I noticed the name Jack Tucker at the bottom of the page and started to laugh. This file, at least, had nothing to do with Onslow's illicit financial dealings. Jack Tucker was one of the gangsters Tiffany had created to populate her novel.

CHAPTER 14

Over the weekend, when the workmen were off and it was quiet in the house, I spent two productive days going over clients' manuscripts and trying to read a bit more of Tiffany's novel. It was slow going, and the research files I sampled weren't much better. I could only do a little bit at a time. The more I read, the more I began to doubt my earlier convictions. Surely the police knew their business. I plodded on, but with less and less enthusiasm for my self-imposed task. I found it very easy to abandon the project when Calpurnia demanded her fair share of attention.

Once I'd set Tiffany's files aside, I didn't go back to them. Instead, since the renovations on the second-floor bath were complete, I spent Sunday evening adding the finishing touches. Calpurnia followed me as I entered this large room located just at the top of the stairs and began her own inspection of the premises. She's always been fond of bathrooms. In our house in Maine, she used to sit on the edge of the tub and bat at the bubbles in the water.

"It's smaller than I remembered," I told her, "but it's big for a bathroom. It was probably a bedroom in the original floor-plan, before they added indoor plumbing." The house was built early in the twentieth century, probably around 1908.

There was plenty of space for a nice old dressing table with a three-section mirror. I'd bought it at an auction years ago and refinished it myself. A wide, padded bench went with it. Both had been crowded into my bedroom for the last few days to give the plumber room to work. Once those two items were back in place, I got out the picture hangers and put up several framed nineteenth-century fashion prints. I completed my decorating efforts by adding a trio of colorful scatter rugs and hanging matching curtains at the single small, square window.

Every once in a while, nostalgia catches me by surprise. It washed over me then, as I stood staring across the short distance between my house and the one next door. Although the neighbors had their lights on upstairs, the curtains were closed and there was nothing for me to see. That hadn't always been the case.

"I was a snoopy kid," I said aloud.

For once, Calpurnia looked interested.

"From what was my bedroom, the room that's now going to be my office, I used to spy on our neighbors on the other side. They had a nephew living with them, and he used to make out with his girlfriends in the hammock that was right under my windows."

I glanced over my shoulder to see if Calpurnia was listening. She was in the sink, looking hopefully at the faucet. She much prefers running water to what I put in her bowl.

"Pay attention. I'm confessing my sins here."

After I obliged her by starting a thin stream of water flowing into the sink, I returned to the bathroom window and was hit by another flashback. I'd been standing in this exact spot, and I remembered the whole embarrassing incident with crystal clarity.

When I was growing up, the house on this side had belonged to a middle-aged widow named Cora Cavendish. As many people did in those days, she'd taken in a roomer or two during the summer. Later, she'd converted her entire second floor into an apartment. I was in high school the year she rented it to our new music teacher. Everyone was curious about him, so I'd had no qualms about stationing myself at this vantage point in the hope of catching a glimpse of him.

That was the first time I truly understood the meaning of "be careful what you wish for." While I watched, the teacher and his wife walked into their bedroom. A moment later, they were locked in a passionate embrace. This wasn't just necking in a hammock. This was hard-core. They tumbled onto the bed and started tugging at each other's clothes. My cheeks were burning, but I couldn't look away. I was both disappointed and relieved when they broke apart long enough for him to turn off the light, plunging the room into darkness and putting an abrupt end to the peep show.

It's a good thing I wasn't musical. I didn't have to see that teacher in class or chorus or even work with him on the school-wide musical. The one time his wife asked my mother if I was available to babysit for them, I came up with an excuse to get out of it. I could no longer remember what I'd said, but my reason must have been a doozy. Mom was never one to let me shirk responsibility, and she was a firm believer in the theory that young people should earn their spending money.

Even back then, I mused, I hadn't been particularly fond of taking care of little kids, no matter how well their parents paid me. It hadn't been much of a stretch to decide I didn't want any of my own.

I started to turn away from the window when a new thought struck me. I don't know why it had never occurred to me before, but I suddenly realized that if I had found it so easy to spy on the neighbors, then they must have had an equally good view of what went on inside our house. When I took another look out the window, it seemed to me that the house next door was even closer than I remembered. I suspected that the same was true of the distance between my house and the one on the other side. No wonder one of my mother's most frequent warnings when we argued was: "Keep your voice down. Do you want the neighbors to hear?"

"We were spoiled living where we did in Maine," I said to the cat.

Our nearest neighbor had been on the opposite side of busy U.S. Route 2, and his house was set well back on his lot. No other houses were close to our place. It was surrounded by open fields and a forested hill-side.

You wanted to come back to Lenape Hollow, I reminded myself. *This is the compromise.*

I felt certain I'd get used to the lack of privacy, just as I'd grow accustomed to living on one acre instead of twenty-five. At least the present-day crop of neighbors seemed to be pleasant people. The house I'd just been staring at had been converted back into a one-family dwelling. The folks living there were a family of four, the O'Days. The parents, Tom and Marie, both worked and their teenage children appeared to participate in every extracurricular activity known to man.

The house on the other side of me also housed a single family, the Frys. The adults were quiet and kept to themselves, but their three kids had the run of the neighborhood. They were loud, boisterous, and prone to cutting across my backyard to get to a friend's house at the other end of the block. I'd done the same thing in reverse when I was their age and never understood at the time why that had made old Mrs. Mintz so livid. She used to stand just outside her back door and yell at me to get off her property. Naturally, I ignored her. She died when

I was seven or eight and the Rosens — the ones with the nephew — moved in.

Calpurnia stropped herself against my leg. I scooped her up and carried her out of the room. Then I did an about-face to shut off the faucet. It was getting late, and it had been a long day. The next week was scheduled to begin as early and as noisily as the last. Sleep beckoned.

"Remind me to close the curtains before I turn on the light in the bedroom," I instructed the cat. "Kids are terrible snoops."

I was smiling as I carried her across the hall. I had not entirely outgrown that tendency myself, but I was fairly certain that I'd no longer be embarrassed by anything I saw.

CHAPTER 15

Ten o'clock Monday morning found me back in my makeshift downstairs office with the pocket doors closed. Above my head the carpenter, Charlie Katz, was installing built-in floor-to-ceiling bookshelves in the real office. It was going to be an ideal place to work when it was finished, but in the meantime all that pounding was distracting.

Not only was there activity upstairs, but Matt Adams, the plumber, was hard at work on the downstairs bath that shared part of a wall with the dining room. He was a gruff, no-nonsense individual who hadn't said more than three words to me since the first day of renovations, but his thumping and clanging was loud enough to wake the dead. It was not good background music for someone struggling to find a politic way to tell a client that he needed to throw out the first three chapters of the novel he'd been slaving over for the past six years.

145

I jumped when someone knocked on the opaque panes in the pocket doors and slid one side open far enough to poke his head into the room. It was George Finkel, the electrician, a man on the lean side but with a compact build. His plain, square face was dotted with old acne scars and topped with wispy brown hair that was slowly giving way to baldness. I couldn't begin to guess his age, other than to say he was long past being a teenager and not yet close to retirement.

"Hello, George," I greeted him, proud of myself for finally putting names and faces together. "Is there a problem with the wiring?"

"Not anymore, but it's a good thing you decided to upgrade. Mice sure made a mess of the old wires."

"Mice!"

I managed not to add "Eek!" or jump up on my chair, but I have to admit that I've never been fond of rodents. Calpurnia, of course, enjoys a tasty mouse now and again, and regularly went on hunting expeditions in the cellar of our house in Maine. She was always generous when she caught one. I can't begin to count the number of times I found *parts* of a mouse she'd left for me, usually by stepping on them in my bare feet first thing in the morning on my way to the coffeepot.

"The outlets in this house hadn't been checked for at least forty years." George's gaze strayed to the old-fashioned radiator in one corner of the room. "I guess none of the owners were much for changing things."

"Personally, I'm glad no one ripped those out to put in baseboard units. They make it next to impossible to arrange furniture because you always have to be careful not to block the heat."

"Good thing someone decided to replace the old oil burner," George said. "I'd have hated to see an old clunker blow up on you after all the work you've had done on this place."

"Well, aren't you a little ray of sunshine today. As it happens, I remember when that old clunker was brand-new. My father had it installed when I was nine or ten years old. Before that we had a coal-burning furnace. We used to get deliveries. The coal came down a chute and landed in one corner of the basement." After we switched to oil heat, Daddy built himself a darkroom in that space so he could develop his own photographs.

George was shaking his head. "Now if it was up to me, I'd have gone to electric heat, but I could be biased."

I smiled, but I was growing impatient to get back to work. I couldn't figure out why George was still hovering in the doorway.

"Was there something else you need to tell me?" I asked. "Other than about the mice?"

He shifted his weight from foot to foot, looking indecisive. "Mind if I come in for a minute, Ms. Lincoln?"

"Only if you make that Mikki." I waved him toward the only empty dining room chair. The others held stacks of reference books and piles of printouts. Although I usually edit on electronic copies, I like to have a printout, too. Sometimes it's easier to spot errors when I do a read-through on paper.

George closed the pocket doors before perching on the edge of the seat, his hands clasped together in front of him. His expression had turned ominously grim.

"This is probably none of my business," he began, "but I can't help thinking, what with you living here all alone and everything, that somebody ought to warn you."

"Warn me about what, exactly?"

I was touched by his evident concern for my well-being but bewildered, too. As all the workmen had reason to know, since I had to let them in every morning, installing good locks on all the doors and windows had been one of my first priorities when I began renovating the house.

"Not about what. About who."

I bit back my instinctive urge to correct him by saying *whom*. Instead I fixed an encouraging look on my face.

"You got to understand that I didn't mean to eavesdrop, but I was checking an outlet in the living room, and I overheard part of what that guy said to you last week."

"That guy?" For a moment I was puzzled. "Do you mean Alan Van Heusen?"

"That's the one. Smarmy son of a . . . gun. I just want you to know that you shouldn't hesitate to ask any of us working here for help if he shows up again."

"I don't expect he will, but I appreciate the offer." When George started to rise, I gestured for him to stay put. "What I don't understand is what prompted you to make it."

George avoided meeting my eyes. "Just take my word for it, okay?"

In the ordinary way of things, I didn't suppose an electrician had much direct contact with the people he worked for. George was the quiet type, if not as silent as Matt Adams. All his focus seemed to go into doing

149

his job well. That made it all the more extraordinary that he'd decided to speak up. It didn't take a Sherlock Holmes to suspect that he might bolt at any moment. I throttled back the impulse to reach across the distance between us and place a hand on his forearm. If I was reading him correctly, the slightest touch would have made him take off like a scalded cat. I studied him in silence for a moment longer, putting two and two together before I spoke.

"Let me guess. You did a job for Mongaup Valley Ventures, and while you were working there you witnessed something to make you dislike and distrust Van Heusen. Am I right?"

"Something like that," he muttered. "I don't like the way he treats women."

My eyebrows shot up. "Sexual harassment in the workplace?"

As anyone who reads a newspaper knows, disrespecting women is still much more common than it should be. That said, I didn't see how anything George might have witnessed in a business setting could apply to my situation. Van Heusen certainly hadn't been making a pass at me. I felt my lips quirk into a tiny smile at the absurdity of that idea.

"No, ma'am. Mikki." George stammered

a little getting my first name out. "I mean the man's a bully, and so is his boss. It was criminal the way Onslow treated his wife, may she rest in peace."

"Are you telling me that Greg Onslow physically abused Tiffany?"

Abruptly, he stood. "I've said too much. You just watch out for yourself, okay?"

"Wait a minute, George. You can't just —"

But he was already gone. I thought about following him but decided against it. If he was unwilling to provide additional details in private, he wasn't likely to be more forthcoming in front of the other workmen.

Greg Onslow had a lot of influence in Lenape Hollow, and his plans included construction projects. If George had a family to support, he couldn't risk word of his warning to me getting back to Mongaup Valley Ventures. I could fully appreciate his need to earn a living.

At the same time, his criticism of Onslow and Van Heusen brought all my questions about Tiffany's death back to the surface. Instead of returning to my laptop and the editing job that awaited me there, I retrieved two business cards. Alan Van Heusen had given me his the morning he invaded my temporary office. The other had been handed over by Detective Hazlett on the day he came to the house to find out why Tiffany Scott had been in possession of yet another business card — mine — when she died.

That third business card, the one I'd given Tiffany, remained at the forefront of my thoughts. Its bedraggled appearance had nagged at me from the beginning. *Had* it been on Tiffany's body when she drowned? If so, how could anyone believe that her death was an accident?

If she had been murdered, the police were supposed to find justice for her. Had they? I doubted it. I didn't know how homicides were investigated in New York State, but in Maine, unless a suspicious death occurred in the cities of Portland or Bangor, where there were special units to handle such cases, the state police automatically took over. Unlike smaller municipalities, they had the expertise and the facilities to solve major crimes.

The investigation into what had happened to Tiffany Scott appeared to have been conducted entirely at the local level by a very small village police department. I had no idea how much experience or training Detective Hazlett had, but I hadn't heard of any other recent homicides in my old hometown.

As a law-abiding citizen, I was reluctant to think of the police as unqualified or incompetent, and I had no reason to suspect them of corruption, but Hazlett's conclusion that Tiffany's death was an accident did not make sense, not given the condition of my business card.

There was also something off about the intense interest various parties had shown in my dealings with the dead woman, and I'd sensed a definite threat when Alan Van Heusen invaded my home. Receiving George's warning reinforced the wariness I'd already been feeling.

So where did that leave me? I fingered Hazlett's card. It left me nowhere. I was less qualified to investigate a murder than the most poorly trained police officer. The only thing I *could* do was to continue going through the files on Tiffany's thumb drive with a fine-tooth comb.

It occurred to me that I didn't need to hang on to the thumb drive to do that. Since I back up everything six ways to Sunday, one of the first things I'd done was upload Tiffany's files to my laptop. Then I'd copied the material to off-site storage, a spare thumb drive, and what I call my security blanket — the thumb drive that lives in the glove compartment of my car. What can I say? I grew up in the era before there were such things as electronic files. I doubt I will ever entirely believe that written material exists unless I can see and touch it. That's why I print copies of everything I don't want to risk losing and file the pages in manila folders in an old-fashioned metal file cabinet.

The only reason I hadn't yet printed out Tiffany's files had to do with my tight budget. It would require reams of paper and at least one new toner cartridge. Still, I had made all those other backups. That being the case, there was no reason not to turn the original thumb drive over to the proper authorities. I resolved to do so just as soon as an opportunity presented itself.

In the meantime, I needed to get back to work. Like George, I had a living to earn.

CHAPTER 16

One of the not so great things about getting older is that many people, myself included, don't always sleep as well as they once did. Since I have a strong aversion to taking any medication that isn't absolutely necessary, I avoid sleeping pills. I do, occasionally, take naps during the afternoon when the previous night has been a restless one, but that solution was off the table so long as I had workmen in the house.

A few years ago, I read an article about "first sleep" that put an end to any worries I might have had about not sleeping straight through the night. Apparently, hundreds of years ago, it was common practice to go to bed, sleep for a few hours, wake up for a while to talk, have sex, or whatever, and then fall back to sleep until it was time to get up. Ever since, when I've only slept a few hours and suddenly find myself wide awake, I've had no qualms about reaching for the book on my nightstand and reading for an hour or so. If I wake up hungry, I get up and make myself a light snack. Sometimes, against all the advice I've seen elsewhere, I even check my email and browse social media until I feel sleepy enough to crawl back into bed.

The night following my conversation with George, I had trouble falling asleep. It had been a long day in addition to that encounter, and another full one loomed ahead. Matt the plumber had made great progress, but there had not been time for him to finish putting everything back together. The downstairs bath was still torn up and the kitchen sink could only be used with caution. I didn't fully understand the details, but the upshot was that until he got hold of a certain part and installed it, the faucet had to be turned on and off with great care. I managed the trick of it once, enough to get the water I needed to boil egg noodles to go with the baked pork chop and salad that constituted my supper, but after that I left it strictly alone.

When I'd been tossing and turning for a considerable length of time, I decided that "first sleep" wasn't on the menu for that night. My thoughts turned instead to the prospect of a glass of milk and a few crackers. I got up and retrieved the glasses I'd placed on top of the nightstand. I left my hearing aids behind, since I didn't need to hear to find the refrigerator, but I grabbed a small flashlight. Why a flashlight? Force of habit. When I was married I never turned on overhead lights or lamps in the middle of the night because I didn't want to disturb my husband's sleep.

Slightly groggy, my way illuminated by the narrowest of beams of light, I made my way downstairs and entered the kitchen. I hadn't gone two paces before my bare foot landed in a wet spot on the tile floor.

Drat, I thought, freezing in place. *Calpurnia must have thrown up.*

She's a pretty healthy cat, but once in a while something disagrees with her. And, of course, every time she leaves me a present like that, I find it the same way I find mouse parts, by stepping in the mess. At least feet are easier to clean than shoes or socks.

Telling myself I should be grateful she'd hit bare floor rather than upchucking on one of the scatter rugs, I backed up until I could flick the wall switch beside the door. At once, the kitchen was flooded with light.

Flood is the operative word.

Cal had not thrown up. Since her favorite source of water was a faucet, she'd apparently tried to turn on the tap in the sink, the one for which Matt had been short a part. She'd succeeded beyond her wildest dreams, and because the plug was in the drain, the sink had overflowed. Water cascaded down the front of the cabinets, and Lake Kitchen grew ever larger as I watched.

Note to self: Put in hearing aids when you get up in the middle of the night. Had I done so, I'd have been forewarned of the plumbing crisis in progress before I walked into it.

After a moment of stunned immobility, I sloshed through about a half inch of water to turn off the faucet. It was a good thing I'd decided to get up, but my plan to indulge in a relaxing snack was off the table. First I had to schlep a sodden scatter rug through the utility room and out onto my tiny back porch. I hung it over the railing and left it to drip dry. On my way back to the kitchen, I grabbed a mop and a bucket. Sopping and wringing took up the best part of the next hour. At the end of that time I had a very clean kitchen floor.

It could have been worse, I told myself. If I'd slept through the night, there would have been water everywhere. As it was, only a portion of the tile floor had been inundated, and there had been no damage to the contents of drawers and cabinets or to the wall-to-wall carpeting in the hall or, on the other side, the oak flooring in my dining room/temporary office. The floodwaters hadn't even reached the dinette, so I was spared having to move the table and chairs and mop the alcove.

By the time the cleanup was done, I was exhausted. I located Calpurnia, blissfully asleep on the living room loveseat, and carried her upstairs with me. After carefully closing my bedroom door to prevent her from repeating her trick with the faucet, I fell into bed and was out like a light.

I came to, briefly, to find my cat sitting on the nightstand and staring at me. It was just past dawn. As I watched her, Calpurnia delicately extended a paw and tapped me on the nose. Ignoring her, I closed my eyes and drifted off again.

When my alarm clock went off, I smacked it into silence. *I'll get up in a minute,* I promised myself. I had at least an hour until Matt showed up to fix the faucet and finish up in the downstairs bath.

I must have drifted off again. My bed faced east and the sun, higher than it had been at dawn, shone in through light-colored drapes. As I blinked and slowly came awake, I found myself staring at eerie shadows playing across the fabric.

Shadows?

Heart racing, I sat bolt upright and fumbled for my glasses. Putting them on didn't improve matters. The shadows at my second-floor bedroom window were man-sized and rose and fell as I watched.

For a moment the theme music from an old horror movie played in my head.

Calpurnia chose that moment to hop up onto the dresser and shove the curtain aside so she could look out. Part of a jean-clad leg appeared in the gap. In perfect Gothic-heroine style, I reacted by pulling the bed-covers up to my neck.

A millisecond before I embarrassed my-self by screaming or dialing 911, my groggy brain finally started to function. My face heated even as I had to laugh at myself.

"It's Tuesday," I said aloud. "The day my contractor scheduled workmen to remove the old shingles from the porch roof."

They would be replaced, as the roof over the rest of the house already had been, by a nice new metal one. Out of respect for my strained finances, we'd left the front and back porches and the garage until now, since leaks in those locations didn't matter as much.

While my heart rate settled back to normal, I groped for the case holding my hearing aids, pushed the little trap doors closed to seat the batteries, and popped them into my ears. That done, I could finally hear the sounds of demolition.

A glance at the clock told me it wasn't as late as I'd thought. The roofers apparently liked to get an early start on their day. I still had plenty of time to shower and dress before I had to let Matt and George and the other regulars into the house.

"Put the curtain back," I called to Calpurnia, in a fair imitation of a similar command in Mel Brooks's *Young Frankenstein,* and got out of bed to start my day.

CHAPTER 17

Later that day, when I took a late-afternoon break from work, I phoned Darlene. I hadn't heard from her since I dropped her off at her house after her Friday appointment with the eye doctor, and I thought that if she was still in a funk I could cheer her up with a lively account of last night's water sports. If she was feeling more herself, a condition devoutly to be hoped for, then I could use her as a sounding board for my suspicions about Tiffany's death.

"How are you doing?" I asked when she answered.

"Fine." She sounded listless.

Oh-oh. That was not her usual response. Tendrils of concern snaked through me. "Okay if I stop by later?"

Instead of her accustomed invitation to "come on over," she put me off. "This just isn't a good time."

"I've got a story that will make you laugh."

Enough time had passed that I'd begun to see the humor in both my middle-of-the-night flood and early-morning panic attack.

The roofers, having removed all the old shingles, put down new tar paper, and cleaned up the mess created by the demolition process, had already left for the day. They'd be back first thing in the morning to put a new roof on the porch — metal this time so that the snow would slide off and I would never again have to make use of a roof rake. The day after that, they'd start on the garage roof, and they'd finish up with the roof over the small back porch off the utility room.

There was a long pause before Darlene answered. "Thanks, but . . . not today, okay?"

"Well, sure," I said. "I don't want to intrude. Is there anything I can do for you? Pick up groceries? Walk the dog?" Darlene and Frank had an aged schnauzer who spent most of his time asleep in his favorite sunny spot in their fenced-in backyard. "I'm just looking for an excuse to get out of the house," I added with a laugh that didn't come out sounding anywhere near as natural as I'd hoped.

"I don't need any help." Listlessness morphed into impatience. After the briefest of goodbyes, Darlene ended the call.

I stared at the phone for a long moment before I put it down. The friend I'd come to know again in the last couple of months had been unfailingly upbeat. She'd always been ready to chat on the phone or spend an hour or two together at her place. Sure, everyone has a bad day now and again, but I couldn't help but feel there was more to it than that.

Sometimes I think better when I'm moving. As I pondered, I wandered through the downstairs, finally ending up on my front porch. I stepped outside just as the parochial school across the street let out for the day. Primary school children streamed out of the squat, square building. Some headed home on foot. Others were being picked up by waiting parents. Noisy chatter, interspersed with laughter, filled the crisp autumn air. Now and again, a parent called out a name, urging the little darling to hurry it up.

My mind was still on Darlene, but my gaze skimmed idly over the vehicles parked along the opposite side of Wedemeyer Terrace. I didn't expect to recognize any of the drivers, although some of the people who currently had kids in grade school could well be the children of former classmates.

At least they could if both generations had started their families a little later in life.

Seconds after that thought crossed my mind, I did spot someone I knew. At first I couldn't place him. I stared harder. His profile wasn't familiar, but there was something about the way his large hands gripped the steering wheel of the dark blue SUV that rang a bell. Then he turned his head and I bit back a gasp. It was the guard from Wonderful World, the one who'd tried to confiscate my smartphone because I'd dared to snap a few pictures of the scenery.

I took a couple of hasty steps sideways so that I was better hidden by the high railing and low roof of my porch. Since my house faced east and it was a midafternoon in late September, I was safely in shadow.

"Idiot," I muttered, meaning myself.

Just because the guard had hassled me for trespassing didn't mean there was anything sinister about his reappearance in front of my house. He was obviously giving his kid a ride home after school, as were many other parents. While I watched, cars departed one by one until only the SUV remained. It was parked in such a way that it blocked my view of the entrance to the school, so I couldn't tell if a small child had come out of the building and climbed in on the passenger side or not. I assumed one had because the Mongaup Valley Security guy started his engine and drove slowly away. Never once had I seen him glance my way, and yet I couldn't shake the feeling that he'd been watching my house.

"*Paranoid* idiot," I said aloud. Next I'd be imagining that the grumpy woman who'd sat near me at the DMV and given me such an ugly look when we stood at adjoining windows was stalking me. I guess those eerie shadows on my bedroom curtains had affected me more than I'd realized.

I went back inside and returned to fretting about Darlene. I wondered again if her odd mood had something to do with Greg Onslow. If that business deal gone bad had caused repercussions I knew nothing about, anything was possible. Frank and Darlene might well be in serious financial trouble. On the surface they seemed to have an ideal life in their retirement — house, transportation, hobbies — but appearances can be deceiving.

The alternative wasn't any more pleasant to contemplate. What if Dr. Shapiro had given Darlene bad news of some kind? If she hated the idea of surgery as much as I did, she'd be pretty upset about the prospect of having cataracts fixed, assuming that she *had* cataracts. I shook my head. As my own eye doctor had pointed out to me on more than one occasion, these days cataract surgery was no big deal. If Darlene had a health issue, it had to be something more serious than that.

As I wandered through the house, Calpurnia appeared and began to strop herself against my legs. I lifted her up to touch noses with her. "You know what my problem is?" I asked.

She made a little huffing sound, as if to say "What *now*?"

"I obsess about things. That's what James always used to say."

And then he'd insist we talk out whatever it was that was bothering me and, somehow, my worries would always disappear. God, I missed that man! He'd been my rock.

I carried Cal with me into the kitchen, deciding that what I needed to cheer myself up was a nice cup of green tea and a ginger cookie. Cal could have one of her cat treats, and we'd both feel better.

I've got to stop talking to the cat, I thought. Maybe that was my real problem. I hadn't made the slightest effort to make new friends since I'd moved back to Lenape Hollow. Was I so lonely that I'd begun to obsess about other people's problems and imagine scary scenarios that had no basis in reality?

Considering that Darlene was the only person I spent much time with, it was easy to see why I ended up using Calpurnia as a sounding board. That had to stop. I had no excuse save laziness for not cultivating new acquaintances and renewing relationships with old ones.

You'd think I'd learn, but what is it they say about old dogs and new tricks? I'd done the same thing during my marriage. For years I'd relied for companionship on one person, my soul mate, best friend, and husband. I'd been devastated when he died, but I'd also found it ridiculously easy to pull up stakes and move. I hadn't been close to anyone else, not even his sister and her family.

As an only child, I suppose I was always something of a loner. My parents had long since gone to their reward. So had a sprinkling of older first cousins, none of whom had lived near me in any case. It wasn't that I was standoffish. I'd just never gone out of my way to socialize. On reflection, I realized that wasn't a very healthy attitude and was probably one I should change before I turned into a stereotype. I didn't think I was likely to become a hermit or a hoarder, but crazy cat lady was a distinct possibility.

Self-analysis can be painful, but my ruminations ended on a positive note. By starting over in my old hometown, I had the perfect opportunity to change my ways.

I was in the kitchen by the time I had this epiphany, and a glance out the window at the O'Day house next door revealed a chance to seize the moment. Tom and Marie were out in their side yard and looking straight at me. I gave them a little finger wave and hurried outside by way of the back door.

We met over the chest-high fence that separated our two properties. That's chest-high for me. Since they were both taller than I am by a good three inches, this wasn't as awkward as it might have been. They'd obviously been at work. They wore nearly identical suits, his accessorized with a tie and hers with a scarf.

"Good afternoon," I said. "You two are home early."

Together, they owned and operated one of Lenape Hollow's small businesses, an antiques shop located in a building I remembered as a clothing store. I'd been meaning to stop by, if only to be neighborly, but I hadn't yet gotten around to it.

"We leave the kids in charge one afternoon a week after school," Tom said. "Gives them a sense of responsibility."

"And it gives me a chance to work in my garden," Marie added, "although at this time of year there isn't much to do."

She'd created a charming scene in their upward-sloping backyard with flower beds, rock gardens, and winding flagstone walkways, and I told her so. I expected a smile in return for the compliment. Instead, a pained look came over her face. She glanced at her husband in the way that wives do when they want him to be the one to speak up.

Tom cleared his throat. "We've been wondering about your trees."

I followed the direction of his gaze to the virtual forest in my backyard and sighed. "I plan to have most of them taken down, but to be honest, I can't afford to do it just yet. The work on the house itself had to be done first."

Marie sent me a sympathetic look but then delivered a little lecture, the gist of which was that my trees were a fire hazard, created a security risk, and most likely provided a home for the kind of tick that spreads Lyme disease. She was correct on all counts, but there wasn't much I could do about it at the moment.

So much for turning the neighbors into bosom buddies.

I returned to the house to resume my musings on that score. There were at least a dozen people in Lenape Hollow with whom I already had something in common: all those years we'd spent together in grade school and high school. Instead of using Darlene as a lifeline or cultivating the O'Days, I needed to reach out to some of them. I'd already made a beginning with Mike. There had been no progress with Ronnie, but the two of them weren't the only former classmates still living in the area. In fact, I'd just recently encountered another one.

Without further ado, I picked up the phone, found the number I'd made a note of for future reference, and called Dr. Shapiro's office. When Sarah answered, I asked her if she'd like to meet me the next day for lunch.

CHAPTER 18

At noon on Wednesday, I sat alone at a table for two in Harriet's. Sarah Shapiro was late. I should have expected I'd have to wait for her. Back in high school she'd been dubbed "the late Miss Sarah" for her habit of wandering in halfway through a meeting of the yearbook committee or the drama club, babbling away about how she'd mixed up the time or run into someone who'd distracted her or just plain forgotten what time we were getting together. She gave excuses, but she never actually apologized, and she was always laughing about her tardiness, as if she thought we were sure to forgive her because she was scatterbrained and that was just so darned *cute.*

I've become more tolerant in many ways over the years, but my patience for self-centered foolishness has always been in short supply. I found myself wishing I'd remembered Sarah's bad habit before I left the house. I could have finished the editing project I'd been working on all morning.

As I sat there twiddling my thumbs and trying to tamp down my annoyance, I remembered another of Sarah's less than appealing traits. She had dearly loved to know other people's secrets, and she'd never had any qualms about sharing what she found out with all and sundry. I supposed that, these days, doctor-patient confidentiality applied to her on two levels, both as the doctor's receptionist and as his mother. Too bad, I thought. Otherwise I might have been able to ask her straight out if anything had upset Darlene during her visit to the eye doctor.

I sipped coffee as I waited, lecturing myself all the while. Snooping was bad, especially when it involved friends. When Darlene was ready, she'd tell me what was troubling her. Or not. A pal didn't pry into private matters. I'd be there if Darlene needed me — that was the important thing to remember.

To amuse myself and pass the time, I studied the other customers at Harriet's. There were two men at separate tables and two women, a strawberry blonde and a brunette, seated together. I didn't know any of them.

"I hear Greg Onslow is going to take Ronnie North to court over that will," the strawberry blonde confided in her luncheon companion.

My ears perked up.

"He claims he has the *real* will," she continued, "one that leaves all those shares in Mongaup Valley Ventures to him."

"You mean he's saying the one Ronnie has is a forgery?" The brunette wore a baby blue sweater snug enough to emphasize a generous bosom but with a cowl neck to cover the wrinkled skin that was one of the unavoidable signs of getting older. At a guess, she was somewhere in her mid-fifties.

"Are you surprised?" the blonde asked with a laugh. "After all, *Mike* is the one who came up with that will."

Her companion gave a ladylike snort. "Well, then, of course it's a fake. He can't be trusted. Is it true that his second wife threatened to have him arrested for assault if she didn't get a good settlement in the divorce?"

I waited with bated breath for the answer but, of course, with impeccable timing, Sarah chose that moment to arrive. The two women stopped talking to greet her. The blonde invited her to join them, even though they were already halfway through their meal.

"Sorry, Sonya," Sarah said, gesturing at me, "but I've already got a date."

I gave a little wave of acknowledgment.

Sarah was well launched into a familiar litany of excuses for being late by the time she settled into the chair opposite me. I waited until after we'd ordered our soup and sandwiches to ask, *sotto voce,* about the two women at the other table.

The identifications came with full details — age, occupation, family background, spouses past and present. Only one fact stood out in my mind. Sonya, currently Sonya Adler, had once been Sonya Doran. She was my old friend Mike's *first* ex-wife.

"So, did he really assault his second ex?" I thought it unlikely, but people did change in the course of five decades.

"The assault charge was bogus. Totally."

"*Is* Mike an honest lawyer?"

Sarah laughed. "I wouldn't go *that* far!"

"Would he have forged a will if Ronnie asked him to?"

"Well, now, *there's* an interesting question." To my dismay, Sarah turned around in her chair and repeated it for the benefit of Sonya and her friend. "What do you think, girls?"

"Sure, he would," Sonya said, "if he thought he could get away with it."

"You might be a tad biased," I said.

"And you are?"

Sarah spoke before I could. "This is Mikki Lincoln. She used to date Mike in high school."

"Only a few times. Nothing serious."

Sonya's eyebrows shot up. "You're *that* Mikki?" She chuckled. "The one he had such a crush on?"

"I guess." For a moment it was as if I was back in junior high. Then I shook off the feeling of embarrassment, squared my shoulders, and managed a wry twist of the lips that I hoped would pass for a smile. "It was a long time ago."

Sarah gave me a playful slap on the forearm. "Speak for yourself. Just yesterday as far as I'm concerned."

Sonya and her friend, who were both considerably younger than Sarah, hooted at that statement.

"I hope you dumped him and not the other way around," said the brunette. "I'm Betsy Pringle, by the way."

"Nice to meet you. And no, he broke it off with me to take up with Ronnie."

That revelation prompted a renewed round of mirth.

"Nice to know my life is so amusing," I said to Sarah. "Maybe I should consider a new career as a standup comic."

"Is that Mike Doran you're talking about?" asked the old gentleman seated by himself at a window table. He was eighty if he was a day.

"Yes," Betsy answered. "Do you have any good dirt on him?"

"He can't be all bad," the man said. "Not if he's against that stupid theme park."

Sonya stiffened. "What have you got against revitalizing the economy?"

"Yeah. Yeah," the old man said with a sneer. "I've heard it all. Return Lenape Hollow to its former glory as a tourist mecca. It's not going to happen. You can't bring back the past."

"Not the big hotels, no," chimed in the middle-aged man at the other table, "but we've still got fresh air and nice scenery. I bet a bungalow colony could still thrive. And summer camps — remember those?"

"You want to bring back boardinghouses, too? Gone the way of the dodo bird."

"They call them B and Bs these days."

The debate between the two men escalated rapidly. I exchanged a worried look with Sarah when it looked as if they were about to come to blows over the viability of Wonderful World. It was at that point that Ada stepped in.

"Take it outside, boys." She snapped out the command in a no-nonsense voice while at the same time slapping down their checks. She waited, hands on hips, while they reached for their wallets.

After they'd paid their bills and left, everyone in the café turned toward the plate glass window at the front to follow their progress. Crossing the street, the combatants exchanged a few more words, this time accompanied by gestures that left no doubt as to the strength of their feelings. This activity quickly drew a small crowd. I blinked in surprise when I recognized a familiar face. There, standing next to a woman who'd been out walking a pair of poodles, was the security guard from Wonderful World. Again.

Fisticuffs were averted when a uniformed officer came out of the police station. Ada's two customers — I never did catch either of their names — strode rapidly away in opposite directions.

"Whew," I said.

Sarah gave a nervous laugh.

"It was nice to meet you, Mikki," Sonya said as she and Betsy settled their bill and prepared to leave. "We'll have to get together sometime and compare notes."

I smiled but didn't commit myself. I

178

wasn't certain I wanted to make new friends *that* badly.

By the time I turned back to Sarah, she was looking at her watch with an expression of mock horror on her face. "Oh, dear. I'm running late. I've got to get back to work. My Benjie, he kicks up *such* a fuss when I'm not there to greet his patients." Her trill of laughter sounded forced. "He keeps threatening to fire me. Can you imagine? Still, better safe than sorry, y'know?"

And with that, she was gone, leaving me to pay for lunch. Well, I *had* invited her. There was no reason to think we'd split the check, except that women having a meal together usually did. I found myself wondering if she really did have to worry about losing her job. She was my age. If she had nothing but Social Security to live on, she might need to keep working to make ends meet.

Since I had my own work to get back to, I left the café soon after Sarah and hurried up Main Street toward the shortcut — the wide driveway we'd always called the Alley — that would take me straight to my front door. For most of that climb I had an excellent view of my porch roof, an ever-present reminder that as soon as the project was complete, I'd have another bill to pay. With

that dire prospect foremost in my thoughts,
I ruthlessly pushed every other concern out
of my mind.

CHAPTER 19

"I don't understand why people have so much trouble with *farther* and *further*," I complained to Calpurnia later that afternoon. "Farther has to do with distance. It has the word 'far' right in it."

Showing supreme disinterest in one of my pet peeves, Cal continued grooming herself.

I jumped a foot when a deep voice addressed me from the open pocket doors. "Is it really that important?"

"Detective Hazlett. You just scared me out of six years' growth."

"Sorry. The front door was open, and one of the workmen said it would be okay for me to come on in. That *farther/further* thing? Does it really matter so much?"

Former teachers rarely resist the chance to educate someone. I waved him into an empty dining room chair. "Sometimes it does. Sometimes it doesn't. *Farther* and *further* are just one of many pairs of words that writers and news anchors misuse with alarming frequency. I can understand their confusion, especially when two words sound similar and have similar meanings, but it isn't all that hard to use a dictionary."

"These days, most people would Google it."

"If only they would!" I picked up a small red book I always kept near at hand when editing. "See this? It's my ancient copy of the seventh edition of the *Harbrace College Handbook.* It has a convenient 'Glossary of Usage' that I still refer to when I'm uncertain. Then there's this." I hefted another, much heavier book, *The Chicago Manual of Style, 16th edition.* "Publishers rely on this one to settle grammar disputes."

Sadly, right after I bought it, I discovered that it was about to be superseded by the seventeenth edition, available online in a three-year subscription. Since the price would have broken the bank of my fledgling business, that subscription was on the list of "investments" to make once I'd acquired a few more customers.

Hazlett tried to hide his smile. "So you're a stickler when it comes to following rules for writing?"

I shook my head. "To tell you the truth, I'm not. In fact, I believe there are three distinct languages we use all the time, depending upon the situation. Each one has its own guidelines. By my personal definition, what I call 'formal' English is pretty darn picky about usage. It's a must for business letters, scholarly articles, and most nonfiction. The second category is informal English. There, for the most part, rules are strictly adhered to but they can sometimes be broken. For me, fiction falls into this category. And, yes, I have to admit that in informal English, *farther* and *further* are interchangeable."

"And the third language?" Hazlett looked even more amused.

I gave him my best the-teacher-is-speaking-now look before answering. "I make a *further* distinction for spoken English. With the exception of people making speeches or broadcasting the news, speakers have much more leeway. Slang is permitted. So is deliberate misuse of the rules of grammar, usage, and pronunciation, if it is for effect — for example, if the intent is to be funny."

I stopped short of offering examples for fear he'd go glassy-eyed on me. He didn't need to hear me ramble on about how English is a living language in constant flux as new words come into fashion and old ones become archaic.

"We still need rules for formal English," I said to wrap up my mini-lecture. "Otherwise we'd soon reach a point where we couldn't understand each other, but in day-to-day conversation? All bets, as they say, are off. Why are you here, Detective?"

"I had a report that you were stirring up trouble earlier today at Harriet's."

"Me? I wasn't the one arguing the pros and cons of Wonderful World."

"According to what I was told, you sparked the debate by asking intrusive questions."

"Good grief! I was minding my own business, having lunch with an old friend and catching up on local news. I can't help it if she encouraged other people in the restaurant to join in our conversation." I narrowed my eyes. "Who complained?"

He stood without answering. "It's no crime to express opinions in a public place, Ms. Lincoln, but you might want to keep in mind that this is a small town. Word gets around fast when someone starts poking their nose into their neighbor's business."

With that, he departed, leaving the pocket doors open. I stared after him, slack-jawed, remembering only when it was too late to call him back that I'd intended to give him

Tiffany's thumb drive the next time we met. I turned to Calpurnia, who had slept through the whole encounter.

"Some guard cat you are!"

She didn't so much as twitch a whisker.

I closed the pocket doors with a little more force than I'd intended, making the glass panels rattle in an alarming manner. I knew perfectly well that I hadn't said or done one darned thing at Harriet's to deserve a reprimand. That I *was* "poking my nose" into things that were none of my affair was beside the point.

Feeling defiant, I sat back down, exited the manuscript I'd been editing, and opened the folder that contained all the material I'd copied from Tiffany's thumb drive. I resumed reading where I'd left off in her novel.

In spite of a few awkward bits of dialogue, the first few pages held my attention. Tiffany had already introduced a subplot about gangsters buying up property to open a resort in the Catskills, but she hadn't done much with it. Now she revealed that the fictional owner of this resort, a man she'd named Oscar Gregory, was trying desperately to go straight after years of living a life of crime. This ambition was being thwarted by his second-in-command, Matt Brisbane.

I couldn't help but wonder how much Tiffany had based Oscar Gregory on Greg Onslow. And was Matt Brisbane supposed to be Alan Van Heusen? If they were accurate representations of those two men, I might have done Onslow a disservice by suspecting him of dirty dealings. Maybe it was really his henchman who was the crook. Then again, in reading earlier chapters, I'd been certain Onslow was the model for Jack Tucker, a mobster who appeared to be the villain of Tiffany's novel. Was Tucker Onslow? Was he even truly the villain of the piece?

Those questions led me to others. If present-day fact was disguised as fiction, could that have led to Tiffany's murder? Did *Onslow* have mob connections? It wasn't impossible, and if that was the case, then he might well have ordered his wife's death in order to keep her from exposing him.

I drummed lightly on the table with my fingertips and tried with little success to rein in my wildest flights of fancy. It was far too easy to believe in the scenarios I came up with, even the storyline that had Van Heusen acting on his own to protect the interests of Mongaup Valley Ventures.

I buckled down and read on. As I did, in light of my impressions of Alan Van Heusen on the day he'd visited me and the things George had told me about him later, the possibility that Onslow's second-in-command was a mobster's henchman grew stronger.

In Tiffany's book, the character of Matt Brisbane was both a hit man and a womanizer. Sadly, from a literary point of view, he came across as little more than a stereotype of a villain, but that fact did nothing to dispel my suspicions. Most of Tiffany's creations were one-dimensional. The two female characters Brisbane victimized were so close to being cardboard that they could have passed for paper dolls.

Hours later, when I exited the manuscript file, I was no closer to knowing the truth about her husband and his flunky, but I did have an idea where to look next. Onslow had other employees, and some of them were likely to be women. To find out, I went online and called up the website for Mongaup Valley Ventures.

CHAPTER 20

By the following day, I'd collected a fair amount of information about Greg Onslow's business. Tiffany had been a vice president. No one had thought to take down her bio, so I learned that she'd attended Sullivan County Community College before transferring to SUNY Oneonta, where she'd earned a degree in business economics.

Two other women held important positions with the company, one as director of personnel and the other as head of the accounting department. The rest of the pictured executives were all Caucasian males — no surprise there. What did startle me was finding a photo of the security guard I kept seeing around town. He was actually the *chief* of security, and his name was Paul Klein. He'd graduated from SCCC with an associate degree in criminal justice. I hadn't thought private security paid better than working for the local or state police or the county sheriff's department, but maybe it did, especially if you were the head honcho.

While interesting, none of this information seemed particularly relevant. On the surface, Mongaup Valley Ventures was a transparent operation dedicated to advancing the interests of Onslow's adopted community. I couldn't hold it against him that he was originally from California.

Studying those employee bios had made me think about the claims Joe Ramirez had made, especially his insistence that Tiffany had found proof of her husband's wrongdoing. I came to the conclusion I needed to talk to Ronnie North, although I didn't look forward to the meeting.

After I completed a reasonable day's work, I drove to her place. I wasn't sure she'd allow me into her home, let alone speak to me, but it seemed important that I try. At the least, I might be able to discover why Tiffany had put the thumb drive in the mailer with her manuscript.

Ronnie's house looked as imposing as ever. There should have been a uniformed butler to answer the door, or at least a maid in a frilly apron. Instead, it was Ronnie's housekeeper who let me in. Since she was dressed in worn blue jeans and a sweatshirt

189

with the logo of what we in Maine called the "evil empire" — the New York Yankees — the giveaway was the dust rag she still held in one hand. She wore no makeup — a woman after my own heart in that respect — and had a clear, pale complexion that made her look younger than she was. Only the skin on her neck and hands put her true age in the vicinity of sixty. That, and the streaks of gray in her hair.

"I've come to speak with Mrs. North," I announced. "Is she at home?"

"Depends. You got a name?"

I hesitated.

The housekeeper cracked a smile. "Can't remember it?"

I sent her a rueful look. "It's more a case of how Ronnie will react to hearing it. Could you please tell her that Mikki Lincoln has information to share with her about her granddaughter?"

"Poor kid," the housekeeper murmured. Then she gave me a sharp look. "Mikki? Would that have been Mikki Greenleigh back in the day?"

The blank look that went with my nod amused her all over again.

"You don't remember me, do you? Well, why should you? I was a lot younger. Used to tag along after you and Darlene Misner until you pulled that old snipe hunt gag on me. I'm Ann Ellerby. Overweight? Blond braids and braces?"

I stared at her in wordless astonishment, but after a moment I managed to speak. "Small world," I said. "How have you been?"

"Not so bad. Yourself?"

"I'm sorry we were so mean to you," I blurted. "Teenagers can be incredibly self-centered and thoughtless."

Darlene and I had done worse than lead Ann to believe she could join us on other adventures if only she could capture the elusive snipe. When telling her she was too young to hang out with us made no impression on her, we'd resorted to hurtful insults, accusing her of being too fat, too ugly, and too stupid to be our friend.

"Forget it. They say adversity builds character."

Ann's pale blue eyes danced with mischief, making it impossible for me to doubt her sincerity. Our early taunts had apparently toughened her enough that she could endure working for Ronnie North. That was no excuse for bullying, but it did make me feel a little better.

Before I could say more, Ronnie appeared from the back of the house, already looking cross. She did a double take at seeing me. Finding me standing in her front hall did not improve her mood. Her upper lip curled into an expression of distaste.

"Mikki Greenleigh," she said. "Why are you here?"

"Mikki *Lincoln*." The correction was automatic but didn't make so much as a dent in her attitude.

"You didn't answer my question."

"Invite me in and I'll tell you."

The look she sent me was the same one she'd have given a bug she intended to squash, but she waved me ahead of her into the living room. In common with her décor, Ronnie was shined and polished and impeccably turned out in black slacks and a brocaded tunic in the same color. The ensemble made me feel like a hobo in my dress jeans and plain white cotton shirt. Her jewelry wasn't ostentatious, but even my untrained eye pegged the rings, bracelets, and necklace as expensive. She was in tasteful mourning, twenty-first-century style.

We sat. I was on the sofa and she took the wing chair. In a period piece, she'd have rung for tea. Since this was real life and not an episode of *Downton Abbey*, she simply glowered at me, waiting for me to speak. Ann prudently made herself scarce.

I cleared my throat. "You know already that your granddaughter brought a manuscript to me to edit."

She responded with a regal nod, even though that hadn't been a question.

"The police gave the printout to her husband. Since then, both you and he have suggested that Tiffany might have left something else with me. I'd like to know why you think she would have and what you think it was."

"That's none of your business." Ronnie snapped out the words.

"On the contrary. If you want it found, it only makes sense to tell me what I should be looking for."

Thanks to the facelift — possibly more than one — Ronnie always looked like she was wearing a mask. It was a wonder she could still manage to sneer. I wasn't able to tell what she was thinking, but the look in her eyes was anything but friendly. I spoke again before she could order me out of her house.

"As it happens," I said, "Tiffany did leave something with me."

I got a definite reaction to that announcement. Ronnie's right hand twitched, and her eyes widened by at least the width of an eyelash. Verbally, however, I got nothing.

"Your pal Joe Ramirez seems to think Tiffany had proof of her husband's shady dealings."

Ronnie's only response was a continuation of her silent stare. When she finally broke eye contact, it was to open a drawer in the end table beside her chair. She took out a pack of cigarettes and a crystal ashtray.

Taken aback doesn't begin to describe how surprised I was. Most people my age who smoked when they were younger — the ones still alive — had abandoned the habit decades ago. Ronnie lit up and blew a cloud of smoke my way. My obvious discomfort seemed to please her.

"Those things will kill you, you know."

"My business, not yours." She studied me as she puffed. "You know, Mikki. I've never been able to decide what it is I dislike most about you. You were Miss Goody-Two-Shoes in high school. Teacher's pet. Stuck up."

"I was not!" Fifty-plus years later, I could still feel outrage at the unjust accusation. "If you want to know the truth, I suffered from crippling shyness. The only time I could force myself to speak up was if I was sure I knew the right answer to a question in class."

"Obviously, you got over being shy. It took a lot of nerve to come here."

I didn't make the mistake of thinking this was a compliment.

Stubbing out the cigarette, Ronnie stared at the fingers that had held it. An air of discouragement descended over her like a pall.

They say you can always tell age from the hands. I could see that she'd been lucky enough to escape arthritis, but there were plenty of fine lines and the big telltale of prominent veins. Ronnie was fighting a losing battle against getting older and she knew it, just as she knew that her granddaughter's life had ended much too soon.

"Did Tiffany know Greg Onslow was a crook?" I asked. "Is that why she left her shares to you?"

With a movement as simple as straightening her spine, Ronnie once again became the grande dame looking down her nose at the peasant. Instead of answering my question, she asked one of her own. "What did she leave with you?"

"A thumb drive."

"Why?"

"Your guess is as good as mine. I've been reading the files. If she had evidence of wrongdoing, she hid it well." I summarized the plot of the novel, including the fact that thinly disguised versions of Onslow and Van Heusen appeared to be the villains of the piece, and explained that the thumb drive also contained Tiffany's research files. "So far, they all seem to relate to the novel, but it would help if I knew what sort of information to look for."

"Why do you care? Give me the thumb drive, and I'll handle it."

"I've brought a copy for you, but surely another pair of eyes couldn't hurt."

When she held out one hand in a peremptory gesture, I fished the backup out of my pocket and handed it over.

"As to why I care? I liked your granddaughter, Ronnie. She died too young. And maybe, just maybe, it wasn't an accident."

Her mouth worked, the only sign of emotion, as she struggled to speak. "Why . . . ?" She had to clear her throat. "What makes you say that?"

"She drowned."

Ronnie gave a jerky nod, but in her eyes I could see the irritation beginning to build up again.

"Bear with me. Was she wearing a swimsuit?"

"I don't know. I didn't see her body. It was a security guard who found her."

"If she was dressed for a swim, then how

did one of my business cards, one she probably had in the pocket of her slacks, get into the water with her?"

Ronnie's eyes narrowed. "How do you know that it did?"

"The detective asked me to identify it. I could see it had been soaking wet at some point."

Ronnie looked stricken. "She was troubled."

"She sided with you against the theme park."

"Of course she did. Wonderful World is a scam, and everyone who invests in Mongaup Valley Ventures will lose money. That's what she told me. Two days later, she was dead. She was . . . upset by what she'd discovered."

Comprehension dawned. "You think she killed herself."

That would explain why she'd gone into the water fully clothed, but I didn't buy the theory that she'd taken her own life. Tiffany had been on the brink of a new career, or so she'd believed. Feeling as if I was making my way through a minefield, I asked another question.

"If Tiffany had proof that her husband was a crook, why hasn't he been arrested?"

197

"She was the only one who knew the details."

"What about Alan Van Heusen's crimes? Did she have any evidence of what he's been up to?"

Ronnie's brow twitched into what I suppose would have been a furrow if she hadn't had so much work done. "Alan? I don't understand. Greg Onslow runs the show."

"Van Heusen is clearly a bully. It wouldn't surprise me to learn that he has a history of harassment charges, or even assault."

"I . . . those were just unfounded rumors."

"So there *was* something. What?"

Ronnie stared into the middle distance before she replied, as if she was trying to reconstruct another time and place in her mind. "A girl . . . no, a young woman. She had only been working for MVV for about a month. There was some debate about whether she quit or was fired. Tiffany refused to discuss the incident. She and Greg were still newlyweds then. I assumed she kept mum because she had asked her husband to get rid of a female she saw as competition. Tiffany did have a jealous streak." Ronnie made a moue of distaste before she added, "Now that I think about it, I suppose that girl's job put her in far greater contact with Alan than with Greg."

"Do you remember her name?"

"No."

The answer came too quickly, convincing me that Ronnie knew perfectly well who the woman was. For some reason, she didn't want me to find out. Afraid I'd talk to her and get the real story? That was my guess.

"Okay, let's go back to Onslow. Do you have any idea what it was that Tiffany found? Financial records? Incriminating letters? A phony will?"

Ronnie winced at the last suggestion but didn't answer.

Exasperated, I stood. "Maybe there's nothing *to* find. Maybe I'm wrong to suspect foul play."

"Foul — ?" Ronnie sent me a hard stare but I thought I saw a glimmer of hopefulness beneath the antipathy. "What do you mean?"

"Detective Hazlett was looking at the case as a possible murder investigation when he questioned me about my business card. He apparently changed his mind, but I don't think it was because Tiffany killed herself. Maybe there just wasn't enough evidence to go on."

"Or Onslow got to him." Bitterness blended with relief in her voice.

I almost reached out to her, but I could

guess how she would react to any display of sympathy on my part. I clenched my hands into fists to keep them in place.

"Tiffany was a strong swimmer. She'd never have drowned by accident. If it wasn't suicide, and I see now that I was a fool to believe that, then someone killed her."

Having shown her vulnerable side, if only for a moment, the Ronnie I knew of old returned with a vengeance, rising abruptly to her feet to point the way to the exit.

"You've done your good deed, Mikki. You can leave now."

"But —"

"I'll deal with this." She looked down at the backup thumb drive in her hand, staring at it as if it might suddenly come to life and bite her.

"But —"

"None of this is your concern any longer. You've given the right answer in class, as usual, and you've also given me a blinding headache." As her fist closed around the thumb drive, she looked me straight in the eyes. "I want you out of house and out of my life."

"I can help." I meant with searching the thumb drive. I'm not sure how Ronnie interpreted my words.

"You want to help? Go away. Forget we

ever had this conversation."

"But —"

Turning her back on me, Ronnie stalked out of the room, leaving me to find my own way to the front door. I could hear the *tick-tick-tick* of her heels as she ascended the grand staircase in the foyer. Her behavior told me I was missing something, but I didn't have a clue what it was. I went home in a deeply troubled frame of mind.

CHAPTER 21

That evening, after the workmen had all gone home and Calpurnia and I had eaten a light supper, someone knocked at the front door. Since it was full dark by then, I took no chances. On my way to answer it, I grabbed my cell phone and was prepared to speed dial the police station if I felt the least bit threatened by my unexpected visitor.

I relaxed when I looked through the glass panel and saw it was only Mike Doran on the other side. I opened up at once. "Hey, Mike. What brings you out so late?"

He glanced at his watch. "Uh, Mik, it's only eight o'clock."

I felt my face grow warm. I wasn't about to confess how many nights I had already changed into a nightgown and robe by this hour. I don't usually go to bed until ten or eleven, but I like to be comfortable when I'm watching TV or reading or whatever. James always opted for sweats.

"What can I say?" I murmured. "I'm not used to entertaining company in the evening."

It struck me that this was the first time Mike had been in my house since the last time he picked me up for a date. He looked around as if curious to see what changes had been made in fifty-plus years and nodded approvingly.

"There's a lot more to be done," I said as I led him into the living room and indicated that he should take the comfortable armchair. The room was much less crowded than it had been. I'd been able to return most of the excess furniture to where it belonged.

As soon as I plopped myself down on the loveseat, Calpurnia claimed the other cushion. I reached out to stroke her.

"Lucky cat," Mike said.

Now there was a remark best ignored! "Why are you here?" I asked, and immediately flashed on Ronnie asking me that same question.

He shook his head, sending me a reproachful look. "Good old Mikki — straight to the point and no distractions allowed."

I couldn't tell if that was meant as compliment or criticism. Before I could respond, he was speaking again.

"You've been meddling in things that are none of your business."

"I beg your pardon?"

"You heard me. That's not the way to fit in here, Mik."

His tone had me narrowing my eyes at him. "Oh, really? Because no one in this town ever gossips, is that right, Mike?" I was getting a little tired of this refrain.

"Sarcasm? You know what they say about sarcasm."

We quoted in unison from John Knowles's *A Separate Peace,* a book that had been required reading in our senior English class: "Sarcasm is the protest of those who are weak."

The tension in the room eased a little, and we smiled at each other.

"I take it that Ronnie complained to you."

"You've opened up a can of worms."

"Cliché!"

"Whatever. Can't you just let the matter drop?"

"Me? It's your fault — yours and Ronnie's and Greg Onslow's — that I got involved in this in the first place. You're the ones who insisted Tiffany must have left something with me in addition to her manuscript."

"Did she?"

I blinked at him in surprise, wondering why Ronnie hadn't told him about the thumb drive or that she now had her own copy.

More than ever, I missed having James as a sounding board. He'd been a good listener and had almost always steered me in the right direction to solve whatever problem was bothering me. I'd have unburdened myself to Darlene if she hadn't still been avoiding me. I glanced at Calpurnia. She provided comfort but fell short when it came to offering advice. All things considered, Mike was starting to look like a good alternative.

"You have to promise not to tell anyone else what I'm about to confide in you."

"You're swearing me to secrecy?" Mike's lips quirked, but at least he didn't laugh.

"Lawyer-client privilege?" I suggested.

"You're not my client."

Trying to keep the tone light, I fumbled in the pocket of my jeans and pulled out a crumpled dollar bill. I held it up. "Will this do as a retainer?"

He rolled his eyes, but he reached for the bill. "Give me that."

When it had been safely tucked away in his wallet and I had his full attention, I drew in a deep breath and spit out my big confession. "I found Tiffany's thumb drive. She'd left it in the bottom of the mailer that contained her manuscript. There are research files on it, as well as a copy of her book. I've been working my way through both the files and the novel, and I think she may have based some of what she wrote about on criminal activity within Mongaup Valley Ventures."

"Then you need to contact the police."

"There's more. I don't think Tiffany's death was an accident."

Mike did laugh then, but his amusement went into a rapid retreat when he saw that I was serious. "Do you have proof?"

"No. Not yet. And I may be wrong, but I think it's possible. What if she found something that could send her husband to jail? Him or his flunky."

"Van Heusen?"

I nodded and told him about my visit from Onslow's right-hand man. Then I added what I'd learned from George, although I didn't name my source. I finished off with the fact that my business card appeared to have been in the water with Tiffany when she drowned.

"That's a lot of . . . speculation." The way he was being so careful with his words made me smile.

"You think I don't know that? But there's definitely something strange going on. And Ronnie wouldn't level with me, either."

"How much did you tell her?"

"Most of it."

Mike's frown kept me silent while he pondered. When he finally spoke, it was not to say what I wanted to hear.

"It all comes back to what I said earlier, Mikki. You need to stop meddling. You're just asking for trouble if you don't."

"That's your advice as my lawyer?"

"It is."

I sighed. "Okay. Then I guess I'd better go ahead and turn the thumb drive over to the police."

"No!"

"Wow! That was fierce."

He leaned forward, elbows propped on knees, holding my gaze. "Here's the thing, Mik, aside from the fact that the police have closed the case and won't welcome an amateur criticizing the way they did their job, that thumb drive rightfully belongs to Onslow."

"I thought Tiffany made Ronnie her heir. The will is genuine, isn't it?"

He reared back, insulted. "Of course it is, but Tiffany only left her grandmother the shares in MVV. Everything else goes to her husband."

"Why did Tiffany make a will in the first place? I'm willing to bet that most people her age don't have one. And doesn't the timing seem suspicious to you?"

"It was Ronnie's idea," he admitted. "She trusted her granddaughter to vote against the theme park, but she knows better than anyone how fragile life can be."

"What do you mean?"

"She's lost three husbands, Mik."

"I thought she divorced two of them."

"You thought wrong. You understand from your own experience how tough it is to be widowed. Can you imagine going through such a loss three times?"

I bit back my automatic objection to being compared to Ronnie in any way, shape, or form. Besides, *my* marriage had lasted for decades. All of hers had been short-lived. Still, Mike had a point. Losing a loved one is never easy.

"So Ronnie took precautions, and her foresight paid off." I held up a hand to stop his retort. "That didn't come out the right way. Obviously, she didn't want her grand-daughter to lose her life. But what if Tiffany *told* her husband her intentions, and he arranged her death to prevent her from signing that will, only he acted too late?"

"I wouldn't put it past him." Tension radiated from Mike's stiff posture and taut features. "You'll have heard by now that Onslow has produced a second will. He claims the one Ronnie has is a forgery."

"I heard." I didn't tell him who had mentioned it. He had to know that his ex wasn't a member of his fan club.

"My theory is that he found a copy of Tiffany's will after her death and used it as a template for the bogus version. It has the same date and is signed by the same witnesses, but there's one big difference. It leaves everything to him."

"The same witnesses? Then wouldn't they know which will is the real one?"

"All they witnessed was Tiffany's signature. That's standard practice. There was no reason for them to see the contents of the will."

We were silent for a few minutes. "Won't a handwriting expert be able to tell the original from the forgery?"

"Sure, but meanwhile the legal challenge is preventing Ronnie from doing anything with the shares until the case is settled. Even when it is, there will be a long wait while the authentic will is probated. In the meantime, who knows what Onslow will do?"

I was about to ask Mike for his take on

Wonderful World being a total scam when he suddenly stood up, crossed to the love-seat, shoved Calpurnia off, and sat down beside me. He took both my hands in his.

"Listen to me, Mikki. It's not a good idea for you to get on Onslow's bad side."

"Does that mean you think he killed his wife?"

"It means you need to use common sense and stay out of the crossfire. Whether he's a murderer or just a garden-variety con man, he's trouble. Tell you what — why don't I take charge of that thumb drive?"

"No way." I pulled free of his grasp. "It isn't as if he knows I have it. I'm not taking any risks by hanging on to it. Besides, so far it doesn't look as if it contains anything more exciting than Tiffany's manuscript and research files."

"Better safe than sorry."

He looked so concerned about my well-being that I softened my stance. It felt good to have someone worry about me, even though I had no inclination to take on the role of little-lady-in-need-of-protection. "The only file that's been the least bit mysterious is one Tiffany named 'blackmail .doc,' and I'm pretty sure it relates to one of the characters in her novel."

Mike looked startled but forced a smile

when I chuckled.

"Most of the rest of the research consists of newspaper stories about very old crimes," I continued, "although there is one set of notes. She talked with someone who had first-hand knowledge of a Murder Incorporated killing back in the 1930s. Or maybe secondhand, considering how long ago that was." *I should go back and read that file,* I thought. I'd only glanced at the content the one time I'd opened it.

A thundercloud gathered in Mike's expression. "Those old killings were brutal. Why do you want to read about them?"

"I've read worse, and seen the like in living color at the movies."

He was sweet to worry about my delicate sensibilities, but his overabundance of concern was starting to annoy me. I didn't need someone else deciding what I should or shouldn't do.

"Don't worry." I squeezed his forearm in what was meant to be a reassuring gesture. "I don't plan on confronting Onslow or making wild accusations in public, but I am going to read the rest of the material Tiffany left behind. If I find anything that constitutes proof of wrongdoing, I promise that I'll take it straight to Detective Hazlett."

Mike heaved an exasperated sigh. "At

which point you'll probably find yourself in big trouble."

"Why?"

"Ever hear of withholding evidence?"

I sent him a considering look. "You wanted me to give you the thumb drive. What would *you* have done with it?"

"The same thing you're going to," he admitted. "Read the files. Look for anything that isn't fiction." He released me to run one hand through his hair, calling my attention to the preponderance of gray strands among the black. It was thinner than it had been, too.

"And if you found something?" I prompted him.

"I'd be tempted to send it to Hazlett anonymously."

"I could do that, but I'd be afraid that he'd discount it."

Mike forced a smile but his eyes remained deadly serious. "Promise me that if you do come across something incriminating, you won't go to the police on your own. I'll go with you to make certain you stay out of jail."

"You'll be the first to know if I find a clue," I assured him. "Believe me when I say that the last thing I want is to be locked up."

CHAPTER 22

It was Saturday morning before I had a block of time available to spend with Tiffany's files. I had not yet finished reading her novel. Since her plot had grown more convoluted with each succeeding chapter, a little went a long way. The same was true of her research. If I were fascinated by true crime, I might have found the documents she'd collected more interesting, but my tolerance for reading about long-dead mobsters killing each other was limited, and there was a certain gory sameness about the newspaper clippings, not to mention some of the interviews. At first I thought the file I'd just opened was more of the same.

It was the story of someone Tiffany referred to only as "a local man" and detailed how he had gotten away with murder by making the authorities think it was just another mob hit. The real killer had apparently enjoyed a loose connection with a hotel where the gang ran the slots. A note at the end of the account indicated that Tiffany's facts had come from a descendant of this murderous Sullivan County resident.

I should confess that I don't know much about gambling. There are a couple of casinos in Maine, but I'd never visited either of them. The closest I ever came to a one-armed bandit or a roulette wheel was on a ferry ride from Portland to Nova Scotia years ago. Once in international waters, most of the passengers spent their time, and their money, hoping to win big at one of the table games or hit the jackpot by repeatedly inserting money and pulling a lever. I'd found a comfortable chair where I could look out over the water and alternated between watching that peaceful scene and reading a book I'd brought with me. The building of a casino in nearby Monticello might have prompted Greg Onslow to come up with his plan to revitalize Lenape Hollow, but I had zero interest in spending any time in that establishment.

"I'll watch *Ocean's Eleven* if I want to see how gamblers live," I informed Calpurnia as she walked across the table in front of me, momentarily distracting me from my laptop screen.

Just as I started to close the file and move

on to another, a stray thought niggled at the back of my mind. Where was the confirmation Tiffany mentioned? Could it be in the file I'd told Mike about, the one I'd started to read and never gotten back to?

After a few minutes of searching, I found it again. This time I read every word. Tiffany's notes consisted of a collection of quotes that when cobbled together corroborated the details in the file I'd just read. She had taken pains not to identify her source. She hadn't even specified when or where she'd talked to this relative of the man who'd gotten away with what she called "the copycat killing."

Pretty clever, I thought. Murder someone and let the mob take the blame. I wondered if a fictionalized version of the story would appear in the final chapters of Tiffany's novel. That would certainly spice things up.

That thought gave me pause. If the killer's descendant was still around, as it seemed likely he or she must be, he or she might not have wanted this skeleton in the closet exposed. It was one thing to tell a story to a young woman who was interested in the "good old days" and quite another to have your family's deepest, darkest secret appear in print.

How far would a son or daughter go, I

wondered, to ensure Tiffany's silence? Would a grandson or granddaughter care what Grandpa had done? They might. Assuming that Tiffany had been murdered, here was yet another motive and a whole array of new suspects. The person she'd talked to might have been willing to admit the truth in private, but what about other relatives? One of them might not have been happy about sharing the story, let alone the prospect of seeing it reimagined in a published book. A change of name to protect the copycat killer's identity would not have guaranteed that the crime couldn't be traced back to the real murderer.

Instead of opening the next research file, I returned to Tiffany's novel. It contained no front matter, but sometimes writers put acknowledgments and other information about their sources at the end.

And there it was — "A Note from the Author."

Tiffany's files included several interviews. She had talked to a number of local people, members of families who had lived in Sullivan County for generations and had stories to tell about the atrocities committed by Murder Incorporated. Their parents or grandparents had been eyewitnesses to history. The acknowledgments named them all.

I recognized most of the surnames, if not the individuals in question. Only one or two didn't ring a bell, making me wonder if one of them was Tiffany's anonymous source for the tale of the copycat killer.

When I read the author's note the first time, nothing jumped out at me, but on the second pass my editor's eye caught what I assumed was a typo. I frowned. This particular error struck me as peculiar. While Tiffany had occasionally made mistakes in other areas of punctuation, her use of the Oxford comma had been one hundred percent consistent throughout her manuscript. The anomaly I noticed came at the end of a sentence acknowledging several lawyers she'd talked to. If she'd meant to thank them as a group of three, then she should have written "my lawyer friends, Philip Sussman, Lawrence Kruger, and Michael Doran." Instead, she'd thanked "my lawyer friends, Philip Sussman and Lawrence Kruger, and Michael Doran."

There was a tiny but telling difference in meaning, one that could be interpreted a couple of ways. The missing comma could indicate that Mike wasn't really a lawyer, that perhaps he was a fraud. I didn't think that was likely, which left me with the second explanation, that Mike was the source of some specific information, separate from what he might have contributed in his capacity as a lawyer.

Could *Mike* have been the source of the copycat killer story? That was a leap, I know, but once I considered the possibility, I began to remember details from his past that seemed to corroborate the theory.

Mike's father died when Mike was just a baby. He'd been a lot older than most of our classmates' parents — old enough to have murdered someone back in the 1930s. Had he left behind papers telling his story? Or had Mike's mother known what he did and passed that knowledge on to her son?

Frowning, I stared into space. If I was correct, why hadn't Mike mentioned that Tiffany had talked to him? The answer to that question was easy enough to come by. It probably embarrassed him to have a killer for a father, even if the murder did take place a long time ago. Perhaps it was his desire to keep his father's secret under wraps that prompted his offer to take charge of the thumb drive.

My frown deepened. If that was the case, why had he shared his father's story with Tiffany at all? He was an old family friend. That meant that Tiffany had known him all her life. Perhaps she'd picked up bits and pieces of the story over the years. That would explain the way her notes were written — as if they'd been compiled in a number of separate sessions. Had Mike even realized he was being pumped for information?

So, I thought, assuming that Mike's father was the copycat killer, did that give Mike sufficient motive to murder Tiffany? Nonsense, I told myself. Mike wouldn't have killed Tiffany to stop her from revealing his family secret. He'd have threatened to sue her to stop publication of her novel, and that was only if she'd actually intended to use the story. I couldn't confirm that she'd included it until I finished reading her book.

I dedicated the rest of the day, when the absence of workmen bathed the house in peace and quiet, to completing that task. Nowhere in the text did she mention a copycat crime. I closed the file with a sense of relief.

So much for that theory! I shook my head, amused by the way my overactive imagination had gone off on a tangent. To fall back on clichés, I'd been grasping at straws. Even my identification of the copycat killer as Mike's father had probably been way out in left field. The simplest explanation was that Tiffany had simply misplaced a comma and

Mike had been no more than one of the lawyers she'd talked to.

As for her novel, it had failed to live up to the promise of the first few chapters. In the last third of her book, she had thrown in just about every tried and true plot twist ever to grace a gangster story. Even with input from a good editor, I thought it unlikely she'd have been able to interest a traditional publisher in buying it. Would I have suggested she self-publish? Maybe, but only after a total rewrite. Even then I had my doubts about its potential for success.

It saddened me that Tiffany's dream had not been realized, but I was more disappointed not to have found a clue to her killer's identity in the manuscript. Those thinly disguised caricatures of her husband and Alan Van Heusen? She'd killed them off a couple of chapters before the end.

CHAPTER 23

On Sunday, since Darlene hadn't been in touch and I was concerned about her, I went to the one place I was certain to find her: worship services at the First Presbyterian Church of Lenape Hollow. I inserted myself into the pew next to her and gave her my widest smile. I received a decidedly guilty look in return.

As soon as the recessional began, I addressed the elephant in the room. "You've been avoiding me, kiddo. Don't you think it's about time you told me why?"

She closed her eyes for a brief moment, gave a theatrical sigh, and conceded my point.

I followed Darlene's van back to her place. Since Frank was at the golf course, we had the house to ourselves, but she insisted on making sandwiches before we settled down to talk. By the time we were seated at her kitchen table with plates and glasses in front of us and the smell of recent baking — apples and cinnamon — in the air, I'd lost patience with her delaying tactics.

"So?"

"I guess you're wondering why I've been so uncommunicative all week." She inscribed random patterns on the tabletop with the tip of one finger and avoided meeting my eyes.

"I guess I do. I've been worried about you. I know darned well something is wrong. You haven't been yourself since the day I took you to see the eye doctor."

The hint of a smile curved her lips at that statement. "Gee, you should have been a detective."

"We'll talk about *that* later."

She cocked her head, inviting me to fill her in then and there. Instead, I motioned for her to continue.

"What can I say? I've been down in the dumps and feeling sorry for myself."

"Why?"

Darlene took a bite of her chicken salad sandwich, delaying the next part of her confession. I followed suit, trying to pretend I wasn't about to explode with curiosity. Darlene makes a mean chicken salad with homemade mayo and tiny bits of Vidalia onions and green peppers, but for once I didn't take the time to savor the taste.

When she spoke, her words came out in a rush. "I thought I was losing my eyesight. That day you took me to Dr. Shapiro it wasn't just for a checkup, and the tests didn't go well. He told me I needed to see a specialist. He said there was a possibility that I might go blind."

The food I'd just put in my mouth instantly turned to sawdust. With an effort, I finished chewing and swallowed. "Oh, Darlene, I —"

She spoke right over my attempt to comfort her. "Dr. Shapiro set up an appointment for me with a guy in Middletown. I drove myself to the appointment and had more tests."

"You didn't have to go through this alone. I could have —"

"Yes, I did. I didn't want anyone to know." She shrugged. "I didn't even tell Frank. I can't stand the thought of being pitied."

There was nothing I could say to that. She wouldn't believe me if I claimed that no one would feel sorry for her.

"Anyway," she continued, "when the specialist looked over the list of medicines I take, he picked up on something that Dr. Shapiro missed. The scare was a false alarm. Or to be more specific, the problem was caused by one of my arthritis medications. Lucky me. I get to choose between living with pain and losing my sight."

Although she was trying to make light of the scare she'd had, I could imagine how frightened she must have been. "I just wish you'd told me sooner. At the least I could have offered moral support."

"I didn't want to talk about it. To tell you the truth, I didn't even want to think about it. I still don't, really, but you deserved an explanation for my behavior."

"I get why you clammed up. I do." I reached across the table to place my hand over hers. It was vibrating with tension. "The thought of not being able to see would scare the bejesus out of me, too."

There was no need to say more. After a moment, we went back to eating lunch.

"So," Darlene asked when only crumbs remained on her plate, "how was your week?"

"Interesting," I said, and filled her in on what I'd been up to.

When she laughed at the saga of Lake Kitchen, I knew our friendship was back on an even keel.

"One of these days, I've got to meet this cat of yours," she said.

"Any time. Just don't bring the dog." I

reached down to ruffle Edmund's ears as he gazed up at me with adoring but blood-shot eyes. "Calpurnia would beat the crap out of him."

CHAPTER 24

By ten o'clock on Monday morning, the noise level at my house was more than I could endure. Even removing my hearing aids didn't help. Once again, men were working directly over my head in what would eventually become my office.

Leaving Calpurnia to cope — she appeared to be able to sleep through an earthquake — I packed up my laptop and headed for Harriet's. If J. K. Rowling could create Harry Potter in a coffee shop, surely I could edit a manuscript in one.

I should have known better.

"There she is — my favorite rabble rouser." The greeting was ambiguous, but Ada's wide grin reassured me that she wasn't planning to ban me from the premises. As soon as I was settled at a table, she brought me coffee. It was already doctored the way I like it with two Splendas and a dash of half-and-half.

"Why do I suddenly feel as if I'm living in an old sitcom?" I asked of no one in particular.

"*Friends?*" Ada's smile widened. "I always liked the atmosphere in Central Perk."

"I was thinking of *Cheers,*" I told her, "where everybody knows your name."

"And your business."

"That, too."

As I sipped my coffee and nibbled a blueberry muffin, I checked out the other "regulars" at Harriet's and realized with a mild sense of surprise that I *did* know most of their their names. Somehow, in the last few weeks, I had become part of the community again. So much for all those warnings about making myself unpopular by meddling. Everybody loves a good gossip!

I nodded to Sonya Adler, Mike's ex, and her friend Betsy, avoided making eye contact with Clarice Cameron, the minister's wife, and tried to figure out why the young man in blue jeans and a faded "Feel the Bern" T-shirt looked so familiar. I had a sneaking suspicion it was because I had known his father when he was that same age. Or maybe his grandfather. Sometimes I forget how long ago some of my contemporaries started their families.

"Well, will you look at that," Sonya exclaimed.

Everyone turned to stare through Harriet's plate glass window at the police station. A woman was being helped out of the backseat of a cruiser. She wasn't handcuffed, but there was something about the alertness of the uniformed officers on each side of her and the way Detective Hazlett was keeping a close eye on the proceedings that suggested she hadn't volunteered to come with them.

The prisoner kept her head down and had the collar of her jacket turned up, but it only took a glimpse of her face in profile to identify her.

Clarice gasped. "My goodness — they've arrested Ronnie North!"

"Who says she's under arrest?" Ada asked.

"Why else would she be taken to the station in a police car?"

The words were barely out of her mouth when Mike Doran pulled in behind the cruiser, flung himself out of his vehicle, and raced inside.

Sonya gave a snort of laughter. "The charge can't be too serious if she called a divorce lawyer to get her off."

"Murder is about as serious as you can get," Clarice murmured.

Everyone turned to look at her.

"Do you know something the rest of us don't?" I asked. "Maybe Ronnie just got pulled over for speeding."

"Ronnie attends my husband's church," she reminded me, "and so does her housekeeper. Poor Ann. She's been in a terrible quandary, uncertain whether or not she should speak to the police. Naturally, she went to her pastor for guidance."

"Does he share confidences with you, or did you eavesdrop?" Sonya asked.

There was no love lost there, a story I promised myself I'd pursue some other time. For the moment, I awaited an answer as eagerly as everyone else in the café.

Clarice Cameron ignored Sonya's question, but she was only too eager to share what she knew. There was an undercurrent of glee in her voice, making me wonder what Ronnie had done to make an enemy of the minister's wife.

"Ann heard grandmother and granddaughter quarreling the morning of the day Tiffany died."

I looked at her askance. "That's it? Hardly grounds to accuse someone of murder."

"I heard Tiffany Scott drowned," the young man said. "An accident."

Sonya looked thoughtful as she toyed with a spoon. "She was a very good swimmer.

She was in the water almost every day. Back before her husband announced his big plans for the property, people thought he might have bought Chestnut Park just so she could have the lake all to herself."

Clarice was nodding like a bobble-head. "She'd *never* have drowned by accident. I'll bet you anything that the tests they did on Tiffany's body came back to say she was drugged before she went into the water, and who would have been in a better position to doctor her food? She had lunch with Grandma almost every day."

While the other patrons at Harriet's continued to speculate, I kept my thoughts to myself. Foremost among them was denial. I could think of no reason why Ronnie would to do away with her own granddaughter. Despite the fact that we'd all seen her taken into police headquarters, I couldn't believe it was because Detective Hazlett thought she'd killed Tiffany.

Maybe Ronnie and Tiffany *had* quarreled that morning, but that didn't mean much. Clarice didn't appear to know what they'd argued about. Her interpretation of what Ann had told her husband was obviously colored by her personal dislike of a woman who enjoyed lording it over others. I sympathized. I didn't care for Ronnie either, but that didn't mean I would blithely sling accusations her way.

Revolted by the increasingly wild guesses Ada's patrons were voicing about Ronnie's relationship with her granddaughter, I gathered up my laptop, paid my bill, and headed for my car. I did not go home. Instead I drove to Ronnie's house. I wanted to hear the story of her quarrel with Tiffany from the horse's mouth.

CHAPTER 25

When Ann opened the door at the North house, I could tell she'd been crying. Suddenly, I felt awkward. I was intruding at an emotional time, and when you got right down to it, Ronnie's removal to the police station was none of my business. Despite my reservations, and before I could talk myself out of asking, I blurted out my question.

"Has Ronnie been arrested for murder?"

"They took her in for questioning." Ann swiped at her damp cheeks. "It's all my fault. I should have kept my big mouth shut."

My mind was whirling. Had the police, contrary to what they'd led everyone to believe, continued to investigate Tiffany's death as a possible homicide? They did tricky things like that all the time in the movies, but I always assumed that the screenwriters made them up.

Ann turned away from the door, leaving it open, and headed down the hall toward the back of the house. I took that as an invitation to follow her and caught up with her in a spacious, gleaming kitchen that smelled more strongly of Clorox than it did of cooking.

"It's not your fault, Ann. You had to tell the police what you knew."

Abruptly, the floodgates opened. I slung a comforting arm around Ann's shoulders and guided her to a kitchen chair. The least I could do was offer tea and sympathy while she cried. I bustled about, finding everything I needed in logical places, and in short order had placed two steaming cups of Earl Grey on the table in front of us. Ann sniffled and sipped and looked grateful for the pampering.

"I hear you overheard a quarrel," I said when I'd taken a few swallows from my own cup. I'm not a big tea drinker, but anything hot is soothing when you need to calm down.

"Hard not to," Ann said with a shrug of her bony shoulders.

"Loud, huh?"

"They always were." A tiny smile curved the corners of her mouth upward. "Tiffany inherited her grandmother's temper."

"Were they often at odds?"

"Often enough." She ran a finger around the rim of her cup.

"What were they arguing about this time?"

Ann shook her head. "I stopped paying attention years ago."

I gave her a sharp look.

She took offense. "I'm an employee in this house. I don't get paid to listen in on conversations."

"So you didn't hear anything unusual? No threats?"

"The boss lady was always threatening to cut Tiffany out of her will."

So much for not listening.

"If you didn't hear anything incriminating, why are the police questioning Ronnie?"

"Mostly because I didn't tell them about the quarrel until yesterday. That detective got pretty huffy about me withholding evidence, but I told him I wasn't sure it was important. Besides, if they'd asked me the right questions at the beginning, I'd have told them sooner. It's not like Mike Doran mentioned it, either."

I felt myself tense. "Mike was here that morning? While they were shouting at each other?"

"Sure was."

I had no idea what to make of that revelation, nor could I figure out why the police had taken Ronnie down to their headquarters instead of just questioning her at home. It didn't sound as if they had much to go on . . . unless Clarice's theory about the autopsy results was right on the money. I was trying to think of a subtle way to ask Ann if she knew what medications Ronnie had in the house when the back door slammed open with a crash and, preceded by a whiff of Emeraude, Ronnie stalked into the kitchen.

She was breathing fire even before she spotted me. My presence sent her right over the edge. "What the hell are you doing in my house?"

I stood up in a rush, prepared to make a run for it. Even though I didn't believe Ronnie had killed anyone, I was suddenly very much aware that there were a number of dangerous weapons in the room, everything from carving knives to cast iron skillets.

"Now you just settle down, Ronnie North," Ann said.

We both stared at her. Given the state she'd been in only minutes earlier, I couldn't have been more surprised if a garden gnome had spoken.

"Mikki and me, we were just chatting. Did

you know we used to play together when we were kids?"

"You were gossiping." Ronnie snapped out the accusation. "I won't have it."

Having cowed her housekeeper, she turned on me. In contrast to her red face and burning gaze, her words were ice cold. She enunciated each one with a precision that left me in no doubt about how serious she was.

"Get out of my house, Mikki, and this time don't come back. You'll never be welcome here."

CHAPTER 26

There was nothing about reopening the investigation into Tiffany Scott's death in the next morning's newspaper, but all that day my mind kept returning to the case. Much as I disliked Ronnie, I disliked even more the idea that an innocent person could be suspected of murder.

By three o'clock that afternoon, I'd given up trying to accomplish anything to do with editing. The thumb drive weighed heavily on my conscience. That the police had questioned Ronnie suggested that they had changed their minds about Tiffany's death being an accident. If that was so, any potential evidence belonged in their hands.

If they were focused on Ronnie as a suspect, they'd be disappointed. There was nothing in the files I'd looked at to indicate that she had any reason to harm her granddaughter. There weren't even any mature female characters, evil or good, in Tiffany's novel.

I had a brief, unworthy moment when I considered delaying just to make Ronnie sweat, but petty vindictiveness is an unattractive trait. I had to do what was right, no matter how she'd behaved toward me. Since I had it in my power to help clear her of suspicion and point the finger in a more likely direction at the same time, I could no longer shirk my civic duty.

I tried to keep my promise to notify Mike first. I phoned him before I left the house, but my call went straight to voice mail. I didn't leave a message. Despite his warning, I felt certain I didn't need a lawyer.

Detective Hazlett kept me waiting for forty-five minutes and looked harassed and out-of-sorts when I was finally admitted to his inner sanctum. He did not get up. "What can I do for you today, Ms. Lincoln?"

"It's what I can do for you, Detective Hazlett." I placed the thumb drive on the only relatively uncluttered spot on his blotter.

"What's this? No." He held up a hand. "I can see it's a flash drive. Why are you giving it to me?"

"It belonged to Tiffany Scott."

I lowered myself into the visitor's chair so that we were at eye level. His eyes narrowed

238

and the rest of his face turned to stone, giving me an uh-oh moment and making me wonder if I should have waited until Mike could come with me after all. Since it was too late to contact my lawyer friend, I sat with my hands primly folded in my lap and waited to hear what Detective Hazlett had to say.

"Did you have this when I interviewed you after her death?"

"I did, but I didn't know it. I discovered it much later, inside the mailer that contained her manuscript. It was buried way down at the bottom, easy to overlook. If I didn't recycle packing materials, I'd never have found it at all."

There, I thought. That didn't stretch the truth by much. If he asked me directly *when* I'd found the thumb drive, I'd tell him, but I saw no point in making trouble for myself. Let him assume that I'd just now come across it and had brought it straight to the police station.

Hazlett picked up my offering and turned it over and over in his fingers. Obviously, he wasn't planning to dust for prints. I had the uneasy feeling that he didn't quite believe my story. I wanted to jump in to defend myself, but common sense warned me to keep quiet. I'd do better to wait and see what developed.

"You were reusing the mailer?" he asked.

"Not exactly. I had tossed it into a bin with other padded envelopes good enough to reuse. It was because people kept asking me if Tiffany had left anything with me besides her manuscript that I went looking for it."

"People?" Only by the slightest shift in position did he indicate that my words had piqued his interest. "What people?"

"Well, Ronnie North, for one." It wouldn't do to let her off the hook entirely. "And Alan Van Heusen, on behalf of Gregory Onslow." I briefly described the visit from Van Heusen, emphasizing his threatening manner and my discomfort in his presence. "I didn't think to check the mailer right away, but when I did, I found the thumb drive."

Hazlett's steady stare was starting to make me nervous. "What's on it?"

"You're assuming I looked at it?"

He very nearly cracked a smile. "I can't imagine that you didn't, Ms. Lincoln, and you wouldn't be here handing it over if you didn't have some reason to think I'd be interested in the contents."

"I don't know if you will be or not. All the files appear to be related to research for Tiffany's novel, and the novel itself in on there, of course. I just . . . I thought you should have it."

Belatedly, I remembered that I'd already given Ronnie a copy of Tiffany's thumb drive. I wondered why she hadn't mentioned it to Hazlett. From his reaction to the original, it was clear that this was the first he'd heard of its existence. Of course, considering the way Ronnie felt about me, it wouldn't have surprised me to learn that she'd tossed her copy in the trash without even looking at it.

"I see," said the detective. "Very well, Ms. Lincoln. Thank you. I'll take charge of it."

"You really should read the files. And the novel."

He shot me one of those "give me patience" looks. "Why is that?"

"There are characters in the book that, uh, seem to be based on real people."

He waited.

"On her husband and his flunky, Alan Van Heusen. They're both portrayed as crooked businessmen. Mobsters. Onslow may be in there twice, as the prototype for two different characters, both of them villains."

"Murderers, I suppose?"

"Well, the novel is set in the heyday of Murder Incorporated." I couldn't quite keep the sarcasm out of my voice.

"I'll take that into consideration." When I made no move to leave, he added in a resigned tone of voice, "Is there something else?"

I tried to think how to ask him if he'd reopened the case. Finally I just blurted it out. I knew before he opened his mouth that he wasn't going to give me a straight answer. He was too polite to order me to get the hell out of his office, but what he did say amounted to the same thing.

"I'm afraid that's a police matter, Ms. Lincoln." He stood to encourage me to do the same.

Accepting that he wasn't going to tell me anything, I reluctantly eased out of the uncomfortable visitor's chair and left. I walked through the police station with all the dignity I could muster. Clearly my help was neither wanted nor appreciated. Why, I wondered, did that sting my pride? I should be relieved to be free of the obligation to set the record straight about Tiffany's death. Hazlett was perfectly correct when he said that some things were better left to the police.

CHAPTER 27

I returned home to find Ann Ellerby sitting on my front porch. It was a sunny day and not too cold, and she was warmly dressed. She also had a cup of coffee in one hand and her feet up on the table in front of one of my two wicker chairs.

"Hey," she greeted me.

"Hey, yourself." I eyed her drink.

"That nice George Finkel got it for me when I said I'd wait till you got back. Hope that's okay."

I had told all the workmen they were welcome to put their lunches in my refrigerator, although none of them had taken me up on the offer. I was pretty sure I hadn't said they could use my Keurig, but I wasn't inclined to complain. At least George had been sensible enough not to invite anyone to wait inside the house when I wasn't there.

"No problem." I took the other chair. "What's up?"

"Well, she didn't fire me."

At once I felt guilty. It hadn't once occurred to me that Ronnie might let her longtime housekeeper go just because she'd talked to the police . . . or to me. "Did you think she was going to?"

Ann shrugged. "Not really. Besides, if she did, she'd only hire me back again." Her sudden grin made her look years younger. "Hard to get rid of somebody when they live right in the same house with you."

"An unheated room in the attic?"

"A two-room suite on the third floor with its own bath."

"Nice. How did you end up working for Ronnie in the first place?"

"She saved my life. Really," she insisted when she saw the doubtful look on my face. "I was going through a bad divorce. My almost ex didn't like that I left him. Well, what choice did I have when he came after me with a baseball bat? Anyway, I was staying at the women's shelter, and Ronnie volunteers there. We got to talking, and the next thing I know, she offered me a job. The next time hubby tried to get to me, all kinds of burglar alarms went off, and that was that. No more bail for him. He's in prison now and will be for a good long time, and I'm making excellent money just for keeping

Ronnie's place clean and doing a little cooking."

"If she's been so good to you, why did you go to the police? You must have known it would get her into trouble."

"Did you listen to last week's sermon?"

I had to admit that although I'd gone to church services, I hadn't paid much attention to Pastor Cameron's words. He has one of those droning voices that causes listeners to tune out and, in some cases, fall asleep.

"It was all about telling the truth, and I realized that meant more than not lying, and just the day before that the cops had been back at the house asking questions. They said they needed to get the timeline right. You know — figure out when Tiffany was last seen alive."

"Wait a minute. I thought the case had been closed."

"Not so you'd notice, and Ronnie's never bought into the idea that Tiffany's death was an accident. I could tell. Anyway, here's the thing. I hadn't told the cops about the quarrel, but after I listened to that sermon, I got to worrying that knowing about it might be important. I asked Pastor Cameron what he thought, and he said I should tell the detective, so I did, but then he ended up thinking Ronnie was a — what do you call it? — a person of interest. That's just wrong. She's got lots of faults, Lord knows, but she's not a killer."

"No, I don't think she is, either."

"Well, there. See." She jabbed one long, thin finger in my direction. "I knew I was right to come to you."

"About that . . . why *are* you here?" A light breeze wafted into the open porch, blowing a strand of hair into my face. I brushed at it absentmindedly, until it was once more tucked behind my ear. It was Ann who held my attention.

"Because you're one smart cookie. Always were. I remember that from when we were in school." Her tone suggested that this explained everything.

"There were *lots* of smart girls in my graduating class." Nine of the top ten, in fact.

Ann waved this objection aside. "None of the others came to talk to me after Ronnie was taken to the police station. You did. You wanted to know about the quarrel. I don't think you were just being snoopy."

"It was nosiness, at least in part. I have to be honest with you, Ann. I've never been all that fond of Ronnie."

"Maybe not, but you don't want to see her railroaded for a crime she didn't commit. I can tell. And I think you've been giving Tiffany's death a lot of thought ever since you heard about it."

Her insight made me uncomfortable. "My husband used to say I obsessed about things."

"You say that like it's a bad thing."

She'd succeeded in coaxing a smile out of me, and that was followed by the reluctant admission that I didn't want to stop searching for the truth. "If Tiffany *was* murdered," I said aloud, "there were at least two people in her life who were far more likely to have had a reason to kill her than Ronnie."

"The husband, right? Because the husband or wife of the victim is always a suspect."

"The husband, yes, but mostly because Tiffany was opposed to what he was planning. She left those shares in Mongaup Valley Ventures to her grandmother as a way to stop him. I'm a little unclear on what he's been up to, but if he was afraid he'd end up in jail because of what she knew, that's a pretty good motive to get rid of her."

"You said two people."

"The other is Alan Van Heusen, Onslow's right-hand man."

"Huh." All of a sudden, Ann became intensely interested in her empty coffee cup.

"Huh, what?"

She shrugged.

"You came to me," I reminded her. "I assume that's because you think I can help clear Ronnie's name. I won't be of any use to you if I don't know what's going on." I wasn't sure how much I could do in any case, but it was clear that Ann was holding something back, and I wanted to know what it was.

Ann fiddled with the only jewelry she wore, a plain gold pinky ring, twisting it around her finger as she spoke. "The name Alan might have come up during that quarrel."

"The quarrel you didn't listen to?"

"That's the one."

"Okay." I could feel my brow furrow as I tried to work out why Ann thought this was so important. "That can hardly be surprising if they were arguing about something to do with Mongaup Valley Ventures."

"It was . . . more personal than that."

"Don't tell me Tiffany was cheating on her husband with his flunky!" I started to laugh, but the sound died in my throat when I got a good look at Ann's face.

"Not Tiffany," she said in voice rife with disapproval.

"I don't understand."

248

Ann huffed out an exasperated breath. "And here I thought you'd be quick to pick up on hints. It wasn't Tiffany who was defending Alan Van Heusen. It wasn't Tiffany who's been having afternoon tea with that jerk two or three times a week for the last couple of months."

"Van Heusen . . . and Ronnie? Are you talking about a . . . a romantic relationship?"

My mind boggled at the very thought, but that scenario certainly explained Ronnie's peculiar reaction on the day I'd given her a copy of Tiffany's thumb drive. I'd suggested that either Greg Onslow or Alan Van Heusen, or both, might be guilty of sexual harassment in the workplace. She'd seemed shaken by the idea, even while admitting it was possible.

"I don't think they were actually doing the nasty," Ann said in a surprisingly prim voice, "but Ronnie sure acted like she was fond of him."

"Fond enough to defend him to her granddaughter, if Tiffany made accusations against him?"

Ann nodded. Her face crumpled into a mask of misery. "Maybe even fond enough to keep his name out of the investigation, even if that means making herself look guilty."

CHAPTER 28

That evening I phoned Darlene.

"I need you to come out of retirement," I told her. "I want to tap into your research skills."

"Librarians never really retire," Darlene informed me. "They just stop handling patron requests and stick to looking up stuff that interests them."

"Will you help me hunt for more information on Alan Van Heusen and Greg Onslow?"

There was a long silence on the other end of the line. "What do you want to know?"

"Anything shady. Where do we start?"

"Online first." She hesitated. "I've done some poking around already, back when we had our problem with Onslow. People where he lived before coming to Lenape Hollow weren't willing to talk to us."

"What about the locals? What happened to the folks whose businesses he bought?"

"I can try connecting to some of them, but between the threat of being sued and the fear of physical violence . . ." She let her voice trail off.

Physical violence? I didn't like the sound of that. I'd been hoping that Darlene was joking when she hinted that busted knee-caps weren't out of the question. I toyed with the phone cord of my landline, considering. I'd worm the details out of her next time I saw her in person. Right now I needed her to get busy digging up dirt. If Onslow, Van Heusen, or Mongaup Valley Ventures had broken the law in any way, I was set on finding proof of it.

"We need a list," I said. "If we look at all the projects Onslow and Van Heusen have been involved in, we may be able to find a weak link."

"I'll see what I can come up with."

I ended the call feeling much more optimistic than I had been. I picked up Calpurnia, gave her a hug, and informed her that she was due for a treat. While she chowed down on cat candy, I helped myself to three scoops of maple walnut ice cream with double-chocolate sauce on top and considered what I already knew from my own research.

I'd thought at one point that the fate of

the character based on Onslow would provide me with a clue to his real-world dealings, but in the end Tiffany had whitewashed him, making him as much victim as villain. It was a neat plot twist, and it pointed to Alan Van Heusen as the real evildoer. Then she'd killed off his character, too. Proof she didn't like him? Or just her awkward attempt at a surprise ending?

As much as I wanted to, I couldn't trust fiction to accurately reflect fact. Some things in Tiffany's book seemed to fit reality. Others decidedly did not.

Darlene must have stayed up all night, because she called me first thing the next morning, before I was even out of bed, to report on what she'd uncovered. "Can you come over?" she asked. "I can email the links, but I already have printouts here, and if we're face-to-face I can connect the dots for you much more efficiently."

If I knew Darlene, she'd already annotated the pages and added footnotes.

"Start the coffee. I'll be there in ten minutes."

Once I was dressed and had fed the cat, all I had to do was call the carpenter to let him know that I'd leave the front door key in the mailbox for his crew.

Darlene's husband was just leaving as I

arrived. "Golf again?" I called as I got out of my car.

Frank just grinned and waved. He was a good-looking guy, tall and trim with a killer smile. He still had all his hair, too. It crossed my mind, for just an instant, that almost daily golf games would make a good cover for a guy who was running around on his wife. Then I mentally slapped myself upside the head. I had never had any reason to think Frank and Darlene weren't the devoted couple they seemed to be. It appeared that my recent interest in crime was making me mistrustful. I'd have to watch myself or I'd turn into one of those nasty old ladies who is suspicious of everyone.

When I reached the kitchen, Darlene already had the coffee poured and was dropping dollops of pancake batter onto a griddle. In short order, she placed a short stack in front of me and supplied me with butter and maple syrup.

"It's from New York," I complained, catching sight of the label. "The best maple syrup comes from Maine."

"People living in New Hampshire and Vermont would disagree. Besides, you're a resident of the Empire State now. Get used to it."

"Where's your sympathy?" I complained

253

in a mock show of disgruntlement. Then I chowed down. Darlene makes a mean pancake.

When we'd eaten and she'd cleared away the dishes and refilled our coffee mugs, she covered the kitchen table with the newspaper articles she'd printed out. They came from six different towns in three states.

With Greg Onslow's whole sordid history spread out in front of me, I didn't need much help to connect those dots. The pattern was clear. Onslow went into a small town, set up shop, had one or two successes, and then, on the biggest of his deals, declared bankruptcy. His investors lost their money.

"How could this go unnoticed?" I asked. "Didn't anyone check his credentials when he came here?"

"He wasn't a new hire at a local company. He set up his own business, and he was rich enough to make the operation look impressive. Who, exactly, would investigate? Besides, in person he's persuasive. If asked, he steers investors toward his successes and away from his failures."

"I'd think his temper would be a tip-off."

Darlene shook her head. "That quarrel he had with Joe Ramirez in the cemetery? That's the first time I've ever seen him that riled up. He's usually got perfect control of himself."

"Where did the start-up money for Mongaup Valley Ventures come from? If he declared bankruptcy, shouldn't he have been broke?"

"You'd think so, but somehow he always seems to come out ahead. He probably used his business losses to his advantage at tax time."

"I'd think that the banks would stop lending him money at some point. When the average person defaults on a loan, their credit rating goes straight into the toilet."

"I guess it's true that the rich are different." Darlene sounded bitter, and I couldn't blame her.

I gathered the printouts into a stack, squared the corners, and set them aside before meeting Darlene's eyes across the table. "Will you share the details of what happened to you and Frank? It might help me to understand how Onslow operates."

She sighed, took a long swallow of coffee, and nodded. "You may as well know. You're already privy to most of the embarrassing things that have happened to me, the ones in the distant past, at any rate."

I had to smile at that, remembering a couple of incidents from our high school days, but this was not the time to reminisce.

"Do you remember the old tannery?" Darlene asked. "The one out on Collins Road?"

I was at a loss and said so.

"It doesn't matter. The important thing is that the building hasn't been in use for decades. When the last owner defaulted on taxes, the town took over the property. They got some kind of grant to clean up the site — toxic waste and all that."

I nodded, encouraging her to continue, and took another sip of my coffee. I had no idea where this story was headed.

"Everything was looking good. The town sold the property to Greg Onslow with the idea that he'd tear down the old building, put up a modern structure, and lure new businesses to the area. There were rumors about a call center and hundreds of jobs." She paused to gulp down more of her own excellent brew. "Anyway, when Onslow opened up the project to investors, it sounded like a sweet deal. Everything was promising . . . on paper. Frank and I weren't the only local people who thought so."

"What went wrong?"

"What didn't?" As she talked, she began to fold her napkin into accordion pleats, a sure sign that she was stressed. "The biggie was that there was asbestos in the walls of the old tannery building. The town should have checked for that years ago, but somehow it slipped through the cracks. Onslow discovered the problem early on, along with just how much the cleanup was going to cost. It's specialized, you know, with all kinds of rules and regulations attached, and guaranteed that the project was sure to lose money. Knowing that, he kept that information to himself and continued to encourage people to invest. Meanwhile, he quietly unloaded his shares in the project. By the time word of the asbestos problem finally leaked out, Onslow was in the clear and only the people he'd talked into joining him in the venture were left holding the bag."

"That's appalling. And unethical. And if it's not illegal, it should be."

Darlene abandoned the mauled napkin to clench both hands around her mug. "We could have taken him to court, but it would have been a long, drawn-out, expensive battle with no guarantee of success. Onslow's high-priced lawyers would have run circles around anybody we could afford to hire."

I frowned at the stack of printouts. "Given the pattern established elsewhere, shouldn't that have been the point where he folded his tent and disappeared into the night?"

"There was a difference this time. He'd just married Tiffany Scott."

"But after that shady deal, why would anyone around here do business with him? How did he find investors for Wonderful World?"

"I don't know about anyone else, but Frank and I were embarrassed that we'd been so gullible. We weren't anxious to have anyone find out about it. Then, too, Onslow sent Van Heusen around with some cock-and-bull story about how sorry he was for our losses. Underneath the sympathy the message was crystal clear: Make waves and we'll sue *you.*"

"For what?"

"Libel. Or is it slander? I can never keep those two straight."

"Libel is in writing. Slander is spoken. But since you'd have been telling the truth, he'd have no grounds to accuse you of either, let alone any hope of convincing a judge."

"Maybe, but it would still involve a long, drawn-out lawsuit. Onslow could afford that. We couldn't. Plus he was already earning good will for his downtown revitalization project. People didn't want to listen to any criticism of him."

"You mean those businesses he bought up? But people seem to know that some of the owners didn't want to sell. You mentioned it. So did Ada Patel. The Thai restaurant, right?"

Darlene stared into her now empty mug for a long moment before she answered. "There were a few . . . accidents on the premises. As far as I know, no one ever reported anything to the police, but Frank liked to have lunch there, so he witnessed one of them. He arrived to find the owner badly bruised and bleeding. The guy *said* he'd taken a fall, but Frank had just seen Alan Van Heusen leaving by the back door. He's pretty sure Van Heusen beat up the owner, and I know for certain that two days later he sold the place to Mongaup Valley Ventures. Right after that he left town."

A chill ran through me when I remembered the way Van Heusen had invaded my personal space. That sort of intimidation fell far short of physical violence, but I had no trouble believing the man capable of hurting someone to convince him to co-operate.

"I wonder if we can track them down. The owner of that restaurant, I mean."

"I can try." Darlene sounded doubtful. And tired.

I gave her a narrow-eyed look. For the first time, I noticed the dark circles under her eyes. "Did you get any sleep last night?"

"My neck was bothering me. I wouldn't have slept anyway."

"Your eyelids are at half mast." I stood, gathering up the stack of printouts. "Go lie down and have a nice long nap. I'll take this stuff home with me and —"

"Leave it here. I'll take the nap. I will," she insisted when she saw my skeptical expression. "After I get up again I want to keep going with this. I've left matters too long as it is. Frank and I can't get our money back, but at this point I'll settle for the sweet taste of revenge." Suddenly she didn't look so wiped out anymore. She fixed me with a steely gaze. "What I don't get is why you're so determined to bring Onslow down."

For a moment I was stumped. Why *was* I taking such a personal interest? I'd barely met Tiffany. I certainly didn't owe Ronnie any favors. I hated to think I'd only gotten involved because I was nosy. Then I once again pictured Alan Van Heusen looming over me in my own dining room.

"I don't like bullies. And I think the cops are barking up the wrong tree."

Darlene frowned. "Can you elaborate a little on that?"

I'd told her already about the visit from

Van Heusen and the interest everyone had expressed in the mysterious something they'd all thought Tiffany had left with me. Darlene also knew about my discovery of the thumb drive and, in general, what it contained. When I'd recapped all that, especially my conclusion that thinly disguised versions of both Onslow and Van Heusen appeared as characters in Tiffany's novel, I added the new bits.

"Tiffany was at odds with her husband over Wonderful World. She left her shares in Mongaup Valley Ventures to Ronnie, although Onslow is contesting the will. Then yesterday, I found out that Tiffany and Ronnie quarreled on the day Tiffany died, which is why the cops now think that *Ronnie* might have been the one who killed her."

"Whoa! Who said anything about killing? I thought Tiffany's death was an accident."

"That's what everyone thought, but it seems Detective Hazlett didn't close the case after all."

"Wow."

"Indeed. There's something else, too, although I'm not sure how it fits in. Ronnie has been seeing Alan Van Heusen."

"Seeing?"

"Socially. Ann Ellerby — you remember Ann? — told me that Van Heusen has been a frequent caller at Ronnie's house. I've no idea what he's really up to, but according to Ann, he's been acting like he's courting her."

"Isn't he a little young for her?"

I gaped at her. "Really? That's your take on this? Darlene, it's got to be a con, or maybe Onslow ordered him to butter her up to undercut her opposition to Wonderful World."

"I'm surprised you care. Ronnie was awful to you in high school. Come to think of it, I'm not sure I'd put it past her to have murdered someone."

"Not her own granddaughter. Besides, back in the day her weapon of choice was always the well-aimed taunt. Words hurt, but they aren't usually fatal. I don't believe Ronnie killed Tiffany. In fact, from what she said to me, she actually thought Tiffany might have committed suicide."

"Whoa. Hold on. When did you talk to Ronnie?"

I filled her in on our encounters and then repeated my suspicion that Onslow, or maybe Van Heusen, might have murdered Tiffany to keep her from ruining whatever scam they were running with Wonderful World.

"I suppose Onslow could have drowned

his wife to protect his business dealings," Darlene said, but she sounded doubtful. "He's a creep and a crook, but that's a long way from being a cold-blooded killer."

"Anyone can kill, given enough provocation."

She shook her head. "No. I don't buy it. I don't think he'd want to get his hands dirty. He'd delegate."

"To Van Heusen?"

"More than likely."

"If they entered a conspiracy to commit murder, then they're both guilty."

A wry smile played at the corners of Darlene's mouth. "I like that scenario, but we have no proof that it's true."

"Then your next task is to find out more about the flunky."

"Petty revenge. I love it."

"I don't know *what* you mean," I objected, although of course I did.

"You just want to bring Van Heusen down as payback for scaring you and stepping on Calpurnia's tail."

I made a face at her but took it as a good sign that she was able to apply a bit of dark humor to the situation. "Maybe so," I admitted, "but I'll tell you one thing. Something is definitely off-kilter with the Wonderful World project, and your experience with Onslow and the tannery suggests that the outcome is not going to be good for Lenape Hollow. We may not turn up anything to advance the homicide investigation, but I'd say we have as good a chance as anyone of uncovering proof that the men running Mongaup Valley Ventures are as crooked and twisty as Storm King Highway."

Darlene gave a snort of laughter at the comparison. Pasting her best effort at an evil grin on her face, she rubbed her hands together in anticipation. Neither of us voiced the sobering thought that must have occurred to us both — that when Tiffany had found that proof, she'd ended up dead.

CHAPTER 29

With Darlene sleuthing online, I made an attempt to do a little detecting in the non-cyber world. Ronnie, however, refused to talk to me. She'd left orders with Ann not to let me in.

When I left the North house, I drove to Wonderful World. I'm not certain why. I certainly wasn't going to risk trespassing charges or another encounter with Onslow's goon, Paul Klein. I guess I just wanted to remind myself that it was a real place, and to eyeball how close it was to Ronnie's house. That proximity must have doubled the annoyance factor for her. Bad enough her grandson-in-law wanted to build a theme park, but the fact that he intended to put it right next door to her home had to be galling in the extreme.

When I got back into the car, I noticed I was getting low on gas, so I drove downtown and pulled into the gas station across the street from our old school. I could still remember a time before it was built. There had been an old abandoned house on the lot. Feeling very brave, I'd crept inside with a couple of friends — I can't remember which ones after all this time — and spent an hour or so wandering through the empty rooms. That was the height of daring for my eight-year-old self.

The current incarnation was at least twice as large as the gas station I remembered from the 1960s. Back then, I'd often stopped in on my way to school to buy chewing gum or candy. I don't imagine my parents knew about that.

The rack of goodies had been kept in a tiny office that also contained a desk and a cash register. There had been an adjacent two-bay garage where the owner did minor repairs. In those days, most people paid for their gas with cash. Credit was a local matter, extended on a person-to-person basis.

There were three pumps available, all of them self-service. I got out of my car and stared at the screen in front of me. Intellectually, I know that buying gas with a credit card is a simple process, but I'm one of those people who always inserts the card upside down first and then backward. Third time's the charm.

Embarrassing as that is, it's nothing compared to my clumsy attempts to stick the nozzle into the gas tank, and that's assuming I can get the gas cap unscrewed in the first place. I consider my efforts a success, however, if I don't end up sloshing gasoline on my clothing. Back in Maine, there are still plenty of places that offer "full service." They pump your gas for you, wash your windshield and rear window, and take cash in payment. Boy, do I miss that.

I was still glowering at the slot where the credit card was supposed to go and muttering under my breath when someone came up beside me.

"Good morning," Joe Ramirez said. "Problem?"

"Only with my being fumble-fingered and old-fashioned. I hate having to pump my own gas."

He grinned. "Maybe you should have bought a place in New Jersey."

I stared at him with a blank look on my face. I'd heard what he said, but it didn't make any sense.

He relieved me of my credit card, inserted it correctly, and worked whatever magic was necessary to get the system to accept it. "In New Jersey, by law, customers aren't allowed to pump their own gas. You have to

have the gas station attendant do it for you."
After returning my card, he reached for the
nozzle. "Allow me."

"Thank you. You're a lifesaver."

He shrugged. "Naw. I'd just hate to have
a customer go away mad. This is my place."

"Oh, I see." I didn't know whether to be
embarrassed or doubly grateful. The latter
was easier. "So, tell me, since no one else in
town seems willing to pump gas for little
old ladies like me —"

He smirked at my self-identification, making me like him even more.

"How do people with disabilities manage?" I finished.

I was thinking of Darlene. With her arthritis, she'd have more trouble than I did with
the whole process.

"My employees are always glad to assist,"
Ramirez assured me. "All you need to do is
go inside and ask for help."

A glance through the windows at the front
of Joe's business showed me what amounted
to a convenience store. Rows and rows of
goodies were available for purchase, everything from potato chips to toilet paper.

"What if getting in and out of the car is a
hassle?"

His smile broadened as he gave a couple
of final squeezes to make sure my tank was

full and extracted the nozzle. "If you sit here by the pump long enough, I'm sure someone will be curious enough to come out."

My receipt popped out, and he handed it to me.

"I appreciate this," I told him.

"No problem. We like happy customers." He started to turn away.

"For what it's worth, Darlene Uberman and I have started digging into Greg Onslow's and Alan Van Heusen's past business practices. We're hoping to come up with something that will stand up in court."

I expected praise. I got a frown. "You be careful," he warned before he continued on into the store. "Either one of them would make a bad enemy."

CHAPTER 30

On Friday, Mike asked me to have lunch with him. My first thought was that it wouldn't hurt to have a lawyer on standby, and Mike was the perfect candidate. There was certainly no love lost between him and Onslow, and as Ronnie's attorney, surely he'd be interested in any evidence that would help get his client off the hook.

I slid into the passenger seat of his car prepared to launch into a lengthy account of what Darlene and I had been up to, but he barely gave me time to say hello before he took charge of the conversation. During the twenty-minute drive to the restaurant he'd chosen, Mike talked nonstop, mostly about what great food they served there.

I wondered why he was trying so hard to impress me, but after the first mile or so I was content to let him ramble. Belatedly, I remembered that he'd warned me against snooping. He might not be as happy as I'd hoped to hear that I'd ignored that advice.

When we were seated and the waitress had taken our orders, I started to speak. The words caught in my throat when I noticed the way Mike was staring at me. The troubled expression on his face did not bode well.

"Something bothering you?" I asked.

"It's that thumb drive you found."

Too late, I recalled that there was something else Mike didn't know. Despite the promise I'd made to him, I had given Tiffany's thumb drive to Detective Hazlett. That I'd tried to phone Mike first and couldn't reach him was no excuse. I could have waited until we could go to the police station together. Since I hadn't, the least I could have done was to confess as soon as I was able to reach him.

That ship had sailed. Attempting to sound innocent, I asked, "Do you think there's something on there that will clear Ronnie of suspicion?"

"My concern has nothing to do with Ronnie."

"Then what? You obviously have something weighing on your mind." When he didn't answer me right away, I drew a deep breath. "Either Greg Onslow or Alan Van Heusen killed Tiffany. I'm more certain of it with every passing day."

His whole body tensed. "Proof?"

"If I had any, I'd have taken it to the police, but there are plenty of hints in Tiffany's novel. She barely disguises either of them, and the characters based on them are crooks. The one who is clearly Van Heusen is a hit man."

"In fiction," Mike reminded me.

"The thumb drive also contains research files, one or more of which might yet prove to be evidence of wrongdoing."

I would have said more. I certainly intended to confess that Detective Hazlett already had possession of the original, but the expression of distress on Mike's face stopped me cold. Instead, I closed my mouth, frowning. What on earth did he find so troubling about that statement?

The answer came to me in a rush, causing me to make a small sound of distress. Of course he was concerned about the possibility of the police reading those files. He must think Tiffany had identified his father as a murderer. I made my voice as gentle as I could.

"I don't think anyone will make the connection. It's only because I know you and some of your family background that I did."

His eyes narrowed. "What are you talking about?"

Although he was trying to sound clueless, I was convinced that he knew exactly what I meant. I explained anyway, telling him about the clue in the Oxford comma and the details in Tiffany's files that had led me to believe that he was the anonymous source of Tiffany's account of the copycat crime.

"I can understand why you don't want your father's story made public," I added. "Obviously Tiffany didn't intend to tell anyone about it. Neither do I. You have my word."

The arrival of our meal gave Mike an opportunity to process what I'd told him. By the time the waitress left us alone again, he'd regrouped. He sent me a rueful smile. "I'll hold you to that promise."

"Cross my heart and hope to die." The childhood oath and the gesture that went with it came easily, but the laughter that followed had a hollow sound. "But, Mike, if you didn't want anyone to know the truth, why did you share the story with Tiffany?"

"I didn't. Well, not intentionally. My second wife was friendly with her mother, and of course I knew her father, so Tiffany was at our house a lot when she was a kid. She was interested in true crime even then." He shook his head. "I'll never understand how such a well-brought-up young girl came to be so fascinated by the stories of a bunch of low-class mobsters, but she was. One day when she was at the house she was going on about this one murder — the one I had reason to know something about — and before I knew what I was saying I told her that the police got it wrong. I stopped before I said too much, but she was always a sharp kid, and she was relentless. Every time she saw me after that, she tried to worm more details out of me. In the end, bit by bit, she had the whole story. I thought I'd been clever about it. I said I knew the truth because the man's son was a client of mine, but she guessed early on that I was talking about my own father."

"How did you hear the story?" I asked. "I mean, you never knew him. I remember that much. You used to say that he died when you were still in diapers."

"My mother told me how he used to boast about getting away with murder. Can you believe that? To prove what a big man he was, he gave her all the details. She was appalled, of course."

So appalled that she'd shared the story with her only child? People are strange. And I still didn't understand why Mike had told

274

even part of that ghastly tale to a young girl, no matter how macabre her interests.

"How much is on the thumb drive?" Mike asked.

"Not your name. Or his. Tiffany's notes reflect the way she gathered the information — separate pieces that she was later able to put together to make a whole. She was thorough in her research once you gave her enough to go on, but she must have realized you wouldn't want the story to spread any farther. She didn't use a copycat killing in her novel."

Looking relieved, Mike forked up a generous portion of the lasagna he'd ordered. I tucked into my coquilles St. Jacques. The wonderful smells wafting up from the food had been tempting even while the topic of conversation had threatened to rob me of my appetite. We ate in silence for a few minutes before he spoke again.

"You can understand why I was reluctant to let the police see the contents of Tiffany's thumb drive. If she'd named names, they might have thought I had a reason to silence her."

"Don't even joke about it."

"I'm not kidding. It would seem logical to them that someone in my situation could be desperate to keep Tiffany quiet."

Unwilling to admit to that brief moment of doubt I'd had when I'd first suspected that Mike was Tiffany's source, I sent him a bright smile and spoke in a bracing tone of voice. "You would never kill anyone."

"Of course not, but I'm glad all the same that I have an alibi for the time of Tiffany's death."

I mimed wiping sweat from my brow, but I was dead serious when I said, "I'm very happy to hear it." After a moment's hesitation, I added, "I gather they've been investigating Tiffany's death as a homicide all along."

"It looks that way. Something appears to have cropped up as a result of the autopsy, something that makes Ronnie a person of interest to them."

"Aren't they looking at anyone else?"

"I imagine they are, but they don't confide in me."

"They need to do more to investigate both Onslow and Van Heusen, and there *could* be information to help with that on the thumb drive."

Mike's fist slammed down on the tabletop, startling me and drawing the attention of other restaurant patrons. A dark red stain crept up his neck and into his face as he hissed at me. "Will you stop obsessing about that damned thumb drive?"

"Sorry."

He held up a hand. "No. I'm the one who should apologize. I overreacted. Tell you what — let's drop this subject entirely and simply enjoy the rest of our meal. Okay?"

"Sounds like a plan," I agreed, relieved that I wouldn't have to admit that I'd already given Tiffany's files to the police. I suppose I needed the respite from talk about murder and other crimes as much as he did.

CHAPTER 31

When renovations began on my house, I gave myself permission to sleep as late as I wanted to on weekends. Saturday and Sunday were the only two days I could be certain that no workmen would show up first thing in the morning.

It wasn't yet light out on the day after my lunch with Mike when something jerked me out of a sound sleep. I lay there, heart pounding and breath coming in short gulps, trying to figure out what had awakened me. It was Saturday, so it couldn't have been the alarm clock. I stared blearily at its illuminated dial. I'm nearsighted without my glasses, so the numerals were fuzzy, but I could see well enough to determine that it was a little after five in the morning.

I listened hard but heard nothing. I sniffed. No smoke. Deciding that the sound that disturbed my rest had probably been Calpurnia jumping down from the bed, I

278

closed my eyes and willed myself to drift off again. Naturally, that didn't work. Tired as I was, a vague sense of unease kept me from my rest.

"Cal?" I whispered.

No cat appeared.

That she wasn't nearby was odd. She usually slept at the foot of my bed . . . when she wasn't trying to insinuate herself under the covers for warmth.

I rolled over and thumped the pillow into a more comfortable shape, but it was no use. I wasn't going to be able to go back to sleep until I figured out what had caused me to wake up. Odds were good that it was something Calpurnia had done. Maybe she'd knocked something over. If it had broken, there'd be a mess to clean up, and she might have been spooked into going into hiding.

I hoped she hadn't flooded the kitchen again, but that, at least, seemed unlikely. Matt the plumber had gotten a good laugh out of my story, and then he'd fixed the faucet so that anyone lacking opposable thumbs would have found it impossible to turn on.

With a sigh, I threw the covers back, thinking that I might as well check for damage now as later. I fumbled on the nightstand for my little flashlight and the cases containing my glasses and hearing aids.

From force of habit, I didn't turn on the bedside lamp, but by the time I'd shoved my feet into slippers and pulled on my robe, I was awake enough to remember that I didn't have to worry about waking anyone else. Once I'd tied the sash, I flicked the wall switch. I had to close my eyes against the sudden glare when the overhead light came on.

"Cal?" I called again, raising my voice.

Still no cat.

Beginning to be alarmed, although I couldn't have said why, I headed for the stairs, turning on more lights as I went. The landing was noticeably colder, so much so that I glanced toward the window, wondering if I'd opened it during the day and forgotten to close it again. I couldn't think why I would have. The weather hadn't been *that* mild, and now that it was October the nights could get downright nippy.

Then it hit me — the obvious source of the chill. I pelted down the stairs and skidded to a stop at the bottom.

"Oh, no," I whispered.

My front door should have been closed and locked. I'd checked it right before I went to bed. I knew I had. I always did. I squeezed my eyes shut but when I opened them again nothing had changed. The door still stood open.

I eased forward until I could peer around the jamb. The screen door, too, was ajar. Whoever had left that way hadn't cared if the latches caught. Suddenly I was more angry than afraid. I'd been so careful about keeping the outside doors closed. I'd had to be. Ever since I moved into this house, Calpurnia had been trying to escape to explore the big wide world beyond the windows. Fearful for her safety, I'd gone to great lengths to make sure all the workmen knew that she was an indoor cat.

The realization that Calpurnia was still among the missing threw me into confusion. I guess I wasn't as wide awake as I'd thought I was. I dithered, unable to decide what to do first. What if my cat *hadn't* escaped? Barring the possibility of a poltergeist, it was obvious someone had broken into my house. That was bad enough, but if they'd hurt Cal . . .

I didn't stop to think that I might be running into danger. Calling Calpurnia's name, I raced from the downstairs hall through the archway that opened into the living room. Stopping only long enough to turn on the lights and peer under the furniture, I crossed to the pocket doors, flinging them wide and scrabbling at the light switch for the dining room. My heart was thudding so loudly that I was sure the neighbors could hear it. My hands were shaking, too.

I took one step into the room and froze. My jaw literally dropped at the sight that met my eyes. Someone had tossed papers everywhere. They'd pulled files out of my file cabinet and emptied the bin where I kept mailers for recycling. Worse, my laptop was not in its usual place on the dining room table. It wasn't anywhere.

"Calpurnia!"

No cat appeared, but I spotted my cell phone lying on the floor. Grateful that the thief hadn't stolen it, I picked it up and punched in 911.

After I reported the break-in and the theft of my laptop, I went on to check the kitchen. Still no cat. By the time a police car pulled into my driveway, I'd turned on every light in the house, indoors and out. I kept calling Calpurnia's name, but she didn't come running. I didn't realize I was crying until the young policewoman who was first on the scene handed me a box of tissues. By that time, another officer, this one male, had arrived and was checking the house to make certain the thief wasn't still on the premises. I could have told him there was no one there, but I suppose he had to see for himself.

"She's never been an outdoor cat." I dabbed at my eyes. "I'm afraid she'll get lost. Or hit by a car. Or run into an animal bigger than she is."

"We'll keep an eye out for her, ma'am. Now I think you need to sit down and tell me what happened here." She coaxed me out onto the porch and into one of the wicker chairs, settling herself in the other one . . . just where Detective Hazlett had been sitting when he told me Tiffany was dead.

My gaze slid to her name tag. It said Blume. Old English teacher that I am, a literary connection popped out of my mouth. "Not Judy?" That just shows how rattled I was.

Fortunately, she understood the reference. "Ellen," she said. "I'm a cop, not a writer, but I loved her books when I was a kid."

"Some lowlife stole my laptop," I said after a moment.

"Is anything else missing?"

"I . . . I haven't really looked. I think the television and DVD player are still there."

"Do you feel up to taking a look now?" Her partner had completed his search and signaled that it was safe to go back inside.

We walked from room to room. At night I take my purse, with my credit cards and cash, into the bedroom with me, so I knew they were safe. As it turned out, nothing was out of place anywhere except in my temporary office. It was a mess and getting messier by the minute as the male officer applied a coat of fingerprint powder. When the magnitude of the cleanup job I faced sank in, I felt tears well up all over again.

"You run a business from here?" Officer Blume asked.

Her brusque question helped put me back on an even keel. I sniffled once, blew my nose, wiped my eyes, tightened the sash on my bathrobe, and focused on answering her question. "Yes, I do. Editing services. Losing my laptop would ruin me if I didn't have —"

"Insurance?" Blume asked.

"I was going to say backups, but I do, in fact, have insurance." I could see the policy from where we stood. It was on the floor along with other carelessly tossed documents that should have been neatly stored in my file cabinet. What I did not see was the fireproof storage box designed to keep my electronic copies safe.

I was cussing under my breath as I conducted a frantic but thorough search of the ransacked room. It was a futile effort.

"I don't get it," I said. "The box is clearly labeled BACKUPS. I keep the key in the lock. All the burglar needed to do was open it to realize that there was nothing of value inside."

Unless the copies of my electronic files were what he was after in the first place.

I staggered back into the living room and collapsed onto the loveseat. After a moment, I looked up to meet the sympathetic but bewildered gaze of Officer Blume. She'd been efficient and helpful, but she wasn't the cop I wanted to talk to.

"You need to call in Detective Hazlett."

"He'll see the report, ma'am."

"Please don't call me that. I'm not even seventy yet. And you're missing the point. This break-in is connected to the murder of Tiffany Scott."

Blume's eyes widened, although she still sounded doubtful. "You want me to wake the detective?"

I could understand her reluctance, since it was still an hour or so short of sunrise, but I insisted. She let me listen in when she phoned him. I caught enough of his side of the conversation to comprehend that Hazlett was not a morning person. Concluding that he'd need coffee when he arrived, and aware that I could do with a jolt of caffeine myself, I headed for the kitchen. As I went, I was glad to hear Officer Blume mention that the case also involved a missing cat.

Fifteen minutes later, I heard my front door open and close. There was a short, muffled conversation in the hallway, and I braced myself for a difficult interview, but as I turned to greet the detective a huge wave a relief washed over me. Cradled in his arms, apparently unharmed, was Calpurnia.

"Where did you find her?" I took her from him, holding her tight, heedless of the fact that she was filthy.

"Her eyes reflected my headlights when I pulled into your driveway. She was hiding under the porch. She's probably been there the whole time."

"I wish you could talk," I said to Cal.

She squirmed, making it clear she wanted to get down to inspect the contents of her food and water bowls. Reluctantly, I let her go, fixed the detective an oversize mug of coffee, and settled in at the dinette table to explain why I'd been so insistent that Blume call him.

"I have a confession to make," I told him. "I loaded the entire contents of Tiffany Scott's thumb drive onto my computer. I'm convinced that's what the person who broke into my house tonight was after, since the only things he took were my laptop and a box of backups."

"He?"

I took a deep breath. "There are two people who may have something to fear from what's in Tiffany's files. One is Greg Onslow. The other is Alan Van Heusen, who works for him."

"Mr. Onslow has no reason to go to such lengths to get a look at the contents of that thumb drive," Hazlett interrupted. "He already has possession of the original."

"You *gave* it to him?"

"He's his wife's heir. Do you have a problem with that, Ms. Lincoln?"

"You know he's a crook, right?"

"I know Mr. Onslow is . . . unpopular in some circles."

"That's a careful answer."

"I'm a careful person. Before I arrest anyone, I need proof of guilt, and I prefer to get the go-ahead from the district attorney, too. Otherwise, any judge worth his salt is likely to refuse to hear the case and dismiss it out of hand."

"Then it's a pity you didn't bother to read Tiffany's manuscript and her notes."

For just a second, something that re-

287

sembled amusement flickered in Hazlett's eyes. He wasn't about to admit that he'd made a copy of the thumb drive before he turned it over to Onslow, but I was positive that he had. His next words made me even more certain of it.

"Is there something specific in those documents that you'd like to call to my attention?"

"Three of the characters in Tiffany's novel are thinly disguised versions of Onslow and Van Heusen, two of Onslow and one of Van Heusen. Anyone who reads the manuscript and knows both men can spot the resemblance." A light bulb went off. "Oh. That could be why Onslow stole my laptop and backups, or ordered Van Heusen to. He wants *all* the copies, not just the one you gave him. He intends to destroy them."

"And why would he imagine that you made copies, Ms. Lincoln?" Hazlett asked. "I certainly didn't tell him, since I didn't know."

"You suspected. Don't try to convince me you didn't. And so would he. Suspect, I mean. Onslow may be a lot of things, but he's not stupid."

"Breaking in here and calling attention to your electronic files strikes me as a pretty dumb move."

"Nobody's perfect." I felt as if I was banging my head against a brick wall. "Let me tell you about some of the shady deals he's been involved in."

He listened attentively and even took notes while I filled him in on everything Darlene and I had discovered about Onslow's past business dealings, but he remained stone-faced throughout. I had to wonder how much of it he already knew. He didn't ask me any questions about the material on Tiffany's thumb drive. I couldn't decide if that meant he'd already read it, or that he intended to go back to his office after he left my house and take another look at the copy he'd made, or that he didn't think my suggestions were worth the time it would take to follow up on them.

"Don't you think this information is suggestive?" I demanded when he returned his notebook to his pocket. "Especially when you add in the fact that Tiffany sided with her grandmother against her husband?"

Instead of answering my question, he said, "We'll keep an eye out for your laptop, but I don't hold out much hope of getting it back. If you had personal information stored on it, you should change your account numbers and passwords."

"I didn't." My faith in cybersecurity

doesn't extend to using electronic banking or bill paying. I don't store passwords online, either, and my address book is the old-fashioned handwritten kind. "I only use the laptop for work and email. Fortunately, I have backups of my clients' files off site, and there are printouts of most of them in that mess scattered all over the floor of the dining room."

Hazlett's voice grew stern. "I trust you don't have a printout of Tiffany Scott's novel."

"Of course not. I gave you the only manuscript copy." I didn't mention the thumb drive I keep in the glove compartment of my car or that Tiffany's files were also backed up in that nebulous thing called the cloud. Detective Hazlett had no need to know that just as soon as I got my hands on a new laptop, I would have access to all the information she had left behind.

He stood, looming over me as I sat at the dinette table. "Ms. Lincoln, we will investigate this burglary and do our best to recover your property, but I think it highly unlikely that this crime has anything to do with Ms. Scott's death. Whether it does or not, you need to stop meddling in matters better left to the police."

"I only —"

"You've been investigating Mr. Onslow's business dealings."

"Well, yes, but —"

"Stick to your editing, Ms. Lincoln. The Lenape Hollow Police Department can do its job without your assistance."

CHAPTER 32

The next morning I skipped church and went shopping for a replacement laptop. I stocked up on thumb drives, too. Then I spent the rest of the day trying to find various functions in the newest incarnation of the word processing software I use. Can you say frustrating? I come from a long line of folks who believe that "if it ain't broke, don't fix it." The computer industry has obviously never heard that saying.

By nightfall, I had everything installed. Downloading files from the cloud had hit a snag — why didn't that surprise me? — but I'd successfully copied them from my glove-compartment backup and was back in business.

I went to bed late and got up early in the hope of putting a dent in the work I'd let slide over the weekend. It was Columbus Day, but when you work for yourself, there are no holidays. On the bright side, the workmen had the day off, and the house was deliciously quiet. I was so pleased with my progress by noontime that I decided to treat myself to lunch at Harriet's.

Since the weather was fine and I needed the exercise, I walked there, relishing the peacefulness of the day. There was no hint of the winter to come, just a light, refreshing breeze and the faint smell of mulched leaves.

At the café, nothing was calm, quiet, or peaceful.

"Did you hear?" Sonya called to me from a table she was sharing with three of her friends. "Ronnie North has been arrested for Tiffany's murder. They took her into custody last night."

To say I was startled would be putting it mildly. I'd been hoping for an arrest, but it was not supposed to be Ronnie who was carted off to jail. I'd expected Detective Hazlett to get the goods on Greg Onslow or, failing that, to find charges to bring against Alan Van Heusen. I'd been so confident of Ronnie's innocence that I couldn't quite take in the news of her arrest. My thoughts swirled as I picked my way through the lunchtime crowd to a small table in the corner.

Ada materialized at my elbow. "You look

like you could use a drink."

"For once, I wish you had a liquor license."

"Coffee?"

"That'll have to do."

Maybe it would help clear my brain. I couldn't seem to think straight. Why on earth had they arrested *Ronnie?* What could they possibly have found to use as evidence against her?

While I sat there waiting for my hit of caffeine, I tuned in to the conversations at the other tables. One thing was immediately obvious: It was impossible to separate fact from speculation. Turning in my chair, I addressed Sonya, who seemed to have the best connections for local gossip.

"What happened to make the police take such a drastic step?" I asked.

"They searched her house. I guess they found something." The words themselves were ambiguous, but Sonya spoke in such an authoritative tone of voice that most people who heard her were convinced that she knew what she was talking about. The three women sitting at her table, none of whom I knew by name, all nodded earnestly.

I remained skeptical. "Found what, exactly?"

"No idea, but it must be pretty good."

"A bloody knife?" I asked. "Poison? A signed confession?"

Sonya did not appreciate my sarcasm. She retaliated by ignoring me, and her friends did the same. Despite the cold shoulder, I might have tried to engage her in further conversation had Ada not set a steaming cup of coffee in front of me. My nose wrinkled as I caught a whiff of something that was *not* half-and-half or Splenda. At my startled look, she winked and walked away.

My first cautious sip told me I'd been right. The coffee had been enhanced with a jigger of whiskey. I'm not much of a drinker, but in these circumstances I was grateful for the nip. I'd downed more than half of the drink when I sensed a presence beside me. I looked up to find Joe Ramirez awkwardly shifting his weight from foot to foot.

"Would you mind if I joined you, Mrs. Lincoln?"

"Not at all." At first I assumed he was asking because all the other tables were full, but a surreptitious glance around Harriet's told me that wasn't the case. There were more people than usual in the café, but a table by the window was free. Curious, and well aware that Ramirez was one of Ronnie's biggest supporters, I smiled at him and waved him toward the chair opposite me.

He plopped himself down and picked up a menu. When we'd both ordered soup and sandwiches, I sent him a speculative look. "What do you think of today's news?"

"Mrs. North is being railroaded. No question in my mind."

"Detective Hazlett must have found something pretty damning. He's not the type to go off half cocked."

"Mrs. North didn't do it," Ramirez said in a low voice.

"I don't think she did, either."

"Maybe you can help her."

"Me? How?"

"Figure out what really happened. She talked you up to her housekeeper, you know. Ann repeated some of what she said to me."

"Ronnie said something positive about me?" I was astonished.

Ramirez nodded. His expression was solemn, but a spark of amusement lurked in his dark eyes. "Come to think of it, it might have been more like a complaint. She told Ann that you were good at solving puzzles. Back when you two were in high school, you were the one who was the fastest at figuring out the word problems in math class and diagramming sentences in English. Apparently you were a whiz at algebra, too."

I made a face. "I hated math. I just happen to have a good memory and the ability to spot patterns. No big deal."

"It was to Mrs. North. She told Ann that she had to struggle to keep up with you." He chuckled. "Sounds to me like you two were rivals back in the day."

I was surprised to hear that Ronnie had seen me as competition. I'd always thought she looked on me as a lesser being. She'd certainly made enough derisive comments about me, picking on my clothes, my hairstyle, and any other shortcomings she could identify. I was still mulling over this new insight when our food arrived. By then the crowd had thinned out some.

After a few bites, Ramirez renewed his effort to get me on board the "free Ronnie" train. "You told me you and Mrs. Uberman were trying to dig up dirt on Greg Onslow. If anyone killed Tiffany Scott, he did. Have you found anything to point the cops in his direction?"

I shook my head. "Nothing criminal, just unethical, but you already know he's a sleaze-ball."

As I took a bite of my roast beef on a kaiser roll and chewed, I realized that there was something Joe Ramirez did not know.

I'd never told him about Tiffany's novel or her research files. While we ate, I quietly filled him in on the essential details.

"On the surface, those files have nothing to do with Greg Onslow, but I'm certain she based characters on him and Van Heusen. Why would she do that unless both of them are more than just run-of-the-mill swindlers?"

He didn't look any more convinced than Detective Hazlett had.

Having finished eating, I stacked my soup bowl on top of my sandwich plate and shoved both to one side so I could put my elbows on the table and lean closer to Ramirez. I was conscious of the other café patrons nearby, but none of them seemed to be interested in our conversation, and Sonya and her cronies had already left.

"No matter what Ronnie may have said about my problem-solving abilities, no matter how smart Ann thinks I am, the fact remains that the police had enough evidence to make an arrest, and it isn't Onslow who's sitting in jail right now."

"Are you saying you've changed your mind? You think Mrs. North is guilty?"

"I'm saying we don't know all the facts, and we could be wrong about her. I've heard it said often enough that anyone can kill given the right circumstances. I'm afraid we need to consider the possibility that the police are right, and she did murder Tiffany."

"No way would she harm a hair on that girl's head."

"They had an argument on the morning of the day she died."

"Who doesn't fight with their relatives once in a while?"

He had a point, but someone had to play devil's advocate. "What if Tiffany backed out of her promise to help oppose Wonderful World? I keep thinking of that will Onslow produced. Who's to say it isn't the real one?"

"Nothing would have made Mrs. North murder her own granddaughter. Besides, Tiffany would never have written a will in favor of that crook she married. Once she figured out what he was up to, she and Mrs. North had only one goal, to stop him."

"When?"

"When what?"

"When did Tiffany switch her allegiance? I met her a few days before she died, and I did not get the impression that she and her husband were on the outs."

"It was recent," Ramirez admitted, "but there's no question about how she felt. Like

I told you the other day, she discovered proof that he was a crook. That's what made her turn against him."

"Proof she didn't share with anyone."

"Right." He stared morosely into his empty soup bowl. "What I can't figure out is why she stayed with him as long as she did. She was a smart girl. She should have caught on a lot sooner than she did."

"Maybe she was in love with him," I suggested. "Or she'd liked being married to a rich, powerful man. Some women value those attributes enough to turn a blind eye to what they don't want to see."

Ramirez didn't look pleased by my suggestions. I wasn't happy about them, either, especially when I considered Tiffany's novel. She had not written that book overnight. At a guess, she'd spent at least a year on it, and if she modeled her villains after her husband and his flunky, then she knew full well what kind of businessmen they were.

Why, then, had she stayed with him?

I found a likely answer in Onslow's temper. I'd witnessed it for myself in his clash with Ramirez at the cemetery. It wasn't much of a leap to conclude that Tiffany might have been afraid to leave him.

"I've told you about Tiffany's novel," I said aloud. "What I haven't told you is that someone broke into my house early Saturday morning and stole my laptop." I explained my reasons for thinking Onslow was behind the theft. "Who else would want to make certain that all the copies of the novel and the notes for it disappeared?"

"You think he recognized himself in her story?"

"Maybe, although I've read that most people that writers use as models for their characters never spot the similarities between themselves and the fictional versions. It could be that Onslow saw something I missed in the research files, but if Tiffany's proof was on that thumb drive, it was well hidden."

"Huh," he said, frowning.

"What?"

He shook his head but he looked shaken. "It's this business of Tiffany writing a novel. That means she was making stuff up, right?"

I nodded.

"That's an awful lot like lying."

"So it is. What are you getting at?"

"That quarrel you say Mrs. North had with her granddaughter — what if it was because she found out Tiffany had been deceiving her? I hate to say it, and I'm not sure I believe it, but what if she'd been working with her husband all along and was trying to con her grandmother into making some concession that would make it easier for them to build the theme park?"

We stared at each other across the table, neither of us liking the conclusion to which this reasoning led. Faced with such a heinous betrayal by her own kin, Ronnie *could* have been driven to murder.

CHAPTER 33

When I left the restaurant I headed north along Main Street, taking the shortest route home. I'd spent far longer than I'd intended over lunch. There was still a steep hill to climb, but it was the one that led straight to my house. When I was a kid, this route — the Alley — was a handy shortcut to and from school. It was also the quickest way to get to the grocery store.

Somewhat to my surprise, that store was still in business, although it had changed names and hands any number of times. I remembered it best as an A & P. I'm not sure there are any of those left anymore.

Once I'd huffed and puffed my way up the lower section of the Alley, where I'd almost come to grief on a sled one winter, the grade leveled off a little. I was still climbing, but walking took less effort. Preoccupied with Ronnie's arrest and its implications, I paid no attention to my surroundings until the low growl of a car engine and the crunch of tires on the loose gravel at the side of the paved section penetrated my consciousness.

The vehicle sounded alarmingly close. I glanced over my shoulder and my heart leapt into my throat. The bumper of a full-size SUV was less than a foot behind me. Pulse racing, I jumped smartly to one side, fearing that, in another second, it would run right over me.

Once off the tarmac, I stumbled through high grass as I turned to give the driver a piece of my mind. One glimpse of his face drove all thought of yelling at him right out of my mind. I recognized the enormous hands grasping the steering wheel and the hard eyes boring into me as the nostrils beneath flared. That resemblance to a bull about to charge confirmed his identity. It was Paul Klein, the security guard who'd hassled me for taking pictures at Chestnut Lake.

I knew I was in serious trouble when he veered in my direction. The truck followed me into the field.

Cue the theme from *Jaws* and substitute a dark blue SUV for the shark. I had no idea why Klein was trying to run me down, but his intent was crystal clear. I zigged. He zagged. In desperation, I looked around for a place to take shelter. I didn't think I could outrun the truck long enough to reach the safety of my house.

Still bobbing and weaving, desperate to put some distance between myself and the metal monster behind me, I cut across the grassy area we'd used as a playground when I was a kid. There was a house on the far side. When I was young, I spent a lot of time with the children who lived there. We'd scare ourselves silly playing a game we invented in which every car that drove along Wedemeyer Terrace at dusk with its lights turned on was a monster. We'd shriek and hide behind parked vehicles until the danger was past. The reality version on my tail wasn't nearly as entertaining. I was panting with exertion, and perspiring freely, and my legs felt as if they might give out on me at any moment.

With my last reserves of strength, I headed for the Edgar house. Back in the day, there was a sort of tunnel where we'd played another of our games. Intertwined branches over our heads had shielded us from the outside world. I had no idea if it still existed, but I prayed that it did. So far, I'd avoided being hit by the SUV less by my agility than because the same ruts that kept trying to trip me up were also making the truck veer off course.

I glanced over my shoulder and felt a jolt of panic. Klein was steering straight at me. I dove for the entrance I remembered, positive I could feel the heat of his engine scorching my back.

Even at eight years of age, I'd had to stoop to walk under the boughs. Squirming in beneath them at sixty-eight required executing an ignominious belly flop. As soon as I landed, I started to crawl like a soldier under fire. My heart was pounding so loudly that I could no longer hear if I was being pursued.

The ground was hard packed and cold. Twigs caught at my clothes and hair, but I kept going, praying all the while that the idiot behind the wheel wouldn't decide to plow into the barrier of branches to get at me.

It didn't take long to reach the other end, although it seemed an eternity. I popped out next to a very familiar tree. It was much bigger now, but those limbs were the ones on which we'd perched to pretend we were birds sitting on our nests.

Off to my left, I heard Klein gun the engine of the SUV. A moment later, tires squealed as they hit the hard surface of the

Alley and the vehicle sped away. I lay there panting, only dimly aware that a woman had come out of what had once been the Edgar house. It startled me when she spoke.

"Are you okay?"

"I'll live."

I rolled over and sat up, knowing I must look a sight. I was glad I hadn't bothered with a purse for the short walk to Harriet's. I'd have lost anything that wasn't attached during my mad flight. As it was, my keys, cell phone, and a little cash were safely tucked into the pockets of my jeans.

I looked down at the cowl-neck sweater I'd put on over a long-sleeved cotton tee. It had once been a lovely shade of pale green. Now it was covered in dirt, leaves, and twigs and ripped in at least a dozen places.

"Mikki?" the woman said. "Mikki Green-leigh?"

Surprised to hear her address me by my maiden name, I stared at her. She was about my age, so I'd probably known her years ago, but I had no notion who she was.

"I'd heard you bought your old house," she said, and then helpfully added, "It's me — Cheryl Edgar. Well, Cheryl Soretto now."

"Oh, for goodness' sake!" I used a handy branch to haul myself upright.

Cheryl was one of the seven Edgar children. All but the eldest had been younger than me, but I'd played with all of them when I was small. Cheryl had been the next to youngest. When I was a little older, and had outgrown such pastimes, she had continued to stop by the house to ask if I could "come out and play." I'd ignored her and left it to my mother to gently turn her away. I felt a little guilty about that now. I'd abandoned old friends for new. And then, a little later, I'd discovered boys.

"What happened to you?" Cheryl looked me over with a critical eye, but her lips twitched as if she was trying not to laugh.

"Long story. I owe you an apology," I added in a rush.

"For what?"

"For not telling you in person that I'd gotten too old for 'Birds' and 'Monsters' and all our other games."

She laughed. "We're all a lot older now. And you're bleeding. Do you want to come inside and get cleaned up or go home to do it?"

I looked down at my hands, which had taken the brunt of the abuse not borne by my sweater. Now that the adrenaline rush was wearing off, my knees stung and my back and shoulders were none too happy with me. "I think I need to sit down."

The interior of the Edgar house looked very different from the way I remembered it. I don't know why that surprised me. It had been close to sixty years since I'd last been invited inside. Cheryl had changed, too. Hair that had once been golden brown was now a gorgeous silvery gray.

While she fussed over my minor injuries and got me a glass of water, Cheryl chattered on about how she'd stayed on in the family home after the rest of her siblings moved away. She'd married, had a brood of children of her own, and been widowed about a year before I was.

I drank the water, submitted to her ministrations, and stayed largely silent.

"There, that should do it." She closed the first aid kit and placed it on the end table.

We were in her living room, near the front window. Just as I looked out, I saw a familiar vehicle cruise by — a dark blue SUV. I couldn't see the driver, but a chill ran through me. It had to be Paul Klein. Was he looking for me? Would he come after me again?

Following the direction of my gaze and seeing the shudder, Cheryl compressed her lips, put her hands on her hips, and fixed me with a look that brooked no denial and made me wonder if she'd gone into teaching, too. "Spill."

"That SUV tried to run me down."

"In the Alley?"

I nodded. "When did they make it a through street?"

"It isn't, although some people treat it that way. They put barriers up during recess, just to be on the safe side, since the children from the Catholic school play on the tarmac. Why was someone trying to kill you?"

"That's a good question." I fumbled in my pocket to retrieve my cell phone, relieved that it did not appear to have been damaged when it, and I, had been merrily bouncing along on the ground. "Excuse me a moment, Cheryl," I said with extreme politeness. "I need to call the police."

CHAPTER 34

Once again it was Ellen Blume who responded to my complaint, meeting me at my house some twenty minutes after I phoned the police station. Seated on the loveseat in my living room, she took my statement without comment, but there was something in her manner that suggested she had her doubts about my reliability as a witness.

"How is it that you recognized the driver?" she asked. "Do you two have a history?"

"Not much of one. I only met him once, when he was working as a security guard at Chestnut Mountain."

From my chair, arranged at a right angle to her perch, I watched her face, all the while continuing to stroke Calpurnia's soft fur. A cat in the lap is the best medicine on earth for jangled nerves.

"And this previous encounter? When was that?"

"Last month. Mr. Klein caught me trespassing on Mongaup Valley Ventures land and escorted me back to my car."

She lifted a questioning eyebrow at me, sensing there was more to the story than I was telling her. When I didn't elaborate, she prompted me with another question. "Is that the place where they're going to build a theme park?"

"That's what I hear."

"And you didn't encounter this man again after that incident?"

"Not . . . directly."

"What does that mean?"

"It means that I've seen him a couple of times, and now that I think about it, there could be a reason for that." I frowned, trying to remember just when and where I had noticed Paul Klein lurking. "If he doesn't have kids in the Catholic school, then he was watching my house the other day when he was parked across the street. And I think he might have followed me to Harriet's on another day, although I suppose that could have been a coincidence. I have no idea what kind of hours he works."

"Are you telling me you think he was stalking you?" She tried to hide her disbelief, but it came through loud and clear.

"No. I'm saying I saw him a couple of

times, and then he tried to run me down."

"Why would he do that?"

"If I knew, believe me, I would tell you."

"And you're certain it was deliberate? You didn't just panic because the SUV got too close to you before you noticed it? You were walking in the middle of the road."

Her attitude was beginning to annoy me. "Okay, first of all, it's not a road or a street, it's a private drive. There's not supposed to be through traffic. Second, if you go look at that field you'll see the tire tracks where he followed me. There's no way that was unintentional."

"And you got a good look at the driver?"

"I told you I did. Well, enough of one. He's a big guy. Huge hands." I stopped short of adding the flaring nostrils. That detail would only help identify him if he was angry at the person confronting him.

"Hair color? Eyes?"

"Sorry. I have no idea what color they are. The only time I was close enough to have noticed, I was busy getting the bum's rush."

"Yes, you did say you were trespassing."

"Can I take back that confession? I wouldn't want you to have to arrest me."

My attempt at humor went over like a lead balloon. I sighed and waved off whatever she was about to say.

"Officer Blume, I'm telling you the truth. I don't know why this man came up behind me in the Alley in his SUV, but he did, and when I moved off the pavement and onto the grass, he chased me all the way to Cheryl Soretto's property line. When I swerved, he swerved. He was definitely trying to hit me."

"You're *certain* you haven't had any other encounters with him?"

"Yes." Then I reconsidered. I'd spent some time during the last week or so driving around Lenape Hollow, revisiting old stomping grounds and promising myself I'd come back to certain spots when I had more time. "Once or twice there might have been a blue SUV in my rearview mirror, but it's a popular vehicle. I can't swear to you that it was the same one."

The theory that Paul Klein had been following me didn't cut any ice with her. I bit back a sigh. It's no fun when someone doesn't believe you. I wanted to remind her that I was the victim here, but sarcasm wouldn't help my case.

I took a couple of deep breaths and told myself to look at the situation from Officer Blume's point of view. She undoubtedly found it difficult to imagine anyone stalking an old broad like me. To be honest, an account of someone thrown into a panic by a vehicle suddenly coming up behind her doesn't sound like much when it's written up in a report. You had to be there.

I wondered how quickly grass sprang back after someone drove over it. If my accusation was dismissed for lack of evidence, I'd be labeled "the senior citizen who cried wolf" at the Lenape Hollow police station, and no one there would ever take me seriously again. If I were to call in another complaint, they might not even show up to investigate. They'd assume it was a false alarm.

"The break-in the other day was real," I reminded Officer Blume, "and so was today's incident. I was nearly run over. Maybe Paul Klein didn't mean to hurt me, but he was definitely trying to give me a scare."

"Why?"

"I wish I knew."

The only theory I could come up with — that he'd been ordered to follow me — was one I didn't think I should share with a police officer who already had a skeptical look on her face. She'd hear any accusations I made against Greg Onslow or Alan Van Heusen as the paranoid, possibly senile ravings of a batty old lady.

Officer Blume managed a tight-lipped

315

smile. "I just want to make sure of the facts before I start questioning people, Ms. Lincoln. Is there any possibility that you could be mistaken? It doesn't sound like you got that good a look at the driver."

"I saw enough."

"And you say it was an SUV? Blue?"

"Yes. Dark blue."

"Not black?"

"Blue," I said firmly.

"But you didn't notice the license number?"

"Would you, under the circumstances?" Once again I held up a hand to stop her from replying. "Never mind. You're probably trained to look for things like that. Well, I'm not. I was too busy trying to save my skin."

"Okay. Well —"

"You're very young," I blurted.

"Excuse me?"

"How old are you, if you don't mind my asking?"

The unexpected question seemed to throw her off her stride. "Twenty-five."

Something else struck me then. "Did you grow up in Lenape Hollow?"

"Yes, I did." She started to rise, but I caught her arm.

"Humor the nosy senior citizen. Did you

go to school with Tiffany Scott?"

"What does that have to do with anything?" I heard a thread of annoyance in her voice and released my grip before she could shake me off.

"I have no idea, but it was the fact that she wanted me to edit the novel she'd written that brought me to her husband's attention, and Paul Klein works for Mongaup Valley Ventures."

"Tiffany wrote a novel?" The idea seemed to surprise her.

"She did, and a lot of the people in her life appear in it only thinly disguised." That was stretching the truth, but my lie was rewarded. Ellen Blume's eyes widened. "It's a murder mystery," I added, "so of course police officers show up as characters."

A distinct worry line appeared in her forehead. "Why are you telling me this? Am I in it?"

"I don't think so, but I do wonder what you thought of Tiffany."

"She was a spoiled brat." This time Blume succeeded in getting to her feet. "Excuse me, Ms. Lincoln. I'm going to take a look at that field now."

I watched her progress from my front window. She drove her police car into the Alley, parked, and stood staring down at the grass with her hands on her hips. Then I saw her head turn. Her body assumed a listening stance. A moment later, she was back in the cruiser and had activated both siren and lights.

"So much for that investigation," I said to Calpurnia.

Since my cat had taken over the chair I'd just vacated and was now engaged in a vigorous tongue bath, she did not respond.

Chapter 35

I hadn't been overly concerned about my personal safety after my laptop and backups were stolen. The burglar had gained entry by smashing a pane of glass in the back door and reaching inside to turn the knob on the deadbolt. To keep that from happening a second time, I'd had one of the carpenters nail a sheet of plywood over the hole. It was big enough to cover the remaining panes as well. A new door, without a window, was on my "to buy" list. The front door and screen door hadn't been damaged. They'd simply been left open when the thief chose to leave that way. In a nod to caution, I'd added a security chain.

There were two other entrances to the house. The one through the cellar was protected by both a padlocked bulkhead and a sturdy, windowless door that had a bar across the inside for good measure. The other way in would require the use of a garage door opener, after which an intruder would have two more doors to get through before he could enter the main part of the house. What had once been a small, enclosed side porch was now a tiny sunroom off my temporary office. I suppose someone could climb onto the garage roof and gain access through the balcony over the sunroom that opened into my future office, but I thought that highly unlikely.

All in all, I had no reason to think that my home was not secure. I hadn't been worried about anyone else trying to break in . . . until Paul Klein tried to run me down.

I suspected he'd been acting on orders from his boss. That meant Onslow, or maybe Van Heusen, thought I knew more than I really did. Too bad I was still completely in the dark. I sighed. Was I really safe? Is anyone? I shivered when I thought of the night ahead. Except for my guard cat, who hadn't been much help the last time, I'd be alone in this big old house.

I reached for the phone.

By sunset, I was the proud owner of a brand-new security system. I'd had to dip into my rapidly dwindling financial reserves to pay for it. The premium I'd shelled out for immediate installation on a holiday had further depleted my bank account, but I told myself that my peace of mind was worth the expense. My nest egg wouldn't do me any good if I was dead.

I read the manual while I ate supper, after I'd printed it out from the company's website. Using up that much paper for a poorly written tutorial put me in a grumpy mood, one that didn't improve when I realized that I wouldn't be able to leave my brand-new, super expensive security system activated during the day. With workmen in the house, the thing would be going off every five minutes.

The more I read, the more I wondered if I had just made a costly mistake. It was going to be a pain to remember to reset the alarm every time I was alone in the house. It was certain to go off by accident on a regular basis, if for no other reason than that I hadn't been fast enough to punch in the code. I hadn't yet memorized the random set of numbers, and thirty seconds isn't much time.

I told myself to stop finding fault. At least I didn't have to remember a password that combined letters and symbols with numerals. I found those extremely provoking when they were required by online sites, always for the *customer's* security, of course. For the customer's headache is more like it.

After spending the entire evening with that manual, I had more questions than answers. My biggest concern was whether the system kept working if the power went out. If the material I'd printed out included that information, I couldn't find it. I very nearly phoned the security company and told them to come back and rip out the whole thing. I could always buy a gun to protect myself.

"Right," I said aloud, causing Cal to open one eye. "Not a good idea. I'd be more likely to shoot myself in the foot than I would be to scare off an intruder."

On that cheerful thought, I abandoned the printout and went to bed.

CHAPTER 36

After a restless night, I got up early and lingered over coffee while waiting for the carpenters to arrive. They were nearly done with what had turned into a more complicated project than I'd anticipated. The upstairs hall had always contained a lot of waste space. I'd conceived the idea of reconfiguring the back bedroom — my future office — so that it would incorporate some of that excess. Take out a wall and a door in one place and add the same a few feet closer to the staircase, I said. Easy, right? Wrong. After much discussion of load-bearing walls and other alarming topics, the contractor came up with a plan. I was certain I'd love the result, but it was taking much longer to achieve than I'd anticipated.

By the time I refilled my cup, I'd come to the conclusion that I'd overreacted to the previous day's scare. Officer Blume, no matter what doubts she might have had about my claims, could be trusted to question Paul Klein. After that, he'd know that the police were aware of what he'd done, even if they didn't charge him with anything. If he had any brains at all, he'd realize that if anything happened to me, he'd be the first one they'd suspect.

Had he been trying to kill me? On somber reflection, I doubted it, but if he'd hoped to frighten me into dropping my search for proof that his boss was a crook, and possibly a murderer, he had chosen the wrong way to do it. Nothing would make me happier than finding enough evidence to put the whole crew — Onslow, Van Heusen, and Klein — behind bars.

I considered what I could do to find answers. I'd opened one avenue of investigation, the bullying of female employees of Mongaup Valley Ventures, but had never gotten around to following up on it. I thought back to the little Ronnie had told me when I'd broached the subject with her. She'd recounted what she'd called "unfounded rumors" of sexual harassment at MVV. Then she'd said that Tiffany had been jealous of a woman who worked for her husband, a woman who had subsequently left the company. Immediately after sharing that tidbit, Ronnie had speculated that it might have been Van Heusen who'd been interested in the woman, not Onslow. At the time, I'd felt certain that she knew more than she was saying, and I'd been right. She had been keeping mum about her afternoon teas with Onslow's second-in-command.

I considered trying to worm more information out of George, the electrician who'd warned me that Van Heusen was a bully, but he'd finished his part of the renovations and moved on to another job. Besides, I didn't think he knew anything substantive. He'd just wanted to let me know I could call on him for help if I felt threatened by the man. George had also implied that Onslow mistreated his wife, but that could mean anything from embarrassing her in public to actual physical violence. He'd been short on specifics.

At that point in my ruminations, the work crew arrived. Once they were upstairs, I booted up my laptop and revisited the website of Mongaup Valley Ventures. Their handy photo album of top-level employees was not accompanied by a list of names of those in the lower ranks, but there was something new on the home page. Mongaup Valley Ventures had an opening in their publicity department. Those seeking interviews were told to come to MVV headquarters during regular business hours to fill out an application.

With a bounce in my step and a big smile on my face, I headed for my bedroom. It had been my parents' room when I was growing up, and it has a large walk-in closet. Although I'd tossed most of my "teacher clothes" when I retired, I'd kept a few of the nicer outfits. They were hanging at the back. The first two pantsuits I tried on revealed all too plainly that I'd gained a few pounds since I'd last worn them, but the third ensemble looked well enough. After forcing reluctant feet into low heels, I unearthed a matching purse and headed for MVV.

The headquarters of Greg Onslow's company was housed in what I remembered as a discount superstore that sold surplus goods and fire-sale items. Sometime in the last few years the building had been spruced up and converted into the nerve center of a business empire. The words MONGAUP VALLEY VENTURES were written ten feet tall in bright red letters on a sign atop the flat roof of the building.

I took the time to drive around the parking lot before I went inside, keeping an eye out for a dark blue SUV. Since I didn't see one, I hoped that meant the police had Paul

Klein in custody. Running into him here would be awkward, to say the least.

In the lobby, a pretty young receptionist — dark haired, green eyed, and well endowed — smiled at me and asked if she could be of any help. I fed her my prepared story — I was looking for a job. This appeared to confuse her. I don't suppose she'd seen many applicants with as much mileage on them as I have. She asked me to wait while she contacted the personnel department.

"Is this a good place to work?" I asked when she informed me that someone would be right out to talk to me.

"I like it."

"You're on the front lines out here. Any trouble with irate investors?"

Those big green eyes widened even further. "Why would there be? This is an excellent company doing good work for the community."

"What about the bosses? I won't work for the grabby type. Not anymore. You would not believe what I've had to put up with through the years!"

Although faint color stained her cheeks, I couldn't tell if it was because she'd been forced to deal with that sort of man on the job or because she was too young to appreciate how far women in the workplace have come in the last fifty years. Before she could formulate an answer, a door opened behind her and a deep but obviously female voice boomed a good morning.

"Come on back," she said, gesturing for me to precede her down a long hallway lined with offices. "I'm Ariadne Toothaker, head of personnel. And you are?"

"Michelle Lincoln. Pleased to meet you."

To her credit, Ms. Toothaker didn't bat an eye at my appearance, although she must surely have thought it strange that someone my age was seeking an entry-level position. Once we reached her office, she studied me while I filled out an application. I was fairly certain she was trying to think of a way to let me down easily . . . without running afoul of a charge of age discrimination.

"So," she said when I handed her the completed form, "why is it you want to work for Mongaup Valley Ventures?"

"I need to work. Period." I returned her assessing gaze with interest. Her photo on the website didn't do her justice. She was tall and sturdily built with a no-nonsense haircut and perfectly applied makeup. She wore a dress-for-success skirt and blazer combination in a muted shade of red. Her ivory-colored blouse had a loosely knotted bow at the throat.

"The position we have available is designed to provide opportunities to climb the corporate ladder. The pay is low to begin with, and you'd be expected to put in long hours."

I kept my expression bland and asked myself what I'd want to know if I was really after the job. "Benefits?"

"We have a fairly standard package of health insurance, retirement plan, vacation and sick days, maternity —" She broke off, cleared her throat, and tried again. "We like to hire people who are in for the long haul — individuals who are willing to commit to staying with Mongaup Valley Ventures for the next five, even ten years."

I smiled. "My health is excellent. I expect to live at least another ten years, if that's what's worrying you."

She dropped her gaze to the application and skimmed over my credentials. I'd answered the questions honestly, since there didn't seem to be any point in making things up, although I did omit my current profession as a freelance editor from the list of previous jobs.

"The opening we have is in our publicity department."

"Did someone quit, or are you adding

staff?" I wanted to ask her about the woman Ronnie had mentioned, but since I had no idea how long ago she'd left and didn't know her name, that was a non-starter.

She ignored my question to ask one of her own. "Your last job was as a teacher. Do you have any experience in writing speeches or press releases?"

"A little."

"Any contacts with local media?"

"I know one of the reporters on the local paper." That was stretching the truth. I had been friends with her late mother when we were girls.

"That could be useful," Ms. Toothaker said, in the tone of one trying to encourage a slow learner. "What about video production skills? We are contemplating making our own commercials."

"Sorry, no, but I'm a quick learner, and I have incentive. The alternative to working here is to take a job as a bagger at the local supermarket. That's not exactly stimulating work."

"You're looking for something . . . stimulating?" The idea seemed to boggle her mind.

"Stimulating. Creative." I leaned forward and waited until I could look her straight in the eyes. "I work best in an environment that is congenial and supportive. Nothing good ever comes from a workplace dominated by bullies or prima donnas."

She stared back at me as if I'd grown horns. "I don't know what you've heard, but Mongaup Valley Ventures would never allow anyone who works for us to be harassed or intimidated."

"Good to know." I settled back in the chair. "What's your ratio of male to female employees?"

Instead of giving me an answer, she said, "We are interested in hiring more women."

"Do you pay women as much as you do men?"

Her smile looked forced. "Of course, so long as they are in comparable positions with the company."

I didn't smile back. Putting men in the top jobs provided a handy work-around to the equal pay problem.

"Tell me, does Mr. Onslow take a personal interest in the staff, or does he leave that to the executive in charge of PR? That's a Mr. Van Heusen, I believe. Will he be the one to interview me about the job?"

My rapid-fire questions had Ms. Toothaker's brows beetling. She stood abruptly to signal the end of our meeting. "I have your contact information, Ms. Lincoln. We'll be

331

in touch."

The subtext was *don't hold your breath.*

She walked me back toward the lobby, preventing me from talking to anyone else, but I couldn't help but notice that the secretaries were all female and good looking and that the names on the office doors, except for Ms. Toothaker's, were all male. We were just passing the one bearing Greg Onslow's name when a harried-looking young man intercepted us. After a hushed exchange of words, Ms. Toothaker pointed me toward the exit.

"The door to the lobby is right there. Have a good day."

I took a few steps in that direction but as soon as she was out of sight I backtracked. I had a sneaking suspicion that the personnel department had just received the unwelcome news that their head of security was being questioned by the police. It was perfect timing as far as I was concerned. I poked my head into Greg Onslow's office. The door to the inner room was closed, but a real stunner — ginger hair down to her waist, blue eyes, a figure Barbie might envy — sat squinting at a computer monitor in the reception area.

"Excuse me. Is Mr. Onslow available?"

The redhead looked up, mouth opening

in a startled, lipstick-circled O and heavily mascaraed eyes widening. I wondered if my question had been too complicated for her. Her nameplate identified her as Jenni — yes, with an i — Farquhar. That surname is an old one in these parts and pronounced "Forker."

"Mr. Onslow?" I repeated when she continued to goggle at me without speaking.

"Oh. Sorry. No. He's out at Wonderful World. Hey, do you know anything about computers. My screen just froze."

"Try alt plus control plus delete."

She did, and gave a little shriek at what came up on the monitor.

Rolling my eyes, I eased the rest of the way into the office and stood behind her to read the pop-up. The need to make a decision had apparently thrust her straight into a state of paralysis. I'm no computer genius, but this was basic word processing. With a few clicks of the mouse, I made the required choices, fixed the problem, and earned myself a look of gratitude that would have been more suitable coming from a puppy than from a grown woman.

Planting my rump on a corner of Jenni's desk, I prepared to take shameful advantage of my new status as heroine who saved the day. "I just applied for a job," I said. "Have you worked here long? Do you like it?"

I should have known better than to hit her with more than one question at once. All I got was a blank stare. I switched gears.

"So, what is it you do for Mr. Onslow, besides typing things into the computer?"

"Oh, you know. The usual. I make coffee and answer the phone and run errands."

"Long hours?"

"Sometimes. I've only been here a month, but from what I've seen, he works late two or three nights a week. He's real nice about asking me to stay, though, and then he gives me little gifts to make up for the inconvenience." She stumbled a little over the last word. Too many syllables, I suppose.

"So long as he doesn't take advantage of you."

"Oh, no. I never do anything I don't want to do." She leaned closer and lowered her voice. "He's a widower, you know."

"I do know." Given what appeared to be a 1950s mindset, I suspected she was hoping to catch him on the rebound. Ordinarily, I'd never call another woman a bimbo, but Jenni Farquhar made me think Greg Onslow must have ordered her up from central casting.

"You might want to keep in mind how his late wife died," I said as I hopped down from my perch and headed for the door.

The warning went right over her head.

I'd hoped to explore a bit more, but Ms. Toothaker, having dealt with whatever urgent business had temporarily gotten her out of my way, apparently wanted to talk to the boss about it. She caught me coming out of his office. Her smile noticeably absent, she escorted me all the way to the parking lot. I had the distinct impression that I was not going to be called back for an interview.

CHAPTER 37

Shortly after I got home, I had a phone call from Officer Blume to tell me that she had interviewed Paul Klein. She had not arrested him. Since there had been no witnesses to the incident, it was my word against his that he'd tried to run me down.

Nice, I thought. *He's free to try again.*

She assured me that she was still investigating, but that didn't make me feel safer. As soon as I hung up, I headed for Darlene's house. I wasn't hiding. Not exactly. We'd already planned to compare notes on the information we'd gathered. But I did feel more secure there, right up until the moment when we heard thunderous knocking at her front door.

"Hold your horses!" Darlene yelled, thumping her way toward the entry hall with her walker.

I started to call her back, then told myself not to be such a ninny. It couldn't possibly

336

be Paul Klein. He'd have no way of knowing where I was.

We'd been working in Darlene's living room, so I had a clear view of the person who stepped inside. It still took a moment for me to believe my eyes. Alan Van Heusen was the last person I expected to see.

Papers spread out on the coffee table scattered as I stood, my heart in my throat and my hands already curling into fists. At the sound, Van Heusen turned my way. His eyes glittered with malice when he caught sight of me. "Ms. Lincoln. There you are."

He gave Darlene a shove to get her out of his way and stalked across the room to reach me. Once again, he pointedly invaded my personal space. His face was only inches from mine, and it was not a pleasant sight. Anger never is. If he didn't calm down, he was going to pop a blood vessel.

I could see that Van Heusen was having trouble controlling his temper, but even though I had so recently been in fear for my life, I was strangely unconcerned about my immediate safety. If he'd intended physical violence, I was pretty sure he'd already have hurt me. He loomed, but he didn't touch.

The man was a bully. He was undoubtedly expecting me to whimper and beg his forgiveness, even though I had no idea what

I'd done to upset him. I reminded myself that most bullies are cowards at heart. When he failed to intimidate me, he would fold. He had not yet done so when Darlene, having regained her balance, waded into the fray.

"You've got a lot of nerve barging in here like this." Imitating Van Heusen's technique for capturing attention, she pushed me aside, and none too gently either, and thrust herself into my place. Her walker was at just the right height to give him a painful smack in the abdomen.

Van Heusen winced, but his gaze followed me. "I came to see her."

"Well, see her somewhere else. This is my house, and you aren't welcome here."

"Why don't we all sit down and discuss this calmly," I suggested in what I hoped was a reasonable tone of voice.

The two of them shot identical looks in my direction — the kind that silently asked if I'd lost my mind.

"Let's start slowly," I persisted. "How did you know where to find me?" I couldn't remember having told anyone where I'd be.

"Your car is parked out front."

"Oh."

For some reason, that answer threw me for a loop. I hadn't realized that Van Heusen knew what kind of car I drove. Why would he have troubled to find out? For a moment, I wished I'd parked in Darlene's garage, in the space Frank had left empty. Then I straightened my spine. Why should I hide? I'd done nothing wrong.

Van Heusen had retreated a few steps, but he showed no inclination to take a seat. Darlene and I also remained standing, since it would have put us at a disadvantage to have to look up at him. I hid my hands behind my back to conceal the fact that they were shaking.

"Explain yourself, please, Mr. Van Heusen. I don't understand why you were looking for me. What is so important that it can't wait for a more convenient time?"

His fulminating stare shifted briefly to Darlene, as if trying to decide which of us was the weaker link. Her hands gripped the sides of her walker so tightly that her knuckles showed white and the tension in her jaw offered further evidence that she was upset, but I felt certain she had no intention of letting herself be cowed by the man she called Onslow's flunky.

Van Heusen abruptly returned his attention to me. "You've been snooping around, asking questions. Why are you checking up on me?"

"Is that a problem? Perhaps I'm just interested in investing in Mongaup Valley Ventures."

"Pull the other leg. You're trying to pin something on me. This attack is personal."

"Paranoid much," Darlene said, *sotto voce.*

With his hands fisted, he swung her way. I spoke quickly to divert his attention. "If it offended you that I was asking about you this morning, I apologize. I was actually more interested in your boss, but since the position I applied for was in public relations —"

I broke off when I recognized the expression on his face. It was one of bewilderment.

"What the hell are you talking about?"

"Isn't that why you're ticked off at me?"

"I am ticked off, as you put it, because you were talking in public about investigating me. You and Joe Ramirez at Harriet's. Did you think that no one would overhear? Did you really believe the story wouldn't get back to me?"

"You're in a snit because we've been looking into your past business dealings?" Darlene asked.

I tried to signal her to keep quiet, but her flushed face and the stubborn jut of her chin warned me that she was almost as angry as he was.

"Have you ever heard of freedom of information, Mr. Van Heusen? How about freedom of speech? Surely you're familiar with that one. Mikki can say anything she wants in a private conversation. Furthermore, the last time I checked, there's no law against Internet searches. I was a librarian before I retired. We're big on the idea that everyone should have access to public records."

Van Heusen's glare was venomous. He took a threatening step toward Darlene but pulled up short when Edmund the schnauzer, who had plodded into the room unnoticed, suddenly appeared beside him. Edmund stared up at him with bloodshot eyes and gave a half-hearted woof. Van Heusen reacted by drawing back his leg, aiming what would undoubtedly be a vicious kick at the old dog.

"Don't even think about it." I meant my words as a warning, but they came out high-pitched and panic-stricken.

Until that moment, I hadn't truly been afraid. In a flash, I saw how stupid I was being to think I could reason with this man. It had been beyond foolish to taunt him. We were two women of a certain age and an elderly pooch alone with a potentially violent man who was considerably younger and stronger than we were, a man who might well be a murderer and who looked like he was about to explode.

Van Heusen made an inarticulate sound of rage and struck out at Edmund's head. Edmund evaded the foot, growled, and grabbed hold of Van Heusen's pants leg with the few teeth he had left. When Darlene screamed, I fumbled in my pocket for my cell phone, but before I could retrieve it, the front door flew open and Frank rushed in.

Darlene's husband needed only one glance at the tableau in his living room to realize that drastic measures were needed. Tossing his golf clubs aside, he headed straight for Alan Van Heusen, who had just managed to free himself from Edmund's jaws. Frank seized the younger man by the front of his shirt. He might have been twice Van Heusen's age, but he was in good shape and he towered over him by at least six inches. If they came to blows, it would be a toss-up which one would win the bout.

"You're leaving," Frank said. "Now." To aid Van Heusen's departure, he shifted his grip to the back of his collar and frog-marched him to the door.

Van Heusen didn't fight his eviction. He

only picked on those who were smaller than he was. But he did lob a parting shot at me just as Frank shoved him outside. "If you don't stop interfering in my business, you'll be sorry!"

Frank slammed the door and locked it, then made a production of dusting off his hands. "Good riddance to bad rubbish."

"My hero." Darlene abandoned her walker to throw herself into her husband's arms and reward him with a smacking kiss on the lips.

Edmund, unhurt in the tussle with Van Heusen, tried to insinuate himself between them. I sank down into the nearest chair as my knees abruptly gave out on me.

Frank seemed to enjoy the interlude with his wife, but eventually, about the same time my heart rate settled back to normal, he broke free and demanded an explanation.

It took a while to bring him up to speed. What we told him did nothing to lessen his antipathy toward Van Heusen, and after he'd heard the whole story, he called the police.

They took his complaint much more seriously than they had mine.

CHAPTER 38

After Van Heusen's home invasion, for which he had to spend several uncomfortable hours at the police station but was not arrested, nothing unexpected happened for the rest of the week. I had manuscripts to edit, and since renovations on my house were finally finished, there was plenty of physical labor to keep me busy after working hours. In the evenings, with my new security system giving me peace of mind, I vacuumed up a ton of sawdust, stray bits of insulation, and other debris that the construction crew had missed. They tried. I'll give them that. But their idea of clean and mine differed greatly. Then there was furniture to be arranged and rearranged. I hung pictures and curtains. I unpacked knick-knacks that I'd carefully stashed out of harm's way and put them on display.

Calpurnia enjoyed the boxes and the packing paper.

Before I knew it, it was Friday. Friday the thirteenth, in fact, but I decided to ignore that. I was in the middle of a client's gripping story — her character was trapped in a fallen building after an earthquake — when Officer Blume knocked on my front door.

She tried to turn down coffee, but when I insisted she didn't put up much of a fight. A few minutes later, we were seated at the dinette table with steaming mugs and a package of miniature coffee cakes in front of us. It wasn't exactly gourmet food, or particularly nutritious, but I rationalize that I'm old enough to indulge myself if I want. I also have a stash of Ring Dings in the cupboard.

"So," I said when she had had a sip and a nibble, "what's up?"

"I've come to tell you that we've arrested Alan Van Heusen."

"That's great. And Ronnie North? Has she been freed?" Blume looked puzzled. "Why would she be?"

"But you just said —"

"Oh, I see." She sent me a rueful smile. "No, we didn't arrest Mr. Van Heusen for murder. Mrs. North is still being held on that charge."

"Then what did he do?" I already knew his behavior at Darlene's hadn't rated more than a slap on the wrist.

"I can't give you all the details, but the gist of it is that he has a criminal past as a con man under another name."

"I'm not surprised." I took a long swallow of coffee. "So, you arrested Van Heusen for past crimes," I ventured after a moment. "What about the present? What about here in Lenape Hollow?"

"That's why I came over, to let you know that when we put pressure on Paul Klein, he admitted that Van Heusen contacted him early Monday afternoon, while you were still having lunch, and sent him to watch for you to leave Harriet's. His orders were to put a scare into you."

"Is Klein locked up, too?"

Blume shook her head. "He made a deal to testify against Van Heusen. He isn't in jail, but he's no longer a threat to you."

"Did Klein also break into my house and steal my laptop?"

"As to that, he claims he did not. But you were right about the two instances when you thought he was following you. Van Heusen didn't order round-the-clock surveillance, but he wanted Klein to keep an eye on you. Apparently Van Heusen didn't believe you when you told him Tiffany didn't leave anything here except her manuscript."

I was in information overload. I *had* been followed. It hadn't been overactive imagination or paranoia after all. But if it hadn't been Klein who'd burgled my house, who had it been? "Did you ask Van Heusen about the break-in?"

"He's lawyered up and isn't saying a word about anything. It doesn't matter. We have grounds to hold him on a warrant from another state as well as for what he's alleged to have done in Lenape Hollow. Klein knew other interesting details about his activities here."

I leaned forward, fingers crossed. "Did Klein have anything to say about Greg Onslow?"

"Mr. Onslow is clean." Blume acknowledged my start of surprise by toasting me with her coffee cup. "We can't prove he knew anything illegal was going on, and when we questioned him about his employees, he informed us that he had already fired Mr. Van Heusen. He claims he found out that Van Heusen was using unethical methods to deal with members of the community."

That sounded like a quote and caused my eyebrows to shoot up. "That's his story, eh?"

"It is, and he's sticking to it. We have no evidence to prove otherwise. So far, everything points to Onslow having been taken in by Van Heusen, just like everyone else. We have no case against him."

I stared at her. "You're telling me Onslow is an innocent victim?"

She shrugged. "I'm hardly unbiased on the subject. My mom lost her savings on one of Onslow's deals. She went into it because he was married to Tiffany, and Mom always thought Tiffany Scott hung the moon. I would love to see him end up in the cell right next to Van Heusen's."

I sipped my coffee and considered what she'd told me. Officer Blume concentrated on polishing off the last crumb of her coffee cake. In a minute, she'd leave. She'd given her report to Van Heusen's other victim, me. Her duty was complete.

When she started to rise, I put a hand on her forearm to stop her. "Can I ask you something? About Tiffany?" I remembered that she'd called her a spoiled brat and was curious as to why.

"I guess." She didn't look eager to discuss the dead woman, but she subsided into her chair.

"You and Tiffany must have known each other all your lives." She'd said her mother had been fond of her. That suggested a fairly close relationship between the two girls.

348

"We went to school together, but I wouldn't exactly call her a friend."

Just as I wouldn't have called Ronnie one? I went with that theory. "I suppose everyone was envious of her — rich, pretty, and then she captures an even wealthier husband."

"There wasn't *that* much to be jealous about, especially after she got married. For one thing, Tiffany wasn't as happy as most people thought. I sure didn't envy her being dependent on her husband for every little thing."

"One of the men working on my house, a man who was previously employed by Greg Onslow, hinted to me that Onslow might have been abusive to his wife, psychologically if not physically. When I pressed him for details, he wouldn't say more, but he definitely gave me the impression that all was not well between them."

Blume looked thoughtful. "I never saw any sign that he hit her. And to tell you the truth, she wasn't hurting for spending money. Onslow was generous with her. Anything Tiffany wanted, Tiffany got right up to the end, but she had to *ask* him for it every time. She had nothing in her own name except those stocks she left to her grandmother in her will." She shrugged. "When I heard that, I figured she'd done it to spite him."

"And yet you still think Ronnie is the one who murdered her?"

Blume looked uncomfortable. "I'm not supposed to repeat this, but it will come out at the trial anyway. According to my mother, it's already making the rounds on the Lenape Hollow grapevine. The tests they did after the autopsy turned up traces of one of Mrs. North's medications in Tiffany's body. She was drugged before she went into the water. That's why she drowned, and that's why the charge is homicide. No way was her death accidental."

CHAPTER 39

I brooded for much of the rest of the day while a light rain fell outside my windows and added to the general aura of gloom. I could understand why the evidence made Ronnie seem guilty, but I wasn't convinced she'd kill her own granddaughter. It still seemed to me that Greg Onslow was the most likely murderer. He had a temper. His wife had defied him. And his flunky, Van Heusen, had access to Ronnie's house and, presumably, her medicine cabinet. Then again, if Tiffany's quarrel with Ronnie was over Ronnie's relationship with Alan Van Heusen, and Van Heusen found out about it, maybe he'd acted on his own.

Darn! I really wanted Onslow to be guilty of something. Otherwise, he might still manage to ruin 265 acres that had once provided the community with a swimming hole, a picnic area, a baseball diamond, and thirteen miles of hiking trails. Whether he built his amusement park or not, his machinations were depriving Lenape Hollow of a local treasure.

I doubted the police would listen to my latest theories, but Mike was Ronnie's lawyer. I felt certain he could find some use for the bits and pieces of information Darlene and I had accumulated.

It had been just a week since I'd last seen him. At that time, over lunch, I'd intended to fill him in on everything Darlene had unearthed online. Instead, we'd ended up talking about other matters. Since Ronnie had not yet been arrested, I hadn't felt any urgency about passing along what I knew, especially after he kept warning me against meddling.

I tried phoning him first. His cell went straight to voice mail. Since I didn't think I could leave a coherent message, I disconnected and punched in the number of his landline. I was encouraged by the busy signal. Someone was home, and there was a fifty-fifty chance it was Mike. If he wasn't there, then his wife probably knew where I could find him.

I hopped into my car and drove to Treeline Lane. On the way I realized that he might not be aware that my house had been burgled, or that I'd almost been run down, or that Van Heusen had been arrested. I suppose I should have let him know about those first two incidents as soon as they happened, but it simply hadn't occurred to me.

The Doran house sat on a large lot, but it was nothing spectacular, just a pleasant-looking three-story white clapboard with dark blue shutters on the windows. I rang the doorbell and stood awaiting a response on a tiny front porch that did little to keep me dry. Every gust of wind further dampened my clothes. I made a mental note to buy myself a full-length raincoat, maybe one with a nice warm lining. I was shivering in my short fall jacket and wishing I'd thought to wear gloves by the time Mike finally opened the door.

"Well, this is a surprise."

That much was obvious. He was wearing a ratty old pair of sweatpants and a matching hoodie. When I stepped into the entry hall, I caught a whiff of burnt toast.

"Is this a bad time? I didn't realize it was so close to supper."

He glanced at the grandfather clock in the hall. "It's only five-thirty."

I let that pass. My husband and I both came from families who ate their evening meal as soon as the breadwinner got home from work. We'd kept to that tradition, and

I still did. Ordinarily, I'd already have eaten by this hour. I hoped my stomach wouldn't start growling while I was talking to Mike.

"It's fine," he was saying. "The wife's away for a few days, and I was just catching up on some paperwork."

When I said what I had to discuss was business rather than personal, he led the way to his home office, a room completely devoid of feminine touches. If it hadn't been for the obligatory gold-framed photo of his spouse, prominently displayed on the glossy mahogany surface of his desk, I might have doubted the existence of the third Mrs. Doran. I did a double take when I got a closer look at her likeness. She was bright-eyed and smiling and considerably younger than her husband, but what was most striking was that she bore a strong resemblance to wife number one. I doubted either she or Sonya would thank me if I pointed that out.

Once I was settled across the desk from Mike, I launched into my story, backtracking now and again in an attempt to make certain points clearer. Mike listened without comment, although he did look slightly shell-shocked by the time I finished.

"You've been a busy girl," he murmured.

I'd summarized all the information Darlene and I had gathered about Tiffany's widower and his flunky and combined it with what I'd learned at Mongaup Valley Ventures and from Officer Blume. Unfortunately, that now included the conclusion that Onslow was innocent of any crime.

"It's possible he's not a crook, just a bad businessman who keeps going bankrupt," I said, "but I'm not convinced of that."

"I can tell you how he managed to get startup loans for new ventures," Mike said. "His father was a successful entrepreneur. Onslow managed to convince backers that the acorn didn't fall far from the tree. Daddy's legacy has stood him in good stead for years, but Daddy is long gone now and so is the fortune Onslow inherited from him."

"One of them killed Tiffany," I said, getting back to the most important crime. "If not her husband, then Van Heusen."

Mike rubbed at his chin with the knuckles of his right hand, a nervous habit he'd had as a teenager but one I hadn't seen the adult Mike use until now. "Con men don't usually resort to violence, Mikki. If he thought Tiffany was on to him, he'd have been more likely to take off and start over with a new identity. From what you tell me the police have discovered, he's done that before."

I frowned. "What about Onslow, then? Supposedly, Tiffany had proof that he was guilty of fraud. We *know* she sided with Ronnie to oppose his plans for Wonderful World. Maybe she was getting ready to divorce him." I pictured Jenni Farquhar as I made that suggestion, and my gaze drifted, of its own volition, to the photograph of the third Mrs. Doran.

"Did you find anything to support this theory in Tiffany's manuscript or research notes?"

"Well, no. Not really. I mean, the characters I assume are based on her husband and Van Heusen *are* crooks, but with so many of the details changed to reflect the time period of the novel —" I broke off when he started to shake his head.

"It's a good thing you never gave that thumb drive to Detective Hazlett," Mike said. "He'd have laughed himself silly. Face it, Mikki, there is no *there* there. No proof. Not even a hint about where to look for it. Maybe it's just as well that the original and all the copies were stolen."

"Not all of them. I back up to the cloud."

"Great."

The disapproval in his expression persuaded me that this was not the time to confess that Hazlett did have a copy, as did Ronnie, and that Onslow had the original. Instead I asked, "Do you really think Onslow is innocent? Or that he's so stupid that Van Heusen could have conned him?"

"Anyone can be taken in."

"If Onslow was duped and there's no case to be made that Van Heusen killed Tiffany to keep her quiet about his illegal activities, then where does that leave Ronnie?"

"In jail."

The indifference in his voice puzzled me. I blinked at him in confusion for a moment before the truth reared up and slapped me in the face.

"You think she's guilty! You actually believe Ronnie killed her only grandchild." When he said nothing, I narrowed my eyes at him. "Did she admit it to you?"

"A good defense attorney never asks a question unless he's sure he already knows the answer."

It took me a moment to work that one out. "In other words, you haven't asked her if she's guilty, but you assume she is."

"Innocent until proven guilty, Mikki." A wry smile played across his lips.

"Are you even *trying* to come up with another suspect?"

He sat up straighter, suddenly all stiff-necked and defensive. "I'm not likely to let a client go to prison if I can keep her out. Even a cold-hearted, domineering witch like

Ronnie North deserves top-notch representation. So unless you've earned a degree in law and passed the bar in the last couple of weeks, I'd appreciate it if you'd leave her defense to me."

"I'm trying to help."

He sighed. "And I'm grateful for that. If anything you and Darlene uncovered turns out to be relevant, I'll certainly make use of it."

I must have looked as annoyed as I felt, because Mike pasted on a smile and reached across the desk to pat my hand. In his best soothe-the-little-woman manner he said, "Stick to building your new business and let me handle the lawyering, okay?"

"Do you have any idea how condescending you sound?" I jerked my fingers out of his grasp and stood up.

This time the smile was genuine. "Have a little faith in the legal system, Mik. In the end, it's up to a jury to decide whether or not Ronnie murdered her granddaughter."

CHAPTER 40

By the time I left Mike's house the rain had stopped. It was already dark, and I was tired, discouraged, and beyond hungry. Since my cupboards were almost bare, especially the one that held the cat food, I stopped at the grocery store on my way home. I was wheeling my cart down the aisle with cereal on one side and bread on the other, thinking that it had been a long time since I'd bought a loaf of seeded Jewish rye but that I'd do better to pick one up at the bakery rather than rely on store-bought, when someone called my name. A woman I'd never seen before bore down on me, her gaze avid.

"Didn't I just see your car parked in front of Mike Doran's house?" she asked.

Her question made me uncomfortable, since her words echoed Alan Van Heusen's explanation of how he'd found me at Darlene's. The thing is, my car isn't all that distinctive. It's a very ordinary green Ford Taurus, a few years old but in good condition. It has no bumper stickers and now that the telltale Maine license plates are gone, there's really nothing about it that screams "I belong to Mikki Lincoln."

I may have sounded a bit defensive when I asked, "How is it you know what I drive?"

The woman laughed. "Busted! I saw you leave his place and followed you here."

"Why?"

"You first."

Since I wasn't about to share the truth with a complete stranger, I fudged. "I had a bit of legal business to conduct with him."

Her lips were painted bright red. They realigned themselves into a smirk. "Sure it wasn't monkey business? I hear the current Mrs. D. is out of town. Again."

"Not hardly." Tired of being interrogated, I tried to push my cart past her, but she maneuvered her smaller one into my path, successfully blocking my escape route.

"Are you sure about that?"

Drawing myself up to my full height, I glared at her. "Excuse me, but who *are* you?"

"Can't you guess?" When I declined to play her silly games, she shrugged. "I'm Mike's second ex-wife, Gloria. The one who came after Sonya and before Lindsey."

"Ah," I said. The one who'd been pals with Tiffany's mom. It might have been polite of me to add "nice to meet you," but that would hardly have been truthful. The last thing I wanted was a closer acquaintance with another of Mike's exes.

Now that Gloria had identified herself, I could see the resemblance. All three Mrs. Dorans were well-endowed blondes. Gloria and Sonya also shared an aggressive attitude that I didn't much care for. I tried again to get around her, but she was determined to maintain her blockade. Short of making a scene, I was stuck.

"You two were a hot item in high school, or so I'm told."

"First I've heard of it."

"Really? My source is reliable, at least in this instance."

Belatedly, I caught on. She meant Mike himself. I wondered what else he'd told her about me. Not the whole truth, obviously, since he and I had never done more than smooch as teenagers. I'd been halfway through college before I lost my virginity. Besides, I obviously didn't fit his profile of choice. Back in the day, I was brown-haired, skinny, and decidedly flat-chested.

"Don't believe everything you hear," I advised Gloria as I tried, for the third time, to get past her cart. Once again she shifted to keep me cornered. "What is it you want from me?"

"I want to know anything you know that will make my ex squirm. The man is a total creep. He has as little regard for you as he has for me or Sonya or Lindsey, so come on, girlfriend — share." She leaned closer, sending peppermint-scented fumes my way. "You must know something juicy about his past, the more embarrassing the better."

"Oh, please — are you twelve? Even if I did have a memory that would make him cringe, it would be from five decades ago. Who cares about that now?"

"*He* does. That's the point. With Mike, it's all about reputation."

"Is that why you threatened to charge him with assault? I hear that was the leverage you used to get a better divorce settlement."

"Exactly!" She looked extraordinarily pleased with her own cleverness. "The alimony I got out of him gives me a nice steady income." Her face fell. "Well, it did, till he started pleading poverty. I mean, does that seem likely?"

I was still stuck on the fact that she'd been prepared to lie under oath, and my sarcastic side came out. "Good to know he's not really a wife beater."

"I didn't *entirely* make that up. He *almost* hit me once."

No doubt with provocation, I thought uncharitably. "He's never impressed me as violent. Though it pains me to admit it, I was more of a bully when we were kids than he was." If anything, Mike tended to be over-protective of women, or at least he was with me.

"It was a near thing," Gloria insisted, "and do you know *why* he almost lost control? Because I insulted his sainted mother. That's how I knew he'd cave the minute I threatened his reputation. He's real thin-skinned when it comes to what people think of him, and God forbid anyone should say a word against his family. It's a good thing we never had kids. He'd have put the poor things on pedestals and they'd have had to rebel and then there'd really have been hell to pay."

I gave her a hard look. "Forgive me for prying, but have you been drinking?"

"Only a teeny, tiny cocktail. Or two." She aimed a crooked smile my way. "A habit I picked up from my ex before he went on the wagon. That was after it finally dawned on him that he talks too much when he drinks. Some of his clients didn't appreciate the loose lips."

At her words, an appalling thought shoved its way into my head and refused to be dislodged. "To whom did he talk?"

"What?"

"Did he regret sharing something specific?"

I could tell by her blank stare that I wasn't getting through to her, and I hesitated to elaborate. Surely I was wrong.

"It's been nice chatting with you," I said, "but I really have to get home to my cat."

Cautiously, I eased my cart past the second Mrs. Doran, who was now staring in a bemused way at the many varieties of Cheerios on display.

She came back to life as I fled, calling after me in a loud voice, "You watch out for that Mike Doran. He's a dyed-in-the-wool louse."

The louse and the souse, I thought. *Or maybe the louse and the lush. What a charming couple they must have made.*

CHAPTER 41

Since I already had the basic necessities in my cart — milk, eggs, toilet paper, and cat food — I paid for my groceries and headed home before Gloria could accost me a second time, but although I escaped her presence, I wasn't able to erase what she'd said from my mind.

I should have asked her, I thought. *I should have come right out and demanded to know if Mike regretted telling certain stories to the young Tiffany Scott.*

As much as I wanted to attribute everything Gloria said to the drink, I couldn't quite convince myself that was the case. The upshot was that I had to consider the unthinkable — that if Mike was as protective of his family's reputation as his ex-wife claimed, he was a viable suspect in Tiffany's murder.

He'd made a joke of the possibility when we'd had lunch together, even going so far as to assure me that he had an alibi, but he hadn't been happy that I'd figured out what his father had done.

On autopilot, I carried the groceries into the house and put them away.

Think it through, I told myself. *Mike hasn't tried to harm me. He knows I won't tell anyone. Why would he be afraid that Tiffany would betray his secret?*

What at first seemed an outrageous idea slowly coalesced into an all-too-likely scenario. Maybe I was trying too hard to make the pieces fit, but fit they did, especially when I recalled something Officer Blume had told me. Tiffany hadn't had money of her own. She'd been dependent upon her husband's good will. Mike, on the other hand, if wife number two was to be believed, had told his ex that he was strapped for cash. I hated to think ill of the dead, and I'd liked Tiffany on short acquaintance, but what if that file she'd named "blackmail .doc" wasn't just an innocent part of the story bible for her novel?

I closed my eyes against a sudden urge to cry. Was I right? If I was, then Mike, in the guise of Ronnie's defense attorney, must also be planning to railroad his own client to protect himself. Would he really let her be convicted of a crime he'd committed?

The Mike I'd known long ago would never have done such a thing, let alone add insult to injury by charging Ronnie for his services, but that was the point, wasn't it?

"I don't know him anymore," I said aloud. "People change in fifty years."

Although I hadn't asked a question, Calpurnia answered me with a short burst of cat-speak designed to remind me that I had more important responsibilities than solving Tiffany's murder. First among them was refilling her food dish. Still struggling to put all the pieces of the puzzle together, I obliged her by rote, opening a can and scooping the contents into a clean cat-food bowl. I refreshed her water, too, slopping a little as I returned it to the placemat that kept my kitchen floor marginally cleaner. Like many cats, Calpurnia liked to take her food out of its bowl and eat it off the tile.

I no longer had any appetite for supper. I left Cal to her meal and headed for the dining room. I'd already moved the file cabinets and a number of boxes upstairs, but I had yet to transfer the mess on my dining room table to the desk that had pride of place in my office. I glanced at the ceiling, visualizing the space directly over my head and wishing I could just forget all these newly hatched suspicions and spend the evening settling into the freshly renovated space.

Instead, I sat down at the table and fired up my laptop to take another look at the blackmail file. I'm no math genius, and I know even less about accounting, but in light of what I now suspected it seemed to me that the amounts listed were in line with what a young woman short on funds might reasonably think she could demand from a retired lawyer already burdened with alimony payments. The payments started small, but each one was a little larger than the one before. That would have made it harder for him to come up with the money. To keep Tiffany quiet, he'd been willing to risk the wrath of his ex-wife, but what if she'd asked for even more, and he didn't have it? Would that have given him incentive to get rid of his blackmailer?

I wondered if Detective Hazlett had looked at this file. He hadn't said right out that he'd made a copy of Tiffany's thumb drive, but I was certain he had, and if he had duplicate files, surely he'd read them.

But he'd arrested Ronnie.

I frowned at the columns of numbers on the screen. In crime novels, the police never seem to have any trouble gaining access to people's finances, but "blackmail.doc" didn't list any names, just dates and amounts. If Tiffany had been trying to hide a nest egg from her controlling husband, she'd probably have set up an account at a different bank than the one he used. The police might not have found it.

"And maybe," I said aloud to Cal as she sauntered into the room, "just maybe, I'm letting my imagination run away with me. For all I know, the police collected other evidence from Ronnie's house, something besides the same pills that were in Tiffany's system. Maybe she is guilty and Mike's lack of enthusiasm about defending her is because he has genuine doubts about her innocence."

The flaw in this logic was too big to ignore. Mike had also had access to Ronnie's house, and to her pills. And he'd been there on the day she and Tiffany quarreled — the day Tiffany died.

Mike had said he had an alibi for the time of Tiffany's murder, but he hadn't told me what it was. I had to wonder if he'd been telling me the truth. After all, if he was guilty of murder, a lie would hardly trouble his conscience.

Speculations whirled around and around in my mind until they triggered a dull headache. I shut down the laptop and returned to the kitchen. I needed to eat something, even if I didn't feel hungry. Getting at least eight hours of sleep would be an even better idea, but I didn't see that happening. I opened the refrigerator and stared at the contents, finally pulling out the ingredients for a grilled tomato and cheese sandwich.

I was operating on autopilot until Calpurnia snaked out a paw in an attempt to liberate the cheese I'd just removed from a plastic storage bag. I spoke sharply to her before I lifted her off the counter. She wasn't supposed to get up there in the first place. Then I nullified any hope of training her not to beg by tossing her a small piece of cheddar.

The problem, I decided as I put together a light supper, was that I had thought about my new theory just enough to make myself crazy. I considered asking Mike straight out about his alibi, but if he was innocent he'd be hurt to think I'd suspected him, however briefly, of murder. That was no way to keep a friend. On the other hand, if he was guilty, asking a question like that would be tantamount to setting myself up to be the next one to be bumped off.

I'd polished off the last of my meal before it occurred to me that if the alibi was real, there was someone else who almost certainly knew the details. Before I could talk myself out of it, I picked up the phone and punched in Detective Hazlett's number. When my call went to voice mail, I almost hung up. Only at the last possible moment did I start to speak.

I doubt my message made much sense. I threw a lot in, suggesting that he reevaluate "blackmail.doc" and that he look for a bank account in Tiffany's name and that if the numbers in the file matched her deposits he should also read the files about the copycat killer. I couldn't bring myself to mention Mike by name, but right before I disconnected I asked Hazlett to call me back.

I'd just finished washing the few dishes I'd used that day, a ritual I've always found soothing, when the doorbell rang. I jumped a foot. It was pitch dark outside and I wasn't expecting company. What if it was Mike? I didn't think I was up to facing him. On the other hand, it might be Detective Hazlett, a prospect that was almost as unnerving.

Feet dragging, I made my way to the foyer, flipped on the porch light, and peered through the small window in the front door. I let out a breath I hadn't realized I'd been holding when I recognized Darlene.

"Hold on," I called through the wood. "I have to disarm the security system."

That done, I wrestled with the chain, the

regular lock, and the deadbolt, endeavors that gave me plenty of time to wonder what on earth Darlene was doing on my doorstep. Her arrival was all the more remarkable because my house isn't exactly handicapped accessible. In all the time since my return to Lenape Hollow, she had never once attempted to visit me at home.

"Give me a hand, will you?" she asked as soon as the door was open. She shoved a large rolling suitcase in my direction. Somehow, she'd managed to schlep it up two sets of steps and onto my front porch. "I need a place to stay. Frank and I have had the mother of all quarrels."

"Oh, no!"

"He's pissed off because of that confrontation with Van Heusen in our living room. He says, very unfairly, that it never would have happened if I hadn't been trying to dig up dirt on Onslow. Like he didn't think that was a great idea back when we lost our savings!"

I lugged the suitcase as far as the hall and abandoned it. "You're welcome to stay, but my guest room is tiny, and it's on the second floor."

Using her cane for balance, she went past me, heading into the living room. "A sofa will do. I won't be here long. I'm just giving him time to cool down."

"All I have is a loveseat."

She stared at it, then shrugged. "I can do stairs if I have to. I'm just slow. I left my walker and the scooter in the van. Would you mind bringing them in, just in case I need one or the other in the morning?"

I was surprised she hadn't brought the wheelchair, too. "Give me your keys. I'll move my car out of the garage and put your van in. Then I can unload directly into the house through the sunroom."

It didn't take me long to switch the vehicles around and bring in Darlene's equipment. The scooter was folded up and relatively lightweight. Its battery was heavy, but it was stored in a carrying bag with a handle. I went back out one last time to remove the garage door opener from my car. I locked the Taurus, but since it was parked in the driveway, it was vulnerable. I was taking no chances.

After I relocked all the doors and reset the security system, I reassembled the scooter and installed the battery. I'd seen Darlene do it often enough and thought I'd spare her the trouble. She was obviously upset. It wasn't easy to walk out on a man you'd been married to for half a century. I couldn't imagine anything that would have made me do that to James.

My task complete, I followed the sound of cabinet doors opening and closing to the kitchen. Darlene found what she was looking for in the cupboard where I keep my meager supply of liquor. Holding up a fifth of dark rum, she turned to me with a grin.

"Got any cola?"

CHAPTER 42

It was nearly midnight by the time I'd heard all of Darlene's woes and had filled her in on my new and unwelcome suspicions about Mike. We were in the living room, seated side by side on the love seat with our feet up on the coffee table. I was far from drunk, but I was in a state of pleasant, alcohol-induced haziness.

"I feel guilty even thinking such a thing about Mike," I confided, "and I probably shouldn't have told you what his father did. You've got to promise not to say anything about that to anyone else. Unless the police arrest him, of course."

"Cross my heart and hope to die." Darlene made the appropriate hand gestures to go with her slightly slurred words and then, for good measure, mimed zipping her lips.

"You're not saying I'm wrong."

"How can I? Your theory makes as much sense as Ronnie drugging Tiffany and tossing her into Chestnut Lake."

"Wearing all her clothes and with my card in her pocket."

Darlene shook her head. "Sloppy. Sloppy. Sloppy. Not well thought out. If Ronnie had done it, she'd have been sneakier than that."

"So you don't think she's guilty?"

"Nope. But then, I don't want to think anyone we know could be a cold-blooded killer. I'm finding it hard to believe that Mike is." Darlene punctuated this statement with an enormous yawn. "Sorry." She blinked owlishly at me. "Long day."

"We could both do with a good night's sleep. Does the scooter need to be plugged in?"

"No, but I should probably know where you've stashed it."

"Right next door." I gestured toward the pocket doors.

She hopped up off the loveseat and went to look.

"I remember this room. You used to have all your birthday parties here."

I nodded. "Just the other day I was looking at some of the pictures my father took. It was interesting to see how my mom's decorating changed from year to year."

"And we slept on this floor when you had pajama parties."

"We were a lot younger and more flexible then."

Darlene advanced far enough into the dining room to locate her scooter. Where the sunroom, formerly a side porch, joins the house, the outside wall extends to create the window alcove. I'd tucked her motorized transport into that space. "You put it together!" she exclaimed. "You didn't have to do that."

I shrugged. "It seemed like a good idea at the time."

She climbed aboard, started her up, and amused herself by making *vroom-vroom* noises.

"You've had way too much to drink." I spoke very carefully, enunciating each word so she wouldn't suspect that I was none too steady myself.

Still seated on the scooter, Darlene pointed an accusing finger at the dining room table. "That's got to go. I need maneuvering room."

"Give me a minute."

I made short work of stacking papers on a chair and balancing my new laptop on top of them. Then I attacked the table itself. It had been cleverly constructed so that the leaves tucked under and the sides dropped down until it was less than half the size it had been. Once I'd shoved it up against a wall, there was plenty of open space.

"There," I said. "You've got a clear path from the window alcove all the way to the living room."

I was contemplating whether or not I needed to rearrange some of the furniture in that room when the doorbell rang.

I jumped, and Darlene let out a squeak of surprise. We looked at each other and giggled like a couple of schoolgirls.

"Do you suppose that's Frank?" she whispered.

"Do you think he's come to apologize?"

"I hope so." A faint smile curved her lips.

"Wait here and I'll go take a look. You don't want to seem too eager."

I trotted through the living room and into the hall. A glass-paneled door separates the latter from my tiny foyer. Leaving the security system on, I flicked the switch for the porch light. Then I froze. It wasn't Frank Uberman on the other side of my front door. It was Mike Doran.

I pressed my palms against the wood and shook my head in an attempt to clear the cobwebs away. I hadn't had *that* much to drink, and my recent burst of physical activity had worked most of the alcohol out of my system. *Think, Mikki,* I ordered myself.

I'd turned on the light, so Mike knew I was home. Well, he'd already known that. He could see my car parked in the driveway and that there were still lights on downstairs. What he didn't know was that I suspected him of murdering Tiffany.

When he rang the doorbell a second time, I knew I had to acknowledge his presence. That did not mean I had to let him come inside the house.

"It's late," I called through the door. "I was about to go to bed."

"I need to talk to you for a minute," Mike yelled back, "but I'd just as soon not share our conversation with the neighbors. C'mon, Mik. Open up."

It was the use of the old nickname that weakened my resolve. I hesitated a moment longer, then shut off the security system and unlocked the door, although I did keep the chain on. I peered around the solid barrier of the door, hoping to give the impression that I was already in my nightgown. I feigned a yawn. "Can't this wait till morning?"

Chilly night air eddied into the house, but Mike was dressed for even colder temperatures. He had the collar of a navy blue peacoat turned up, and he was wearing a hat pulled down so low that very little of his face showed. He was wearing gloves, too. It was catching sight of those that gave me the willies. It wasn't *that* cold out.

I tried to slam the door in his face but I wasn't quite fast enough. Mike gave it a mighty kick, breaking the chain and sending me reeling backward. Before I could recover my balance, he was inside. He slammed the door shut with one hand and grabbed hold of my right arm with the other. A moment later he had twisted it behind my back. He spoke directly into my ear, his voice low and ominous.

"I'm really sorry about this, Mikki, but I can't risk having you talk about what you know."

"I don't know anything."

The last word came out on a yelp when Mike tightened his grip. He shoved me forward. I tried to resist, twisting my body in his direction, but that made my arm hurt even more. I could see a small section of Mike's face out of the corner of my eye. The look of grim determination I saw there scared me more than anything he could say.

From the dining room Darlene called, "Is everything okay out there?"

At the realization that we weren't alone, Mike blanched. For just a second, his hold on me loosened.

"Darlene, call the cops!" I shouted as I tried again to wrench myself free.

Mike shifted, wrapping one arm around my neck and pulling me against his chest. I could feel him fumbling in the pocket of his coat with his free hand and the rush of air against my cheek as he shouted, "Don't do it, Darlene!"

The next moment, something hard poked me in the ribs.

"One move toward a phone," Mike yelled, "and I shoot your friend!"

CHAPTER 43

I don't know much about firearms, except that you can kill people with them. My maternal grandfather used to go deer hunting with his pals, but if he ever kept a rifle in the house it was well hidden. Neither my father nor my husband ever owned any kind of gun. All I knew about the one Mike had was that it was deadly. It was probably just a normal-size handgun, but in my imagination it was enormous — big, ugly, and liable to go off at any second.

He pushed me ahead of him into the dining room. Darlene was right where I'd left her, framed by tall windows as she sat on her scooter. When we came through the pocket doors, she lifted her hands to show they were empty.

"I don't have a phone on me. Sorry, Mikki."

"Damn it," Mike swore. "This was supposed to be quick and easy."

"What was? Killing me? Forgive me if I'm not inclined to cooperate."

Although I was trembling all over and not entirely certain how much longer my legs would keep me upright, the sarcasm still leaked out. What was the point of beating around the bush? Mike's intentions were obvious. He was only hesitating to carry out his plan because he'd realized he would have to deal with disposing of two bodies instead of one.

"What's this all about?" Darlene asked.

"Don't pretend you don't know. She probably told you everything." He jabbed me again with the gun, this time hard enough to make me wince.

"I don't know *everything*," I protested. "The least you could do is tell us what you *think* we know before you shoot us."

He released me and gave me a shove in Darlene's direction. When I turned around, I got my first good look at the gun. It wasn't quite as large as I'd envisioned, but it was big enough to terrify me. It took a concerted effort on my part to stop staring at it. The hand holding the gun was visibly unsteady, but that did not reassure me. If it went off by accident, I'd be just as dead.

I started to speak.

"Shut up."

"What? You think we should make this easy for you?" Darlene sounded more irritated than scared. Possibly that was the rum talking.

"I don't think you have a choice."

Whatever condition Darlene was in, I was now stone cold sober and desperately trying to think of a way to talk Mike out of this madness. He hadn't shot us yet. I tried to convince myself that was an encouraging sign.

"So what was the plan?" I asked. "Did you mean to stage an accident for me? A fall down the stairs, maybe? You can't really want to shoot us. That will leave evidence for the police to find. They'll have to investigate a double murder, and if they can trace the gun, you'll be in big trouble."

"That doesn't mean I *won't* shoot you. Where are your backups? All of them this time."

So that was what had triggered this desperate move. I'd told him I still had copies of the files on Tiffany's thumb drive. Then my eyes widened as the penny dropped.

"You're the one who broke in and stole my laptop." It made sense. The break-in had taken place right after I told him that the files contained his father's story. "Is this supposed to look like a second burglary, only this time with a fatality?"

He was scoping out the room. "This is an old house. No one will be surprised when it catches fire and burns to the ground. The only change in my plan is that now two people will be trapped inside instead of just one."

"I don't like that plan," I said. "I just finished the renovations. They aren't even paid for yet."

"Tough."

"Well, that's mature!" I sent him a pitying look. "You're a lawyer, Mike. Can't you think of a way out of this jam that doesn't involve more violence? I can't believe you *intended* to kill Tiffany. You quarreled with her, right? Because she was blackmailing you?"

I got a flicker of reaction to that. He hadn't anticipated that I'd figure out the blackmail angle. I probably shouldn't have mentioned it. I should probably have stopped talking entirely, but what did I have to lose? The longer he delayed killing us, the better our chances that something would happen to prevent that from happening. What that something might be, I hadn't the foggiest notion.

"I can see how you might have lost your temper and pushed her into the water. If she accidentally hit her head on something, you probably left the scene without ever realizing she could drown."

"Nice scenario, Mikki. You should have been a writer. There's only one little problem. It doesn't explain the drugs in her system."

Oops.

"You want to know what really happened? Fine. I'll tell you. I intended to kill that blackmailing bitch all along. And I meant for Ronnie to be blamed for it, too, if the cops couldn't be fooled into thinking Tiffany's death was an accidental drowning. I knew she'd hire me to represent her. No matter how the trial comes out, she's going to pay me enough in legal fees to replace everything Tiffany extorted. Only fair, right?"

"What about your alibi?"

He laughed. "No one ever asked me for one. Why should they? What possible motive could I have had to kill Tiffany Scott?"

Darlene had been silent for quite a while, but now she spoke up. "Why did you pay her, Mike? Wouldn't it have been better to tell her to publish and be damned?"

"Not when my family's reputation was at stake." He snapped out the words in a cold, emotionless voice. His face was equally devoid of expression, showing no regret, no remorse . . . and no pity. "Too bad you had to figure things out. I can't take the chance that anyone else will discover what my father did."

His confession and the plans he had for us should have paralyzed me, leaving me unable to move or speak. Instead, the more he admitted to, the angrier I became. "If you were so anxious to keep that skeleton in the closet, you should never have talked to Tiffany in the first place."

"She was just a kid. She was supposed to think I was making up scary stories to amuse her."

"And you might have been just a little the worse for drink at the time? Said just a little too much? Added just a few too many details?"

He didn't answer.

"It's ironic, you know. I don't think I'd have looked so hard at the files and found the notes on the copycat killer if you hadn't used some of the same tricks when you killed Tiffany."

"What the hell are you talking about?" I had his complete attention now. He had dismissed Darlene, our handicapped classmate, as a negligible threat.

"Oh, come on, Mike. Surely you're aware

of the standard MO of Murder Incorporated — whack someone, tie up the dead body, weigh it down, and toss it in a lake. That's how your father got away with the murder he committed. His crime mimicked a mob hit."

"She was alive when she went into the water, and she wasn't tied up. She drowned."

"She drowned because you got her to eat or drink something that had been conveniently laced with one of Ronnie's meds. What did you use? Painkillers? Sleeping pills?"

"Enough talk," Mike gestured with the gun. "Turn around."

"So you can knock me out?"

My legs still felt wobbly, and there was a decided tremor in my voice. The determined look in his eyes warned me that he was done answering questions. I'd delayed the inevitable as long as I could.

As I turned, I stepped farther away from Darlene. She was still sitting on her scooter. A low hum told me the motor was still running.

The only warning Mike had was a slightly louder whirring sound. Then the scooter shot forward at what Darlene had once laughingly referred to as "ramming speed." It blindsided Mike, knocking him off balance. When he lost his grip on the gun, it flew across the room and struck the stack of printouts I'd piled on a chair, scattering them and sending my brand-new laptop crashing to the floor. The weapon disappeared in a blizzard of white paper.

I dove on top of the pile and began flinging loose pages every which way as I fumbled for possession of the gun. I didn't want to touch the thing, but I couldn't risk Mike getting hold of it again.

On the far side of the room, Darlene continued her assault. Her scooter wasn't heavy enough to keep him pinned down, but as long as she kept giving it power, hitting him with it again and again, he couldn't regain his footing.

He flailed at her, landing a few good blows, and finally succeeded in unseating her. Darlene didn't perform the most graceful of dismounts, but she did manage to roll the scooter on top of him on her way to the floor.

My hand touched cold metal. Panting, reeling a little as I staggered upright on trembling legs, I held the gun by the barrel, my finger nowhere near the trigger. I knew I'd never be able to bring myself to shoot anyone. I didn't even want to point a deadly weapon at another person, but Mike was

crawling out from under the scooter. In another moment, he'd be on his feet. I *had* to
do it.

An instant before I made my move, Darlene took action. She was still on the floor
herself, but she'd landed within reach of my
fallen laptop. Grabbing hold of it with both
hands, she heaved it at Mike just as he came
up on his hands and knees. It whacked him
hard upside the head, and he went down
with a crash.

Cautiously, I stepped closer. He looked
unconscious, but I kept a tight hold of the
gun, just in case.

Darlene used the chair to lever herself to
her feet. Limping a little, she came over to
stand beside me. "Do you think I killed
him?"

"He's bleeding. Dead people don't bleed."
I had no idea how I knew that. I suppose I
read it somewhere.

We stared down at him at a loss what to
do next. Neither one of us had the presence
of mind to find a phone and dial 911. In
the end, it didn't matter. No more than a
few minutes passed before we heard a loud
banging on the front door and the welcome
words, "This is the police! We're coming
in!"

CHAPTER 44

Save for a few memorable highlights, the next couple of hours passed in a blur. I was exhausted, both mentally and physically, but once Mike regained consciousness and was arrested there were a great many loose ends to clear up. Darlene and I went down to the police station to give statements. It was only then that I learned how Detective Hazlett and his colleagues had come to arrive in such a timely manner.

It was my neighbor, Cindy Fry, who saved the day. She'd gotten up for a middle-of-the-night glass of water and while standing at her kitchen sink she had glanced through the window that looked straight into my dining room. Since no one had thought to draw the curtains in the window alcove, she'd gotten an eyeful. The sight of a man holding two women at gunpoint had, quite naturally, prompted her to call the cops.

Detective Hazlett himself interviewed me.

Aside from asking questions, he didn't say much. For some reason, that annoyed me, especially when I remembered that I'd left a message for him, and he'd never returned my call. When he appeared to be about to dismiss me, with no thanks for catching a killer for him, I'm afraid I reacted like a petulant adolescent.

"All the clues to the murderer's identity were right there on Tiffany's thumb drive. If you'd taken the trouble to read her files, everyone would have been spared a lot of grief."

"Ms. Lincoln," he said, "you should know that I took your suggestions seriously. I read every file and I had, in fact, already discovered that the amounts listed in 'blackmail.doc' match deposits to Tiffany Scott's bank account. Given enough time, we'd undoubtedly have found the person who was paying her."

Mollified, I said, "You didn't know the reason behind the blackmail. There was no way you could have, I suppose."

"Special knowledge is always helpful," he agreed. "Most people wouldn't have noticed the anomaly of the Oxford comma. Even fewer would have known enough about Mike Doran's family history to make the connection between Tiffany's anonymous source and the equally anonymous relative who committed a long-ago copycat crime."

The detective and I parted on amicable terms.

When Darlene finished giving her statement, she phoned Frank. He drove us back to my place to collect Darlene's gear and took her away with him afterward. I fell into bed and slept until midafternoon the next day. When I got up, I found I had a voice mail from Detective Hazlett. Ronnie North had been released.

I debated with myself while I fueled up with ham and scrambled eggs, but I really had no choice. I drove to the mansion at the top of the hill. To my surprise, Ann showed me right in.

"I just stopped by to see how you're doing," I said when Ronnie received me in her overly formal living room.

"I'm fine. You needn't have bothered."

"Mike fooled a lot of people."

Her eyes narrowed. "Thank you so much for pointing that out. I am well aware that hiring the real murderer to defend me was not a good decision."

"I didn't see through him, either. Not until I read the material Tiffany left behind." At the odd look that came over Ronnie's face, I added, "On the thumb drive. It was all there. It just wasn't obvious at first."

Ronnie cleared her throat. "Do you have another copy?"

"What happened to the one I gave you?"

"I threw it away." I could see it just about killed her to admit that.

"I'll get one to you. You might even enjoy reading Tiffany's novel. The characters she based on Onslow and Van Heusen all come to bad ends." I hesitated, then said, "I, uh, don't know if anyone told you, but Alan Van Heusen has been arrested on numerous charges having to do with fraud. He was definitely up to no good at Mongaup Valley Ventures."

"So I've been informed."

Her closed expression did not encourage questions or comments, so I kept mum. I told myself, firmly, that it was none of my business what Ronnie's relationship with Van Heusen had been.

"A pity you couldn't pin anything on Greg Onslow," she said after a moment. "He still plans to build his infernal theme park right next to my property."

"Can't you stop him? What about those shares Tiffany left you?"

She made an inarticulate sound of disgust. "They're in limbo until the courts decide which will is valid." The disgruntled look on her face told me there might be some doubt about that. Only natural, I suppose, since it had been Mike Doran who'd produced the will in Ronnie's favor.

Since there didn't seem to be much more to say, I told her to have a good life and left.

CHAPTER 45

Several days later, Greg Onslow called on me. At first, I was hesitant to let him in, but my guardian-angel neighbor was at home and had seen him arrive. Not only that, she went instantly on alert when she recognized him. I waved to signal that I'd be okay, but I made sure I had my cell phone handy when I escorted him into my living room. I had the police on speed dial.

"I owe you an apology, Ms. Lincoln," Onslow said once he'd settled himself on the loveseat.

Since I was uncertain what it was he was apologizing for, I didn't respond.

"I initially discouraged the murder investigation and accepted the verdict of accidental death because I thought Tiffany's death was a suicide and that I'd driven her to kill herself."

This was a startling confession from a man of his I-can-do-no-wrong mind-set. I

396

wondered if he knew that he and Ronnie had both, albeit briefly, shared the same suspicion and the same guilt.

"I'm sure you were relieved to discover you weren't to blame."

The platitude made me wince. What I really wanted was to ask him if he'd realized yet that his controlling ways and Tiffany's subsequent lack of funds to call her own were what had driven her to try her hand at blackmail. I kept that question to myself.

"I bear some responsibility for Alan Van Heusen's activities as well," Onslow continued, "although I can assure you that he acted on his own. I never meant you any harm, Ms. Lincoln. Never."

I took this claim with a grain of salt, just as I remained suspicious of his sudden need to confess his sins. It's true that poor business judgment doesn't equate to criminal behavior, but although Greg Onslow might have been conned and had come out of this whole mess looking like just another victim, he was far from innocent.

"You'll be pleased to know that I have fired Paul Klein. There is no place for such men in my organization."

Bullies? I let that thought pass unspoken, too. I had, however, reached my limit for listening to Onslow pretend to be pure as the driven snow. I stood.

"If that's all you came to say —"

"There's something else."

I remained on my feet.

He got up and cleared his throat. "Tiffany and I didn't always agree on everything, but I'd like to honor my late wife's memory." He gave a self-deprecating laugh that fell far short of convincing. "Once I learned that she'd hoped to have a career as a novelist, I took a look at her book. I'd like to see it published. I want to hire you to edit it."

"Did you read the whole thing?" I had my doubts. Neither of Onslow's fictional alter egos had come to good ends.

"Enough to believe it has promise."

"The first three chapters, then?"

He nodded.

"I'm sorry to have to tell you this, Mr. Onslow, but the rest of the book doesn't live up to its potential." I gave him a brief and honest evaluation of the manuscript, finishing up with my conclusion about its chances of success: "It would have to be completely rewritten before any legitimate publisher would touch it."

"Let me hire you to do that, then. You'd be — what do you call it — a ghostwriter?"

"Thank you, but no." Despite my tight budget, I wasn't *that* desperate for money.

Besides, I wanted nothing more to do with a man like Greg Onslow. There might not have been grounds to arrest him, but he was a crook all the same.

"Why not?"

"I'm not interested in taking on such a long-term, time-consuming project."

I had to repeat my refusal several times before I convinced him I was serious. He stalled again at the front door.

"She was wrong about me, you know."

"Tiffany?"

He nodded. "I do want to restore Lenape Hollow to its former glory. Those downtown businesses will open soon, and so will Wonderful World. It will be the salvation of this community."

He sounded so sincere that I almost believed him. Then my normal skepticism returned, along with a vague sense of alarm. How could I trust anything this man said?

Cindy had remained outside raking leaves the entire time Onslow was inside my house. I was pretty sure this was because she wanted an excuse to keep an eye on my place. She continued to stand guard until Onslow got into his car and drove away.

"Thanks for your help," I called to her once he was gone.

"No problem. Come over for coffee tomorrow morning?"

"I'd love to."

After we set a time, I went back inside, making sure to lock up and set the alarm before I retreated to my second-floor office. I was in a thoughtful frame of mind as I prepared to buckle down and get some work done.

I looked forward to getting to know Cindy better. I intended to carry through on my resolution to make new friends. There would be more visits to Harriet's and quality time with Darlene. But if I was truly to become part of this community, I'd have to do more than socialize.

There was no escape. I would have to find a way to get along with Ronnie North. If Onslow was serious about building his theme park, I'd have to join the campaign to stop him. Only by working together could we hope to keep Wonderful World from "saving" Lenape Hollow.

A RANDOM SELECTION FROM "THE WRITE RIGHT WRIGHT'S LANGUAGE AND GRAMMAR TIPS"

BY MIKKI LINCOLN

If you peek at the peak of a mountain, your interest in scenic views might be piqued.

There is a definite difference in meaning between these two sentences: 1. "The man was hanged." 2. "The man was hung." The rule in formal English is that *hanged* refers to executions and *hung* refers to objects. Therefore a murderer is hanged by the neck until dead but a picture is hung on the wall.

It is easier to decide whether to use "Mother and I" or "Mother and me" in a sentence if you leave out "Mother" and follow the rule for choosing between I and me. Here's an example: "I left the book behind but it was returned to me." Of course, since English is a complex language, there are exceptions. If the pronoun comes after *than, as,* or *but* and there is an additional verb implied by the structure of the sentence, then I is used instead of me. For example, "Mary is older

401

than I [am]." Just to confuse the issue, in informal English (conversation), it's okay to say "Mary is older than me."

Unsure when to use *who* and when to use *whom*? So are most people. Use *who* (or in this case, *whoever*) if it is the subject of the clause: "I respect whoever is elected to that office." In that case, *whoever* is the subject of *is*. Formal writing requires the use *whom* for all objects, as in "For whom did you vote?" In everyday speech, however, it is okay to use *who* rather than *whom*, no matter what its function in the sentence. There is another alternative, too. Formal: "The man whom she admired proved to be a great disappointment." Informal: "The man who she admired proved to be a great disappointment." Sneaky: "The man she admired proved to be a great disappointment."

"How are you?" someone asks. "I'm good" is the reply. No, actually, you're well, although you may feel good. Similarly, you might be a good cook and cook good meals, but you cook well.

"Rein in your enthusiasm for the rain," said the queen who reigned over the country.

Use "each other" for two people and "one

another" for more than two.

Further and *farther* can be used interchangeably when talking about geographic distance, but many writers prefer *farther*. *Further* indicates increased quantity, degree, or time. "The ship is farther from shore than we anticipated. Stay tuned for further developments."

ACKNOWLEDGMENTS

I have many people to thank for their contributions to this first Deadly Edits mystery. First and foremost are Tiffany and Scotti Smith, who generously allowed me to use their names for my victim. Love you guys.

When it came to research, I relied in large part on my own memories of growing up in a town similar to Lenape Hollow. My fictional creation is not — repeat *not* — Liberty, New York. None of the characters are real people from Liberty. Honest. That said, I did make free use of certain floor plans and the arrangement of streets and buildings. My familiarity with the economic situation of towns and villages in Sullivan County, past and present, also came into play in creating the plot. Historian John Conway's excellent articles on Murder Incorporated were extremely useful in imagining the 1930s.

For details of police procedure, I am indebted to Kyle Muthig of the Sullivan County Sheriff's Department for taking the time to answer questions from his mom's old classmate. Any mistakes in this area are mine alone. I also want to thank Kyle's mom, Cheryl Sprague Muthig, for being my friend for so many years.

Other members of the LCHS class of '65, through conversations at various reunions, posts on the "People Who Come From Liberty, New York" Facebook page, and emails, have provided helpful reminders of the way things used to be. A special thank-you goes to Dolores Thompson Gadshian, who went the extra mile and visited the DMV on Mikki's behalf and took pictures, and another to Mary Ellison Grabowski, who is still "Mikki's" neighbor. She and her siblings and I really did play "Birds" and "Monsters" way back when.

My lifelong friend Jayne Benmosche, although she hails from the rival town of Monticello, also helped jog my memory. I am grateful to retired Maine teacher Susan Vaughan for keeping me current on the subject of diagramming sentences. Barb Goffman provided invaluable assistance by reading the manuscript to make sure Mikki didn't do anything to make her unconvincing as a "book doctor." And last, but certainly not least, the incomparable Dina Wilner let me play with her scooter and briefed me on the fine points of getting it into the trunk of a car and maneuvering it in tight quarters.

Although no characters in *Crime & Punctuation* are based on anyone real, Tom and Marie O'Day won the right to name Mikki's neighbors at the charity auction at Malice Domestic 29. Mikki herself got her name from the fact that my parents considered naming me Michelle before settling on Kathy Lynn (Kaitlyn is the name I chose for myself). Mikki has a lot of me in her but she is smarter, stronger, and healthier than I am. Since it takes quite a while to take a novel from concept to print, she also ended up being a bit younger, too. The biggest difference between us is that my very-much-alive husband and I, and our cats, still live on twenty-five tree-studded acres in rural Maine and have no plans to move back to my old hometown in New York State.

ABOUT THE AUTHOR

Kaitlyn Dunnett writes the Liss MacCrimmon Scottish-American Heritage Mystery Series. She also writes under the names Kathy Lynn Emerson and Kate Emerson.

The employees of Thorndike Press hope you have enjoyed this Large Print book. All our Thorndike, Wheeler, and Kennebec Large Print titles are designed for easy reading, and all our books are made to last. Other Thorndike Press Large Print books are available at your library, through selected bookstores, or directly from us.

For information about titles, please call:
(800) 223-1244

or visit our website at:
gale.com/thorndike

To share your comments, please write:
Publisher
Thorndike Press
10 Water St., Suite 310
Waterville, ME 04901